GUARDIAN OF THE GATE

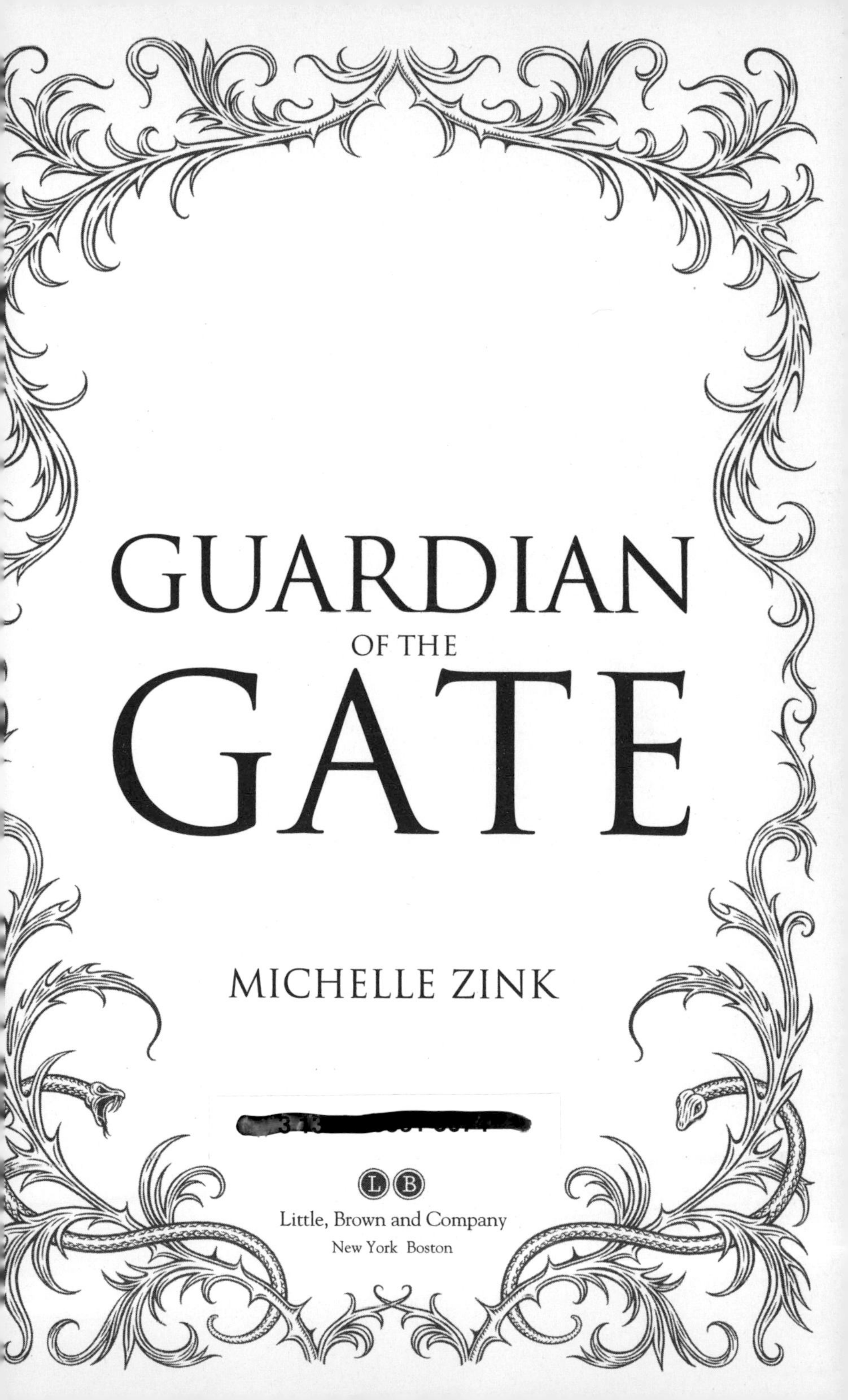

GUARDIAN OF THE GATE

MICHELLE ZINK

LB

Little, Brown and Company

New York Boston

Hand-lettering and interior ornamentation by Leah Palmer Preiss

Little, Brown and Company

Hachette Book Group
237 Park Avenue, New York, NY 10017
Visit our website at www.lb-teens.com

Little, Brown and Company is a division of Hachette Book Group, Inc.
The Little, Brown name and logo are trademarks of Hachette Book Group, Inc.

First U.S. Edition published in August 2010 by Little, Brown and Company
First International Edition: August 2010

Library of Congress Cataloging-in-Publication Data

Zink, Michelle.
Guardian of the Gate / Michelle Zink. — 1st ed.
p. cm.
Sequel to: Prophecy of the sisters
Summary: In 1891 London, sixteen-year-old orphan Lia Milthorpe continues her quest to end an ancient prophecy requiring her to search for missing pages and human "keys" and develop her powers for an inevitable final confrontation with her twin sister, Alice.
ISBN 978-0-316-03447-0 (hc) / ISBN 978-0-316-09139-8 (int'l)
[1. Supernatural—Fiction. 2. Sisters—Fiction. 3. Twins—Fiction. 4. Magic—Fiction. 5. Good and evil—Fiction.] I. Title.
PZ7.Z652Gu 2010
[Fic] —dc22 2009046642

10 9 8 7 6 5 4 3 2 1

Book design by Alison Impey

RRD-C

Printed in the United States of America

For Kenneth, Rebekah,
Andrew, and Caroline.
The heart of my heart.

1

Sitting at the desk in my chamber, I do not need to read the words of the prophecy to recall them. They are embedded in my mind as clearly as the mark that brands my wrist.

Even still, there is something solid and reassuring about holding the cracked binding of the book my father hid in the library before his death. I open the aged cover, my eyes coming to rest on the slip of paper inserted at the front.

In the eight months since Sonia and I have been in London, reading the words of the prophecy has become my bedtime ritual. It is in those quiet hours that Milthorpe Manor is at its most peaceful, the house and servants silent and Sonia fast asleep in her chamber down the hall. It is then that I continue my attempt to decipher the words of the prophecy translated by James's careful hand—to find any new clue that might lead me to their missing pages. And the path to my freedom.

On this summer eve, the fire hisses softly from the firebox as I bend my head to the page, reading, once again, the words that bind me irrevocably to my sister, my twin—and to the prophecy that divides us.

Through fire and harmony mankind endured
Until the sending of the Guards
Who took as wives and lovers the woman of man,
Engendering His wrath.
Two sisters, formed in the same swaying ocean,
One the Guardian, One the Gate.
One keeper of peace,
The other bartering sorcery for devotion.
Cast from the heavens, the Souls were Lost
As the Sisters continue the battle
Until the Gates summon forth their return,
Or the Angel brings the Keys to the Abyss.
The Army, marching forth through the Gates.
Samael, the Beast, through the Angel.
The Angel, guarded only by the gossamer veil of protection.
Four marks, Four keys, Circle of fire
Birthed in the first breath of Samhain
In the shadow of the Mystic Stone Serpent of Aubur.
Let the Angel's Gate swing without the Keys
Followed by the Seven Plagues and No Return.
Death
Famine
Blood

Fire

Darkness

Drought

Ruin

Open your arms, Mistress of Chaos, that the havoc of the Beast will flow like a river

For all is lost when the Seven Plagues begin.

There was a time when the words meant very little to me. When they were nothing more than a legend found in a dusty volume hidden in Father's library before his death. But that was before I discovered the serpent blossoming on my wrist. Before I met Sonia and Luisa, two of the four keys, also marked, though not exactly like me.

Only I have the "C" at the center of my mark. Only I am the Angel of Chaos, the unwilling Gate to my sister's Guardian, a consequence I blame not on nature, but on the confused nature of our birth. Nevertheless, only I can choose to banish Samael forever.

Or summon him forth and bring about the end of the world as we know it.

I close the book, forcing its words from my mind. It is too late an hour to think of the end of the world. Too late an hour to think of my part in stopping it. The sheer burden of it has made me desire the singular peace of sleep, and I rise from the desk and slip beneath the coverlet of the massive four-poster bed that is mine at Milthorpe Manor.

I turn out the lamp on my bedside table. The room is lit

only by the glow of the fire, but the simple darkness of a firelit room does not frighten me as it once did. Now it is the evil hidden in places beautiful and familiar that brings terror to my heart.

It has been a long while since I have confused my travels on the Plane with a simple dream, but this time, I cannot say for certain which one has claimed me in sleep.

I am in a forest that I know instinctively to be the one surrounding Birchwood Manor, the only home I had ever known before coming to London eight months ago. There are those who might say all trees look alike, that it is impossible to tell one wood from another, but this is the landscape of my childhood and I know it for what it is.

The sun filters through the leaves that rise on branches far above my head. It creates a vague sense of daylight so that it might be morning or evening or anytime in between. I am beginning to wonder why I am here, for even my dreams seem to have purpose now, when I hear my name called from somewhere behind me.

"Li-a . . . Come, Lia . . ."

Turning, it takes a moment to place the figure standing just beyond me in the trees. The girl is small and still as a statue. Her golden ringlets glimmer even in the dappled light of the forest. Though it has been nearly a year since I saw her in New York, I would know her anywhere.

"I have something to show you, Lia. Come quickly." The

girl's voice is the same youthful singsong that it was when she first handed me the medallion that bears the same mark as my wrist and is with me wherever I go.

I wait a moment, and she holds out a hand, waving me toward her with a smile too knowing to be pleasant.

"Hurry, Lia. You don't want to miss her." The little girl turns and runs ahead, curls bouncing as she disappears amid the trees.

I follow, stepping around the trees and mossy stones. My feet are bare, yet I feel no pain as I make my way deeper into the forest. The little girl is as graceful and quick as a butterfly. She flits in and out of the trees, her white pinafore drifting behind her like a ghost. Hurrying to keep up, my nightdress catches on twigs and branches. I swat at them as I go, trying not to lose the girl in the forest. But it is too late. Moments later, she is gone.

I stand in place, turning in a circle to scan the woods. It is disorienting, dizzying, and I fight a surge of panic as I realize I am utterly lost among the sameness of tree trunks and foliage. Even the sun is obscured from view.

A moment later, the girl's voice returns, and I stand perfectly still, listening. It is unmistakable as the tune she once hummed as she skipped away from me in New York.

I follow the humming, goose bumps rising on the skin of my arms even under the sleeves of my nightdress. The fine hairs lift at the nape of my neck, but I am unable to turn away. Winding around tree trunks large and small, I follow the voice until I hear the river.

That is where the girl is. I am certain of it, and when I step through the last cluster of trees, the water stretches before me, and the little girl comes into view once more. She is bent over the other side of the river, though I cannot imagine how she crossed such a current. Her humming is melodic but with an eerie undertone that makes my skin crawl, and I continue toward the bank on my side of the river.

She does not seem to see me. She simply continues with her strange song as she runs her palms over the water. I do not know what she sees in its pristine surface, but she stares with singular concentration. Then she looks up and her eyes meet mine as if she is not at all surprised to see me standing before her, across the river.

I know her smile will haunt me even while she offers it. "Oh, good. I'm glad you've come."

I shake my head. "Why have you come to me again?" My voice echoes through the quiet in the forest. "What more could you possibly have for me?"

She looks down, running her palms over the water as if she didn't hear me.

"Pardon me." I try to sound more forceful. "I would like to know why you called me into the forest."

"It won't be long now." Her voice is flat. "You'll see."

She looks up, her blue eyes meeting mine. Her face wavers as she begins speaking again.

"Do you think that you are safe within the confines of your slumber, Lia?" The skin stretching over the small bones of her face shimmers, the pitch of her voice dropping a notch.

"Do you think yourself so powerful now that you cannot be touched?"

Her voice is all wrong, and when her face wavers yet again, I understand. She smiles, but this time, not as the girl from the woods. Not anymore. Now she is my sister, Alice. I cannot help but be afraid. I know well what that smile hides.

"Why do you look so surprised, Lia? You know that I will always find you."

I take a moment to calm my voice, not wanting her to see my fear. "What do you want, Alice? Have we not said everything there is to say?"

She tips her head, and as always, I believe she can see my soul laid bare. "I keep thinking you are going to become wiser, Lia. That you will realize the danger to which you subject not only yourself but your friends. And what remains of your family."

I want to be furious at the mention of my family, *our* family, for wasn't it Alice who pushed Henry into the river? Wasn't it she who consigned him to death at the bottom of it? Yet her voice seems to soften, and I wonder if even she mourns our brother.

When I answer her, there is steel in my voice. "The danger we face now is the price we pay for the freedom we will have later."

"Later?" she asks. "When will that be, Lia? You haven't even found the remaining two keys, and with that aged investigator of Father's, you may never find them."

Her criticism of Philip makes me flush with anger. Father

trusted him to find the keys, and even now, he works tirelessly on my behalf. Of course, the other two keys will do me little good without the missing pages of the Book of Chaos, but I learned long ago that it does no good to think too far into the future. There is only here. Only now.

She speaks again as if hearing my thoughts. "And what of the pages? We both know you have yet to locate them." She looks calmly down into the water, running a hand over it much like the little girl. "Given where you stand in the whole situation, I should think it would be wiser to place your faith in Samael. At least he can guarantee your safety and the safety of those you love.

"More than safety, he can guarantee your place in a new world order. One run by Him and the Souls. One that will happen eventually, whether you aid us willingly or not."

I did not think it possible for my heart to harden further against my sister, but it does. "More likely he will guarantee *your* place in that new world order, Alice. That is what this is really about, is it not? Why you worked in concert with the Souls even while we were children?"

She shrugs, meeting my eyes. "I've never pretended to be altruistic, Lia. I want simply to honor the role that *should* have been mine, rather than the one foisted upon me by the misguided workings of the prophecy."

"If that is still your desire, then we have nothing more to discuss."

She looks back into the water. "Perhaps I am not the best person to convince you, then."

I think I am finished being shocked. Finished being frightened, at least for now. But then Alice looks up, her face wavering yet again. For a moment I see the shadow of the little girl before the vision settles back into Alice. It does not last. Her face ripples, settling on an oddly shaped head and a face that seems to change by the second. I am rooted to my spot on the river, unable to move even as terror overtakes me.

"You still deny me, Mistress?" The voice, once channeled through Sonia as she attempted to contact my dead father, is unmistakable. Terrifying. *Unnatural.* It does not belong in any world. "There is no place to hide. No shelter. No peace," Samael says.

He rises from his sitting position by the river, unfolding himself to a height two times the size of any mortal man. His bulk is massive. I have the very real sense that if he wished it, he could leap across the river and be at my throat in seconds. Movement behind him demands my attention, and I catch a glimpse of the lush ebony wings folded against his back.

And now with my terror there is an unmistakable desire. A pull that makes me want to cross the river and wrap myself in those soft, feathery wings. The heartbeat starts softly and builds. *Thump-thump. Thump-thump. Thump-thump.* I remember it from the last time I met Samael on the Plane and am horrified once again to hear my own heart amplified and beating in time with his.

I take a step back. Everything in my being tells me to flee, but I don't dare turn away. Instead, I walk backward a few steps, keeping my eye on the ever-changing mask that is his

face. At times, he is as beautiful as the most handsome mortal man. And then he changes again and becomes what I know he is.

Samael. *The Beast*.

"Open the Gate, Mistress, as is your duty and your cause. Only suffering follows your refusal." The guttural voice sounds not just from across the river but inside my mind as if his words are my very own.

I shake my head. It takes every ounce of strength I have to turn away. I do it, though. I turn and run, breaking through the tree line on the riverbank even as I have no idea where to go. His roar crashes through the trees as if alive. As if giving chase.

I try to block it out, smacking at the tree branches that scrape my face as I run, willing myself to wake from this dream, to escape from this travel. But I do not have time to develop a plan, for my foot hits a tree root and I fall, hitting the ground so hard and so fast that blackness clouds my vision. Pushing away from the ground with my hands, I try to get back on my feet. I think I will get away. That I will get up and keep running. But that is before I feel the hand grab at my shoulder.

Before I hear the voice that hisses, "Open the Gate."

I sit up in bed, sweat dampening the hair at the back of my neck as I stifle a scream.

My breath comes in quick gasps, my heart thudding against my chest as if still in tandem with his. Even the light streaming

in through a gap in the curtains cannot ease the terror left in the wake of my dream, and I wait for a few minutes, telling myself that it *was* only a dream. I tell myself this over and over until I believe it.

Until I see the blood on my pillow.

Raising my hand to my face, I touch my fingers to my cheek. When I pull them back, I know, of course, what it means. The red stain tells every truth.

I cross the room to the vanity that holds the many pots of cream, perfume, and face powder. I hardly recognize the girl in the looking glass. Her hair is wild, and her eyes speak of something dark and frightful.

The scratch across my cheek is not large, but it is unmistakable. As I stare at the blood staining my cheek, I remember the branches and twigs scraping my face as I ran from Samael.

I want to deny that I have traveled unwillingly and alone, for Sonia and I have agreed it would not be wise to do so, despite the increasing strength of my powers on the Plane. It does not matter that those powers now surpass Sonia's own, because one thing is certain: my burgeoning ability is nothing compared to the will and might of the Souls—or of my sister.

Pulling back the string of my bow, I hold it for a moment before letting the arrow fly. It sails through the air, landing with a *thwack* at the center of the target a hundred feet away.

"You landed it right in the middle!" Sonia exclaims. "And from this distance!"

I look over at her and grin, remembering when I could not hit the target from twenty-five feet, even with the assistance of Mr. Flannigan, the Irishman we hired to teach us the basics of archery. Now, standing in men's breeches and shooting as easily as if I have been doing it forever, adrenaline and confidence surge through my body in equal measure.

Yet I cannot truly relish my skill. It is, after all, my sister I seek to defeat, and it may well be her at the other end of my arrows when it comes time to launch them. I suppose after everything that has happened I should be happy to see her fall, but I cannot manage so simple an emotion when it comes to Alice. Instead, my heart is tainted with a convoluted mixture of anger and sadness, bitterness and regret.

"You try." I smile and try to make my voice cheerful as I encourage Sonia to take her turn at the well-used target. This, even though we both know it is unlikely that she will actually hit it. Sonia's gifts for communicating with the dead and traveling the Plane do not, as it turns out, translate to a talent for archery.

She rolls her eyes, raising the bow to her slender shoulder. Even this small gesture causes me to smile, for not so long ago Sonia would have been too serious for such lighthearted humor.

Threading the arrow, she pulls back on the string, her arms shaking with the effort of holding it taut. When launched, her arrow wobbles through the air, landing silently in the grass a few feet from the target.

"Ugh! I think that's enough humiliation for one day, don't you?" She doesn't wait for me to answer. "Shall we take the horses to the pond before supper?"

"Yes, let's," I answer without bothering to ponder the question. I am not eager to relinquish the freedom of Whitney Grove in favor of the tightly bound corset and formal dinner that await me later this evening.

I sling the bow across my back, packing the arrows within my knapsack, and we cross the archery range to our horses. Mounting up, we start across the field to a glimmering streak of blue in the distance. I have spent so many hours astride my

horse, Sargent, that riding him is second nature. As I ride, I survey the lush openness spread out in every direction. There isn't another soul in sight, and the utter isolation of the landscape makes me grateful all over again for the quiet haven of Whitney Grove.

The fields here stretch in every direction. They give Sonia and me the privacy required for riding in men's breeches and practicing with the bow, both pastimes that would hardly be considered appropriate for young women within the confines of London. And while Whitney Grove's accompanying cottage is quaint, we have thus far used it for nothing more than changing into our breeches and the occasional cup of post-exertion tea.

"I'll race you!" Sonia calls over her shoulder. She is already pulling away from me, but I don't mind. Giving Sonia an edge on horseback makes me feel that we are still on equal footing, even if it is with something as simple as a friendly horse race.

I spur Sargent forward, leaning over his neck as his muscled legs break into a run. His mane licks like ebony fire toward my face and I cannot help but admire his glistening coat and superior speed. I catch up to Sonia rather quickly but pull back on the reins a little, maintaining my position just behind her gray horse.

She holds her lead as we cross the invisible point that has been our finish line through many races. As the horses slow, she looks back over her shoulder.

"Finally! I win!"

I smile, trotting my horse up to her as she comes to a stop at

the bank of the pond. "Yes, well, it was only a matter of time. You've become an excellent rider."

She beams with pleasure as we dismount and lead the horses to the water. Standing in silence as they drink, I marvel that Sonia is not out of breath. It is hard to imagine a time when she was afraid to sit astride a horse, let alone gallop over the hills as we do now at least three times a week.

Once the horses have slaked their thirst, we walk them over to the great chestnut tree that grows near the water. Tying them to the trunk, we sit on the wild grass, leaning back on our elbows. The wool breeches we wear while riding pull at my thighs, but I do not complain. Wearing them is a luxury. In a few hours, I will be laced tightly into a silk dress for dinner with the Society.

"Lia?" Sonia's voice drifts on the breeze.

"Hmmm?"

"When will we go to Altus?"

I turn to look at her. "I don't know. When Aunt Abigail believes I'm ready to make the journey and sends for me, I suppose. Why?"

For a moment, her usually serene face seems to darken with turmoil, and I know she is thinking about the danger we face in seeking the missing pages.

"I suppose I'd simply like to have it done with, that's all. Sometimes..." She turns away, surveying Whitney Grove's grounds. "Well, sometimes all our preparation seems pointless. We are no closer to the pages now than we were when we first arrived in London."

There is an uncommon edge to her voice, and I feel suddenly sorry that I have been so wrapped up in my own difficulty, my own loss, that I have not thought to ask about the burden that is hers.

I drop my gaze to the sliver of black velvet around Sonia's wrist. The medallion. *Mine*. Even on her wrist as it is for my protection, I cannot help wanting to feel the soft dry velvet of the ribbon, the coolness of the gold disc against my skin. My strange affinity with it is both my millstone and my cause. It has been so since the moment it found me.

Reaching out to take her hand, I smile, feeling the sadness of it on my face. "I'm sorry if I don't thank you enough for sharing my burden. I don't know what I would do without your friendship. Truly."

She smiles shyly and pulls her hand away, waving it at me dismissively. "Don't be ridiculous, Lia! You know I would do anything for you. Anything at all."

Her words soothe the worry at the back of my mind. With all the things to fear, all the people to distrust, there is a significant measure of peace in the friendship that I know will always be ours, whatever else may come.

The dinner crowd at the Society is as civilized as any other. The differences lie under the surface and are visible only to those of us in attendance.

As we move through the crowd, my earlier distress slips from my shoulders. Though the prophecy itself is still our secret,

mine and Sonia's, it is here that I come closest to being myself. Aside from Sonia, the Society has been my sole source of companionship, and I am forever grateful for Aunt Virginia's letter of introduction.

Spotting a well-coiffed silver head in the crowd, I touch Sonia's arm. "Come. There's Elspeth."

Catching sight of us, the older woman winds her way gracefully through the throng until she is standing before us with a smile. "Lia! Darling! So glad you could come! And you as well, dear Sonia!" Elspeth Shelton leans in, kissing the air near our cheeks.

"We wouldn't have missed it for the world!" Sonia's cheeks flush pale pink over the deep rose of her gown. After years spent in confinement at Mrs. Millburn's in New York, Sonia has blossomed under the warm attention of others who share her gifts and have many of their own.

"I should hope not!" Elspeth says. "I can hardly believe it was only eight months ago that you two appeared on our door with Virginia's letter in hand. Now, our gatherings would not be the same without your presence, though I daresay your aunt expected a good deal more oversight from me." She winks wickedly, and Sonia and I laugh aloud. Elspeth may have found her calling in organizing the Society's events and social gatherings, but she leaves Sonia and me ample room to be independent. "I must say hello to the others, but I shall see you both for dinner."

She makes her way toward a gentleman I recognize as old Arthur Frobisher, though he is currently attempting to

demonstrate his prowess with invisibility. It is said in the halls of the Society that Arthur descends from a long line of Druid high priests. Even so, his age makes his spells weak, and the faint outline of his graying beard and rumpled waistcoat can be seen through a haze, even as he speaks quite clearly to a younger member.

"You do realize Virginia would have a conniption if she knew how little chaperoning Elspeth has given us?" Sonia's voice is playful at my side.

"Of course. But it *is* 1891, after all. And besides, how would Aunt Virginia ever find out?" I grin at Sonia.

"I won't tell if you won't!" She laughs aloud, nodding to the others milling about the room. "Let's say hello to everyone, shall we?"

I scan the room, looking for someone we know. My eyes light on a young gentleman near the elaborately carved staircase. "Come, there's Byron."

We make our way across the room, snippets of conversation drifting to me on the pipe smoke and incense, thick in the air. When we finally reach Byron, five apples spin through the air before him in perfect time as he stands with his eyes closed, arms at his sides.

"Good evening, Lia and Sonia." Byron does not open his eyes as he greets us, the apples continuing their circular dance. I have long since stopped wondering how he knows we stand before him though his eyes are often tightly closed while he performs some parlor trick or another.

"Good evening, Byron. Getting quite good, I see." I nod toward the apples, though surely he cannot see the gesture.

"Yes, well, it amuses children and, of course, the ladies." He opens his eyes, looking right at Sonia as the fruits drop one by one into his hands. He presents one of the crimson apples to her with a flourish.

I turn to Sonia. "Why don't you stay and ask Byron to divulge the secrets of his... talent while I fetch us some punch?" It is clear from the gleam in Sonia's eye that she enjoys Byron's company—and clear from the look in his that the feeling is mutual.

Sonia smiles shyly. "Are you certain you don't want me to accompany you?"

"Quite. I'll be right back." I am already making my way to the crystal punch bowl shimmering at the other end of the room.

I pass the piano, a tune tinkling with no one at its keys, and try to gauge the player from among those milling about the room. An iridescent wave of energy connects a young woman sitting on the sofa to the ivory keys across the room, marking her as the gifted pianist. I smile to no one in particular, pleased with my observation. The Society offers me endless opportunities to refine my gifts.

When I reach the punch bowl, I turn back to look at Sonia and Byron. Just as I expected, they are deep in conversation. Returning too quickly with the punch would make me no friend at all.

Leaving the parlor, I follow the sound of voices coming from a darkened room down the hall. The door is only half closed, and when I peer through its opening, I see a group congregated around a circular table. Jennie Munn is preparing to lead the attendees through a sitting. I cannot help but be pleased, for Jennie has been schooled by Sonia in the strengthening of the powers with which she was born.

Jennie instructs those seated at the table to close their eyes, and I pull the door farther shut as I pass down the hall, heading for the small courtyard at the rear of the building. I reach for the door, wondering if I will need my cloak, when I notice my reflection in the glass on the wall. I am not one given to vanity. That was always Alice's place. Indeed, I always thought her more beautiful than I, despite the fact that we are identical twins. But now, seeing my face reflected in the glass, I almost do not recognize myself.

The face I once bemoaned as too round, too soft, has sprouted elegant cheekbones. My green eyes, inherited from my mother and always my best feature, have developed a force and intensity not present before, as if all the suffering and triumph and confidence gained in these past months has been cast, shimmering like a jewel, into their depths. Even my hair, before only brown, gleams with health and radiance. My pleasure is a secret rush as I step into the chill night behind the Society's brownstone.

The courtyard is empty, as I knew it would be. It is my favorite escape when we come here to dine. I am still unused to the heavy incense preferred by the more ardent sorceresses and spiritualists, and I breathe deeply of the cold night air. My head clears as the oxygen cuts a path through my body. I make my way along the stone walkway that winds around a garden tended by Elspeth herself. I have never been very good with planting and gardening, but I recognize some of the herbs and shrubs about which Elspeth has tried so mightily to educate me.

"Are you not afraid, out here in the dark?" The deep voice comes to me from the shadows.

I straighten, unable to make out the face or form of the man to whom the voice belongs. "No. Are you?"

He chuckles, and it is like warm wine spreading its fingers through my body. "Not at all. In fact, sometimes I think I should be more afraid of the light."

I pull myself back to the present, opening my palms to the darkness around us. "If that is true, then why don't you show yourself? There is no light here."

"So there isn't." He steps into the dim glow of the half moon, his dark hair gleaming even with so little illumination. "Why do you come into the chill, empty garden when you might be inside, laughing in the company of friends?"

It is odd to come across someone unfamiliar at a Society gathering, and I narrow my eyes in suspicion. "Why should you care? And what brings you to the Society?"

All members of the Society zealously guard its secrets. To those outside our walls we are nothing more than a private club, but the witch hunts of old would be nothing compared to the outcry that would arise were our existence to become widely known. For though there are those in "enlightened"

society who seek the counsel of simple spiritualists, the power that truly exists among our ranks would frighten even the most open-minded individual.

The man steps closer. I cannot discern the color of his eyes, but the intensity with which they survey me is unmistakable. They travel over my face, down the length of my neck, and rest lightly on the pale rise of my breasts above the moss-green bodice of my gown. His eyes skip quickly away, and in the moment before he takes a step back, I feel the heat emanating between our bodies and hear the quick breath in the air around us. I cannot be sure whether it is his or mine.

"It is Arthur who extended the invitation." The warmth is gone from his voice, and he suddenly sounds very much the proper gentleman. "Arthur Frobisher. Our families have known one another for a number of years."

"Oh, I see." My sigh is audible in the night. I don't know what I expected, why I held my breath in fear. I suppose it is difficult to trust anyone when I know the Soul's ability to change shape into virtually anything—most easily a human body.

"Lia?" Sonia's voice calls to me from the terrace.

I have to pull my eyes from the gaze of the man. "In the garden."

Her shoes click on the terrace, growing louder as they approach us on the stone walkway. "What are you doing out here? I thought you were going for punch!"

I wave my hand vaguely toward the house. "It's hot and smoky inside. I needed some air."

"Elspeth has asked that dinner be served." Her gaze drifts to my companion.

I look at him, wondering if he thinks me rude. "This is my friend, Sonia Sorrensen. Sonia, this is... I'm sorry. I don't even know your name."

He hesitates before making a small, formal bow before us. "Dimitri. Dimitri Markov. It's a pleasure."

Even in the dim light of the garden, Sonia cannot hide her curiosity. "I'm pleased to make your acquaintance, Mr. Markov, but we must make our way to the dining table before Elspeth sends out a search party!" It's obvious she would much prefer to stay here and determine what I am doing in the garden with a dark and handsome stranger than go inside for dinner.

I hear the smile in Dimitri's reply. "Well, we cannot have that, now, can we?" He tips his head toward the house. "Ladies, after you."

I follow Sonia toward the house, and Dimitri falls in step behind me. Aware of his eyes on me, I feel a thrill even as I try to banish the whisper of disloyalty to James and, if I am honest, more than a hint of suspicion.

3

Later that night, I sit at the desk in my chambers, fingering the envelope of another letter from James.

It is useless to delay reading it. I already know that it will not get easier. There will be no sudden strength to brace me against the pain I know will come, as it always does, when I read his letters. And allowing it to remain unopened is not an option. James deserves to be heard. I owe him that much.

Reaching for the sterling letter opener, I slide it under the flap of the envelope in one motion, pulling the paper from it before I have time to change my mind.

June 3, 1891

Dearest Lia,

Today I walked by the river, our river, and thought of you. I remembered your hair shimmering in the light and the soft curve of your cheek as you bowed your head, your smile teasing me. It is nothing new that I remember these things. I think of you every day. When you first left, I tried to imagine a secret grave enough to cause you to leave me. I could not, because there is no secret, no fear, no task that could ever willingly keep me from you. I suppose I always believed that you felt the same.

I think I have finally come to accept that you are gone. No, not only gone, but gone in such silence that even my repeated letters bring no word, no hope.

I would like to say that I still believe in you and in our future together. And perhaps I do. But now I am left to do the only thing I can — to take back my life and the loss felt without you in it. So let us just say, then, that we will both go on as we must.

Should our paths cross again, should you desire to come back to me, perhaps I will still be waiting on our rock by the river. Perhaps one day I will look up and see you standing in the shade of the great oak that sheltered us through so many stolen hours.

Whatever happens, you will always have my heart, Lia.

I hope you remember me well.

James

I am not surprised. Not really. I left James. My one and only letter, written to him the night before Sonia and I departed for London, gave no answers. No explanation. It offered only a declaration of love and a vaguely worded promise to return. Those things must seem very empty to James in the absence of a response to his letters. I cannot blame him for feeling the way that he does.

My thoughts travel down a familiar and beloved path. One in which I tell James everything and confide in him as I was unable to do before leaving New York. One in which he stands by my side as I work to bring the prophecy to a conclusion that might allow us, finally, to share a future.

But it doesn't take long to realize that my imaginings are futile. The prophecy has already taken the lives of people I love, and, in many ways, even my own. I could not live with myself if it should take another, least of all James's. It has been unfair to hope that he would wait for me when I cannot even share the reason that I left.

The unwelcome truth is that James is being wise while I have been only naive. My heart twists with the knowledge I have hidden from even myself, stepping around it in the moments when I came too close.

But it has been there just the same.

Standing, I carry the letter to the dying firebox. I think I will throw it in without hesitation. That I will not ponder a future I may not see until the prophecy is laid to rest.

But it is not so simple. My hand stops moving of its own accord, hovering before the firebox and growing warm from its

heat. I tell myself that the letter is only paper and ink. That James may very well be waiting when all is said and done. But the letter is an albatross of memory that I cannot afford. I will only read and reread it should it remain intact. It will only distract me from the matter at hand.

It is this thought that relinquishes my hold, and I cast it into the flame as if it is already on fire. As if it is burning my hand through its very existence. I watch as the edges of the paper curl under the heat. In moments, it is as if I never read the words printed by James's careful hand. As if it was never there at all.

The destruction of the letter lets loose a shaking in my body, and I cross my arms over my chest, trying to force myself still. I tell myself that I am free of the past whether I wish it or not. Henry is dead. James is no longer mine. Alice and I are destined to meet as enemies.

Now it is just the keys, the prophecy, and me.

I do not know how long I have been asleep, but the fire has burned low in the grate. As I scan the darkened room for the source of the sound that awoke me, I see a figure, as ethereal as a ghost, disappear around the corner of my door in a wisp of white fabric.

I swing my legs over the side of the bed. My feet do not reach the ground, but I scoot to the edge and drop to the floor. The lush carpets are soft but cool underfoot as I make my way across the room and out the door.

The hall is deserted and silent, the doors to the other chambers closed. I allow my eyes a moment to become used to the dim light from the wall sconces. When I am able to make out the shapes and shadows of the furniture lining the long hallway, I continue toward the staircase.

The figure, clad in a white nightdress, is descending the stairs. It can only be one of the housemaids who would be up this time of night, and I call out softly, trying not to wake anyone.

"Excuse me, is everything all right?"

Stopping near the bottom of the stairs, the figure turns slowly to meet my voice. It is only then that I gasp aloud into the silent house. Only when I see the face of my sister.

As in my travel, a small smile touches the corners of her mouth. It is a smile both soft and sly. A smile only Alice can manage.

"Alice?" Her name is both familiar and frightening on my tongue. Familiar, because she is my sister. My twin. Frightening, because I know that it cannot really be her, not in the flesh. Her figure is dimly lit, and I see now that her physical body is not here at all.

It cannot be, I think. *It cannot be*. No mortal traveling the Plane can cross the barrier of the physical world. Not visibly. It is one of the oldest edicts of the ancient order of the Grigori, who still set and enforce the rules of the prophecy, of the Plane, of the Otherworlds.

I am still puzzling over Alice's forbidden appearance when she begins to fade, her figure growing more and more

transparent. In the moment before she disappears, her eyes turn steely. And then she is gone.

I grab hold of the banister for support, the room below wavering as the gravity of the sighting hits me. True, Alice is a formidable Spellcaster, dreadfully competent even before my escape to London. But her presence across the miles can only mean that she has grown stronger still in my absence.

Of course, I should never have deluded myself that it would be otherwise. Though I am still discovering the gifts that are mine, I have grown stronger with each passing day. It would only stand to reason that Alice has done the same.

Yet her breaking of the barrier set by the Grigori can only mean one thing: the Souls may have been quiet all these months, but only because they still have my sister working on their behalf.

Only because whatever they have planned, whatever is coming, will more than make up for their long silence.

"Lia. Good morning."

Philip strides into the room, exuding confidence and authority. The fine lines about his eyes are more noticeable than before, and I wonder if it is because he is tired from his travels or simply because he is nearly old enough to be my father.

"Good morning. Please, sit." I settle myself on the sofa as Philip sits on the chair near the firebox. "How was your trip?"

We avoid by tacit understanding certain words, certain phrases, that would make it easy for someone to understand our conversation.

He shakes his head. "It wasn't her. I had high hopes this time, but..." He shakes his head in frustration, leaning back against the chair, exhaustion settling more resolutely over his features. "I sometimes despair that we will ever find the girl, to say nothing of the last, unnamed party."

I suppress my disappointment. Philip Randall has worked ceaselessly to find the two remaining keys. That we have not yet done so is no fault of his. We have only one name—Helene Castilla—from the list Henry so zealously guarded, and we have been unable to locate someone with that name who also bears the mark. The prophecy dictates only that the remaining keys, like Sonia and Luisa, be marked with the Jorgumand and be born near Avebury at midnight on November 1, 1874. Nearly seventeen years have passed since the birth of the keys, and the spotty nature of birth records in the villages of England has done nothing to help our cause.

Helene could reside anywhere in the world by now. She might even be dead.

I try to ease Philip's frustration. "Perhaps we should be grateful. If it were simple, someone else might find them before us." He smiles with something like gratitude as I continue. "I've no doubt we will be back on track in short order."

He sighs, nodding. "There is never a shortage of leads, though once found, they are often endowed with nothing more than a birthmark or scar from a long-forgotten injury or burn. I suppose I'll take a few days to review the newest reports and prioritize them before planning my next trip." His eyes drift to the door of the library before returning to mine. "And you? Have you heard anything new?"

My mood darkens with the question. It is impossible to believe that Aunt Abigail and the Grigori are unaware of

Alice's movements on the Plane and the forbidden use of her power. It is only a matter of time before I am summoned to Altus to retrieve the pages before Alice grows even stronger.

I shake my head in answer. "But I may soon be departing on a journey of my own."

He sits up straighter. "A journey? Surely you don't mean to travel alone?"

"I'm afraid so. Well, Sonia will likely accompany me, and I imagine we will need a guide, but other than that, I suppose I will be quite alone."

"But... where will you go? How long will you be gone?"

It is not often that I must keep something of importance from Philip. Hired by my father before his death, Philip knows more about the prophecy than any other person outside of it save our old coachman Edmund. But even still, I have guarded closely many details in the interest of Philip's safety and mine. The Souls are forbidding, their power immeasurable. It is not impossible to believe they could find a way to use Philip for their own gain.

I smile. "Let us simply say that it is a journey necessary to the prophecy and that I shall return as quickly as possible."

He stands suddenly, raking his fingers through his hair in a gesture of boyish frustration. It makes him look young, and I realize with a start that he may not be as old as I believed, despite the quiet confidence and wisdom that so reminds me of Father.

"It is dangerous enough for you here in London; you cannot possibly consider such a journey." All at once he straightens. "I will escort you myself."

I cross the room, taking his hands in mine. It does not feel at all improper, though I have not touched another man since leaving James behind in New York.

"Dear Philip. That is impossible. I don't know how long I will be gone, and it makes far more sense for you to continue searching for the keys while I see to this other bit of business. Besides, this part of the prophecy must be shouldered only by me, though I heartily wish it were not so." I lean in and brush his cool cheek with the back of my hand. It is an unexpected impulse, though when his eyes darken I see that my surprise is no match for his. "It *is* kind of you to offer your company. I know well that you would join me if I would allow it."

He lifts his hand to his cheek, and I have the strangest feeling that everything said after my brief touch is forgotten. He does not mention my journey again.

That night I travel to Birchwood. I no longer will myself into the Otherworlds, but I do not wish myself back from them either. I know Sonia would be worried to find me traveling without escort, but I am too curious about my sister to relinquish a possible glimpse into her life.

And perhaps a glimpse of James. It is a whisper in my heart.

The sky is inky and endless, with only a sliver of moon to light the tall, swaying grass in the fields. The wind rushes through the leaves in the trees, and I recognize the vacuous calm before a storm, the almost visible crackle of impending lightning and thunder. But for now, at least, it is eerily quiet.

Birchwood Manor is dark and imposing, the steep stone walls rising into the night sky like a fortress. It feels deserted, even from a distance. The lanterns that were once lit near the front door are extinguished, the leaded windows in the library black, though it has long been a habit to keep the lamp on Father's desk aglow through the night.

And then I am in the entry, the marble icy under my bare feet. Though I feel the cold seep into my skin, I am removed from it in a way that I have come to expect while traveling the Plane. The grandfather clock in the foyer ticks quietly as I make my way up the stairs. Even in my travel, I instinctively avoid the fourth creaky step.

Like so many things in my life, the house has become strange. I recognize its outward appearance—the worn, antique carpets, the carved mahogany banister—but something about its chemistry has changed, as if it is no longer made up of the familiar stone and wood and mortar that housed me since birth.

The Dark Room, of course, is still at the end of the hall. It does not surprise me to see the door open, light seeping from its interior.

I make my way toward it. I am not afraid, only curious, for I rarely find myself on the Plane without purpose. The door to my chambers, my old childhood room, is closed, as are Henry's and Father's. I suppose it is only Alice now who matters to Alice. I suppose it is easier for her to forget that we were once a family if all the doors remain tightly shut.

And it is just as well, for I carry reminders of my past, my family, not in the darkest rooms of my heart as one might

imagine, but in its brightly lit corners where I can see them for all they were.

I do not hesitate to step through the door to the Dark Room. The laws of the Grigori prevent me from being seen, even if I did wish it to be different. Even if I did wish to gain control over the forbidden powers Alice seems to have harnessed.

And I do not.

The first thing I see when I enter the room is my sister. She sits on the floor in the center of her circle, the same circle in which I found her all those months before, the one carved into the wooden floor and once hidden under the old carpet. Though my experience as a Spellcaster does not come close to matching that of my sister's, I know enough to recognize the circle as one that strengthens the spell and protects the Caster within it. The site of it causes me to shiver, even in my traveling form.

Alice wears one of her white nightdresses. Trimmed in matching lavender ribbon and once made by the armful, I remember them well. I no longer wear mine, for they are part of another life. But Alice wears hers now, looking strangely innocent and lovely as she rests on her heels, eyes closed and lips moving in an almost-silent whisper.

I remain in place for some time, watching the fine planes of her face fade in and out with the flicker of the candles lighting her circle. Her soft, unnamable words lull me into a strange state of apathy. I find myself almost drowsy, though I am already physically asleep back in London. It is only when Alice opens her eyes that I am forced to alertness.

At first, I think she will gaze into the empty room, but her eyes find mine calmly across the shadows as if she knew I was there all along. She doesn't need to speak the words for me to know they are true, but she speaks anyway, looking right into my soul as only she has ever been able to do.

"I see you," she says. "I see you, Lia. And I know you're there."

I take my time dressing as I ponder my strange trip to Birchwood. Daylight has done nothing to clarify the experience. Reason tells me that I must not have been traveling at all, that it must have been a simple dream, for between the two dimensions of the astral Plane and the physical world is a veil that cannot be lifted. One can only see what is happening on the Plane by occupying it, and clearly Alice was in the physical world while I was on the Plane.

Yet I am certain that I *was* traveling. That Alice *did* know I was there. She said so herself. I am wondering what to do with this newfound knowledge when a knock sounds from the door.

I am not surprised, even in my state of half-undress, when Sonia steps into the room without waiting for me to answer. We stopped standing on ceremony long ago.

"Good morning," she says. "Did you sleep well?"

I reach past the elaborate velvet gowns hanging in my wardrobe, opting instead for something simple in apricot silk. "Not exactly."

Her brow furrows. "What do you mean? What's wrong?"

Sighing, I clutch the gown to my bosom and drop onto the bed next to Sonia. I feel unexpectedly guilty. I have not been honest with Sonia lately. I did not tell her of my terrifying travel to the river the night I saw Samael and awoke with a cut on my cheek. I did not tell her of my vision of Alice the night I saw her on the stairs here at Milthorpe Manor.

And ours is not an alliance that will tolerate secrets.

"I traveled to Birchwood last night." I say it quickly before I can change my mind.

I do not expect the anger that flushes her cheeks. "You are not supposed to travel the Plane without me, Lia. You know this! It's dangerous." Her words are a hiss.

She is right, of course. It has been our habit to travel the Plane together and only when necessary for Sonia to teach me how to use the gifts that are mine. It is for my own protection, for there is always the danger that the Souls might detain me long enough to sever the astral cord that binds my soul to my body. Should that happen, my greatest fear would be realized and I would be stranded in the icy Void for all eternity. Still, Sonia's agitation surprises me, and I feel renewed affection for her in the face of her concern.

I place a hand on her arm. "I didn't go intentionally. I felt... summoned."

She raises her eyebrows, worry creasing her forehead. "By Alice?"

"Yes... Maybe... I don't know! But I saw her at Birchwood, and I think she saw me."

There is no mistaking the shock on Sonia's face. "What do you mean she saw you? She cannot see you when she is in this world and you are on the Plane! She would be in violation!" She hesitates, looking at me with an expression I cannot fathom. "Unless you were the one using forbidden power."

"Don't be ridiculous! Of course I wasn't. I may be a Spell-caster, but I don't have any idea how to conjure such power, nor do I want to know." I stand, pulling the gown over my head and feeling it fall over my petticoat and slide over my stockings. When I emerge from the yards of pale silk, I meet Sonia's eyes. "And I don't think Alice is very concerned about the Grigori right now, though I suppose I should have expected as much."

"What do you mean?"

I sigh. "I believe I saw her. Here, at Milthorpe Manor. I woke up in the middle of the night and saw someone on the stairs. I thought it was Ruth or one of the other maids, but when I called out, the figure turned and it... it looked like Alice."

"What do you mean 'it looked like Alice'?"

"The figure was faint. That's how I knew it wasn't a physical being. But it was her." I nod, surer by the moment. "I'm certain of it."

Sonia stands, walking to the window overlooking the streets below. She is quiet for a long time. When she finally speaks, the mixture of awe and fear are unmistakable in her voice.

"So she can see us, then. And possibly hear us, too."

I nod, though Sonia's back remains turned. "I think so."

She turns to face me. "What does it mean for us? For the missing pages?"

"No Sister of the prophecy would willingly hand over the location of the missing pages to Alice. But if she has been able to observe our progress, she may try and beat us to them, either to use them to her own gain or to keep us from reaching them."

"But she can't cross into this world, not physically. Not for the time it would take to pursue us all that way. She would have to take a ship to London and follow us in person, and that would take time."

"Unless she has someone do it for her."

Sonia meets my eyes.

"But what can we do, Lia? How will we stop her from reaching the pages if she can trace our movements from afar?"

I shrug. The answer is simple and not difficult to find.

"We will have to get there first."

I hope Sonia cannot tell that my words are stronger than my conviction, for the knowledge that I might soon face my sister causes me deep disquiet.

That Alice is ready to meet me, that she seeks to put the gears of the prophecy in motion once again, leaves me only with a sense of foreboding. In the face of my sister's power, my preparations seem meager indeed.

But they are all I have.

5

Sonia and I sit outside on the small patio at the back of Milthorpe Manor. It is not as sweeping as the grounds at Birchwood, or as quiet, but the lush green shrubbery and lovely flowers are a refuge of sorts from the chaos and grit of London. We sit side by side on identical chaises, our eyes closed to the sun.

"Shall I fetch us a parasol?" Sonia asks, I think, out of some semblance of propriety, but her voice is lazy and I know she does not really care whether we have cover from the sun.

I don't open my eyes. "I think not. The sun is fleeting enough in England. I won't do a thing to shield myself from its warmth."

The chaise next to me creaks, and I know Sonia has turned to look at me. When she speaks, I hear the laughter teasing her words. "Surely London's porcelain-skinned girls are cowering for cover on a day such as this."

I lift my head, shielding my eyes. "Yes, well, pity for them. I'm ever so grateful not to be one of them."

Sonia's laugh travels on the breeze floating through the garden. "You and me both!"

We turn in the direction of the house as shouted voices drift to us on the patio. It sounds like a disagreement, though I have never heard the staff argue before.

"Whatever is going—" Sonia does not have time to finish her thought, for all at once there is the scuff of impending boots as the voices become louder and nearer. Rising, we look at each other in alarm as we catch snippets of the argument.

"... quite ridiculous! You do not need to..."

"For goodness sake, don't..."

A young woman rounds the corner first, Ruth quick on her heels. "I am sorry, Miss. I tried to tell her—"

"And *I* tried to tell *her* that it is not necessary to announce us like strangers!"

"Luisa?" There is no mistaking the aquiline nose, the lush chestnut hair, the full red lips, and yet I still cannot believe my friend is standing before me.

She does not have time to answer, for two more figures appear quickly behind her. I'm so surprised that words fail me entirely. Thankfully, they do not fail Sonia.

"Virginia! And... Edmund?" she says.

I stand there a moment longer, wanting to be certain it is

real and not an afternoon dream. When Edmund smiles it is but a trace of the one he had readily available when Henry was still alive, but it is enough. It is enough to shake loose my shock.

And then Sonia and I are squealing and running for them all.

After a round of excited greetings, Aunt Virginia and Luisa join Sonia and me in the parlor for tea and biscuits while Edmund sees to the bags. Cook's biscuits have been known to crack a tooth or two, and I wince as Aunt Virginia bites into one of the granite-like cookies.

"A bit hard, aren't they?" I say to Aunt Virginia.

She takes a moment to chew, and I think I hear her gulp as she forces the dry piece of biscuit down her throat. "Just a bit."

Luisa reaches out to take one. I know there's no stopping her, no matter how much I might like to warn her. Only Luisa's own experience has ever been able to temper her exuberance.

She bites into the cookie with a loud crack, but it only stays in her mouth a moment before she spits into her handkerchief. "A bit? I think I may have lost a tooth! Who is responsible for such a culinary atrocity?"

Sonia stifles a laugh behind her hand, but mine escapes into the room before I can stop it. "Shhhhh! The cook makes them, of course. And be quiet, will you? You'll hurt her feelings!"

Luisa straightens her back. "Better her feelings than our teeth!"

I try to make my expression disapproving, but somehow I know that it is not. "Oh, I *have* missed you all! When did you arrive?"

Luisa sets down her teacup with a dainty clink. "Our ship docked just this morning. And none too soon, either! I was sick almost the entire way."

I remember the rough crossing Sonia and I made from New York to London. I am not as prone to motion sickness as Luisa, but even still, it was not a pleasant journey.

"We would have met you at the wharf had we known you were coming," Sonia says.

Aunt Virginia measures her words. "It was a rather... sudden decision."

"But why?" Sonia asks. "We didn't expect Luisa for quite a few months and, well..." Sonia's voice trails off as she avoids being rude.

"Yes, I know." Aunt Virginia sets down her teacup. "I'm quite sure you were not expecting *me* at all. Certainly not any time soon."

Something in her eyes makes my nerves rattle with fear. "So why *have* you come, Aunt Virginia? I mean, I *am* pleased to see you. It's just that..."

She nods. "I know. I told you it was my duty to remain with Alice, to see to her safety despite her refusal to act as Guardian." She pauses, staring into the corners of the room. I have the feeling that she is not here in London at all, but back at

Birchwood, seeing something strange and terrible. When she speaks again it is in a murmur, almost as if she is talking to herself alone. "I must confess I *do* feel a bit guilty for leaving her, despite everything that has happened."

Sonia shoots me a glance from the wing chair near the fire, but I wait in the empty space of Aunt Virginia's silence. I am in no hurry to hear what she has to say.

She meets my eyes, pulling herself from the past as she speaks. "Alice has grown . . . unusual. Oh, I know she has long been difficult to fathom," she says when she sees my look of incredulity. *Unusual* is hardly a strong enough word to describe my sister in the past year. "But since you left . . . well, she has become truly frightening."

Until recently, I have been largely insulated from Alice's activities, and I find I am hesitant to let go of my relative naïveté, however false. Still, experience has taught me that knowing one's enemy is key to winning any battle. Even if that enemy is one's own sister.

Sonia breaks in first. "What exactly do you mean, Virginia?"

Aunt Virginia looks from Sonia back to me, lowering her voice as if afraid to be overheard. "She practices her Spellcaster craft at all hours of the night. In your mother's old chamber."

The Dark Room.

"She conjures fearsome things. She practices forbidden spells. Worst of all, she grows powerful beyond my imagining."

"Can't the Grigori punish one for using forbidden magic? For using *any* magic here in the physical world. That is what you said!" I hear the hysteria rising in my voice.

She nods slowly. "But the Grigori only have dominion over the Otherworlds. The punishments meted out can only limit one's privileges there, and the Grigori have already banished Alice. I know it's difficult to fathom, Lia, but she is very careful and very powerful. She travels the Otherworlds without detection by the Grigori much as you travel while avoiding the Souls." Aunt Virginia shrugs. "Her disobedience is unprecedented. There is little else the Grigori can do to one who occupies this world. Otherwise, even they would be crossing boundaries that should not be crossed."

I shake my head in confusion. "If the Grigori have banished Alice from the Otherworlds, she should already be in check!" Frustration causes me to practically spit the words from my mouth.

"Unless . . . ," Sonia begins.

"Unless what?" Panic fizzes in my stomach, threatening to make me ill.

"Unless she simply doesn't care." Luisa finally speaks from the sofa next to Aunt Virginia. "And she doesn't, Lia. She doesn't care what the Grigori do or say. She doesn't care about their rules and punishments, and she doesn't need their permission. She doesn't need their sanction to do anything at all. She has grown far too powerful for that."

We fall silent for a time, sipping our tea as each of us contemplates a powerful and unrestrained Alice. It is Aunt Virginia who breaks the silence, though not with talk of Alice.

"There is another reason we've come, Lia, though those I've given are certainly enough."

"What do you mean? What is it?" I cannot imagine anything else that would drive Aunt Virginia across the sea at a moment's notice.

Aunt Virginia sighs, setting her teacup back on its dainty saucer. "It is your aunt Abigail. She's very sick and asks that you come to Altus immediately."

"I had planned to go soon anyway. I had a . . . feeling." I continue without explanation. "But I didn't realize Aunt Abigail was ill. Will she be all right?"

Aunt Virginia's eyes are sad. "I don't know, Lia. She's very old. She has ruled Altus for many years. It may simply be her time. In any case, it is time you go, especially given the developments with Alice. Aunt Abigail is the keeper of the pages. Only she knows where they are hidden. If she passes without telling you where to find them . . ."

She does not have to finish.

"I understand. But how will I find my way?"

"Edmund will be your guide," Aunt Virginia says. "You will leave within the next few days."

"A few days!" Sonia's voice is incredulous. "How will we prepare for such a journey with so little time?"

Surprise touches Aunt Virginia's face. "Oh! I . . . Lady Abigail only requested Lia's presence."

Sonia holds out her wrist so that Aunt Virginia can see the medallion. "I am entrusted with the medallion. I have been Lia's closest confidant for the past eight months. With all due respect, I will not just sit here while Lia faces the danger on her own. She needs every ally, and there is none more loyal than I."

"Well, I wouldn't go that far!" Luisa is indignant. "I may have been in New York while you have been here, but I am as much a part of the prophecy as you, Sonia."

I look at Aunt Virginia with a shrug. "They are two of the four keys. If we cannot trust them with the location of Altus, whom can we trust? Besides, I should like the company. Surely Aunt Abigail would not deny me that."

Aunt Virginia sighs, looking from me to Sonia to Luisa and back again. "Very well. I have the distinct feeling it would be useless to argue the point." She rubs her brow, tiredness seeping into her eyes. "Besides, I must confess the long journey has taken its toll. Let us sit by the comfort of the fire and speak of something more mundane, shall we?"

I nod, and Luisa deftly changes the subject, asking Sonia and me questions about our time together in London. We pass another hour filling Luisa in while Aunt Virginia only half listens. Watching her stare into the fire, I feel a surge of guilt. Speaking of Alice and the prophecy makes discussion of social scandal and fashion faux pas seem pointless and petty.

But we cannot live in the world of the prophecy every minute of every day. Speaking of other things is a reminder that another world still exists—one in which we might someday live. If we are very, very lucky.

"I think it's time you tell me how much you know."

My voice echoes across the floor of the carriage house as Edmund wipes down the carriage by the dim lantern light. He

pauses for a moment before lifting his eyes to mine and nodding in agreement.

If Edmund knows enough to be our guide to Altus, his place in my life and in the lives of my family has obviously been more than that of a family friend and attendant.

"Would you like to sit?" He gestures to a chair against the wall.

I nod, walking across the room and lowering myself to the chair.

Edmund does not join me. He walks to the workbench a few feet away, picking up a large metal tool and wiping it down with the rag. I don't know if it is a necessary task or if he seeks simply to keep his hands busy, but I bite my tongue against the questions swirling in my mind. I know Edmund well. He will begin when he is ready.

When he speaks his voice is low and calm, as if he is reciting a fairy tale. "I knew something was different about Thomas, about your father, from the beginning. He was a man of secrets, and though it was not uncommon for men of his stature to travel widely, he kept close the reasons for his frequent absences."

"But you traveled with him." Father often took Edmund with him, leaving us in the care of Aunt Virginia, sometimes for months, while he journeyed to vaguely referenced, exotic places.

Edmund nods. "That was later. In the beginning, I was like any member of the household staff. I drove for Thomas, managed the workers on the grounds, and saw that the more

laborious upkeep of the house was assigned to appropriate workmen. It was only after your mother became . . . *different* that your father came to trust me with the prophecy."

I remember my mother's letter and her description of her descent into near-madness at the hands of the Souls.

"Did he tell you everything then?" I ask.

Edmund nods. "I think he had to. It was a burden, carrying it alone. Even Virginia, whom he trusted implicitly with those dearest to his heart—you, your sister, and your brother—was not privy to the secrets of the book and his destinations when traveling. I expect he would have gone mad had he not told someone the rest of it."

"What was the rest of it?" I imagine my father all alone and trying to keep his secrets and feel a flash of frustration when Edmund hesitates. "My father is dead now, Edmund. The task of ending the prophecy is up to me. I believe he would want you to tell me everything, don't you?"

He sighs wearily. "After your father hired Philip to find the keys, he took it upon himself to travel each time Philip believed he had found one of them. Thomas wanted to be sure that nothing was overlooked, so he met each potential key himself to either eliminate or confirm them. When he was able to confirm their mark as authentic, as he did with Miss Sorrensen and Miss Torelli, he created situations to see them brought to New York."

I think of Sonia and her sad tale of being sent to Mrs. Millburn's because her parents didn't understand her otherworldly gifts. And Luisa. Luisa who was sent to school at Wycliffe in

New York instead of to England as originally planned. Edmund continues. "By that time, the Souls were already tormenting him with visions of your mother. He wanted to ensure that you had every resource possible should he not be there to help you."

"So you went with him to locate the keys." It is not a question.

He nods, looking at his hands.

"Did you know about Henry? That he was hiding the list of keys from Alice?"

"No. Your father never told me where he kept the list. I always thought it was in the book. If I'd known..." He looks up, his eyes haunted. "If I'd known Henry had it, I would have done more to protect him."

We sit in the silence of the carriage house, each of us trapped in the prison of our own memories. Finally I stand, placing a hand on his shoulder.

"It wasn't your fault, Edmund."

It was mine, I think. *I couldn't save him*.

I start toward the door of the carriage house.

I am halfway there when I think of something. Something I cannot yet answer.

Turning around, I call to Edmund, now sitting in the chair with his head in his hands.

"Edmund?"

He looks up. "Yes?"

"Even with everything my father told you, how is it possible that you can be our guide to Altus? Its location is a closely guarded secret. How is it that you know the way?"

He shrugs. "I've been there many times with your father."

I did not think it possible to be further surprised. Yet I am. "But . . . why would my father go to Altus?" I laugh wryly. "Obviously he was not a member of the Sisterhood."

Edmund shakes his head slowly, meeting my eyes. "No. He was a member of the Grigori."

6

“Everything is packed and ready to go.” Edmund stands near the horses at the front of the carriage, hat in hand.

It has been only a week since Aunt Virginia, Edmund, and Luisa arrived from New York, but it seems like a year. The trip to Altus is no small undertaking. It is a journey that requires horses, supplies, and assistance. When we first discussed the necessary details, I thought it impossible to arrange everything so quickly, but somehow, everything has fallen into place. Philip will continue to search for the keys in our absence, though he is none too happy about my traveling with only Edmund for protection.

I am still reeling from the discovery that my father was a member of the Grigori, but there has been no time for further questions. Clearly there is much I did not know about my parents. Perhaps the journey to Altus will help me find more than the missing pages.

As I descend the steps at the front of Milthorpe Manor, I notice the single carriage and wonder what has happened to the other arrangements made over the past week. "Edmund? Where is the rest of our party? Did we not arrange for additional horses and supplies?"

Edmund's nod is slow. "We did indeed. But there's no reason to make a fuss on our way out of the city proper. Everything has been arranged and the rest of our assemblage will join us at the required time." He pulls a pocket watch from his trousers. "Speaking of which, we ought to get moving."

I look over at Luisa, supervising the loading of the final bags into the carriage, and stifle a laugh. Sonia and I had no trouble packing lightly as suggested by Edmund, but Luisa has not been a part of the preparations Sonia and I have undertaken over the past year. As she watches Edmund load one of her bags, I can almost hear her running down a mental list of packed hats and gloves, though she surely will not wear either after this morning.

I roll my eyes and spot Sonia speaking in hushed tones to Aunt Virginia by the steps leading to the house. Luisa joins me as I make my way to them both, and soon we are all standing in a huddle, each wondering how to begin the difficult task of saying goodbye when we have only just come together again.

As always, Aunt Virginia does everything possible to make the moment easier.

"All right, then, girls. Be on your way." She leans in to kiss Luisa's cheeks, pulling back to look into her eyes. "I enjoyed traveling with you from New York, my dear. I shall miss your spirit; just remember to tame it when safety or prudence requires, hmmm?"

Luisa nods, leaning back in for another quick embrace before turning and making her way to the carriage.

Sonia does not wait for Aunt Virginia. She steps toward my aunt, reaching for her hands. "I'm so sorry to be leaving. We haven't even become properly reacquainted!"

Aunt Virginia's smile is sad. "There's nothing to be done about it. The prophecy will not wait." She casts a glance at Edmund, who looks once again at his pocket watch. "And neither, I imagine, will Edmund!"

Sonia giggles. "I suppose you're right. Goodbye, Virginia."

Having grown up not in a home of her own, but with Mrs. Millburn as her guardian, Sonia is still uncomfortable showing affection to any but me. She does not embrace my aunt, but looks into her eyes with a smile before turning to leave.

Then it is just Aunt Virginia and me. Already it seems everyone from my past is gone, and the prospect of saying goodbye to my aunt brings a lump to my throat. I swallow around it to speak.

"I wish you were coming with us, Aunt Virginia. I am never as sure of myself as when you are with me." I do not fully realize the truth of it until it is said.

Her smile is small and sad. "My time has passed, but yours is just beginning. You are stronger since leaving New York—a Sister in your own right. It is time for you to take hold of your place, my dear. I shall be right here waiting to see the story unfold."

Wrapping my arms around her, I am surprised at how small and frail she feels. I cannot speak for a moment, so swift and powerful are the emotions that crowd my heart.

I pull back, trying to compose myself as I look in her eyes. "Thank you, Aunt Virginia."

She gives my shoulders one last squeeze before I turn to go. "Be strong, child, as I know you are."

I step up and into the carriage as Edmund climbs onto the driver's seat. Once settled next to Sonia with Luisa across from us both, I lean my head out the window, looking to the front of the carriage.

"Shall we, Edmund?"

Edmund is a man of action, and I am not surprised when, instead of answering, he simply flicks the reins. The carriage rolls forward, and without another word our journey begins.

We travel along the Thames for some time. Luisa, Sonia, and I hardly speak within the shadows of the carriage. The boats along the river, the other carriages, and the people walking about all serve to keep our interest until the activity gradually fades. Soon there is nothing but the water on one side and plains stretching to small mountains on the other. The rocking of the carriage and the quiet outside lull us into a sort of stupor, and I doze fitfully against the velvet seat until finally falling into a deep sleep.

I awake with a start some time later, my head against Sonia's shoulder, as the carriage comes to a hard stop. The shadows,

before only gray smudges lurking about the corners of the carriage, have lengthened into a gathering blackness that almost seems alive, as if waiting to claim us all. I shake the notion from my mind as raised voices make their way from outside.

Lifting my head, I find Luisa, as alert as the moment we pulled away from Milthorpe Manor, staring at Sonia and me with something I cannot help but feel is anger.

"What is it?" I ask her.

She shrugs, looking away. "I have no idea."

I did not mean to ask about the noise outside the carriage but about her strange demeanor. I sigh, deciding she is irritable from being left to her own company during the trip out of London.

"Let me find out."

I push the curtain aside from the window and spot Edmund standing near a bank of trees a few feet from the carriage. He is speaking to three men who bow their heads in a show of respect that seems decidedly out of place given the rough nature of their clothing and appearance. Their heads swivel in unison toward something that is blocked from my view. When they turn back to him, Edmund reaches out to shake their hands before they turn away, making their way out of my line of vision.

I sit back in the carriage, allowing the curtain to fall back over the window. We have agreed to keep our identities as secret as possible until we reach Altus, both for my protection and for the protection of Sonia and Luisa as keys.

The dull clop of horses' hooves starts up outside the carriage

and eventually recedes into the distance. It has been quiet for some time when Edmund at last opens the door. Stepping down into the sunlight, I am not surprised to see five horses and a bevy of supplies. What does surprise me is that our horses from Whitney Grove are among the new additions to our group.

"Sargent!" I race over to the ebony horse that has been my companion on so many rides. Wrapping my arms around his neck, I kiss his soft hair as he nuzzles at mine. Laughing, I turn back to Edmund. "However did you get him here?

He shrugs. "Miss Sorrensen told me about your . . . er . . . holiday home. She thought the journey might be easier with familiar mounts."

I look over at Sonia, happily stroking her own horse, and smile in thanks.

Edmund pulls a bag from the top of the carriage. "We should leave as quickly as possible. It would not be wise to stand by the side of the road for long." He hands me the bag. "But first, I imagine you would like to change."

Getting Luisa to don the breeches takes some doing. Though an excellent horsewoman, she was not in London with Sonia and me when we began riding in men's clothing. She argues with us for at least twenty minutes before finally agreeing. Even then, her grumbling is clearly heard as Sonia and I wait outside the carriage, already changed and trying desperately not to look at each other for fear we will burst into uncontrollable laughter.

Luisa finally emerges, holding herself stiffly as she adjusts the suspenders that hold up her breeches. She lifts her chin to the sky and walks haughtily past us toward the waiting horses. Sonia clears her throat, and I know she is stifling a giggle as Edmund hands us the reins to the horses we will be riding through the wood to Altus. He has already strapped our supplies to the horses' haunches. There is nothing to do but prepare to ride.

Still, I stop short of mounting Sargent. It is all well and good for the food, water, and blankets to be transported on the backs of the horses, but there is one thing I must carry myself. Opening the saddlebag on Sargent's flank, I dig around until I find my bow and the knapsack containing my arrows and Mother's dagger. That the knife was once used by Alice to undo the spell of protection my mother cast in my chamber does nothing to dim the comfort it gives me. It was my mother's long before Alice took possession of it.

Now it is mine.

As for the bow, there is no telling if I will have cause to use it, but I have not practiced with the targets at Whitney Grove only to leave our safety to Edmund. I sling the bow across my back and knot the knapsack across my body so that its contents are within quick and easy reach.

"Everything all right?" Edmund, already atop his mount, eyes the knapsack.

"Perfect, thank you." Feeling safer already, I lift myself onto Sargent's saddle.

"What of the carriage?" Luisa asks, turning her horse away from it to follow Edmund.

His voice, coming from up ahead of us, is muffled. "Someone will be along for it later. It will be returned to Milthorpe Manor."

Luisa's brow furrows, and she twists in the seat of her saddle as she looks back. "But... one of my bags is still atop it!"

"Not to worry, Miss Torelli." It is clear from Edmund's tone that he does not expect an argument. "As with the carriage, your extra bag will be returned to Milthorpe Manor where it belongs."

"But..." Luisa practically sputters with indignation, looking from me to Sonia before finally accepting the futility of any debate. When she settles back into the saddle, refocusing on Edmund's back in front of her, the arrows she shoots him are as real as if she were drawing back the string of a bow.

Behind her back, Sonia grins my way as we follow Edmund to the trees bordering the forest. I enjoy the moment of good humor, even at Luisa's expense, for as we leave the brightly lit clearing for the mysterious shade of the wood, I somehow know that from this moment forward, the journey to Altus will be anything but pleasant.

7

"Ugh! I may never sit comfortably again!" Sonia lowers herself carefully onto the rock next to me.

I know just what she means. Riding at our own leisure could not have prepared us for six solid hours atop a horse.

"Yes, well, I imagine we'll get used to it after a few days." I mean to smile but the pain I feel at the rear of my breeches makes me sure it is more of a grimace.

It was a strange day. A day in which we rode silently, hypnotized, it seemed, by the quiet of the woods and the rocking of our horses. Sonia, Luisa, and I rode at the back while Edmund remained at the front by necessity; only he knows where we are going.

Looking over at him, nearly finished setting up the two tents that will be our shelter for the night, I cannot help but wonder at his energy. Though I don't know Edmund's age, he has been a fixture in my life since I was a babe and he seemed fatherly even then. Yet he sat uncomplainingly atop his mount through an excruciatingly long day of riding.

Scanning the camp, my eyes come to rest on Luisa, sitting alone with her eyes closed and her back against a tree. I would like to spend a few moments talking with her, but I cannot tell whether she is asleep and am reluctant to disturb her.

When my gaze comes back to rest on Sonia, she appears close to slumber as well.

"If I do not get moving I fear I will never move again," I tell her. "I'm going to help set up camp."

I feel badly for poor Edmund, stuck in the forest with only three girls for help and companionship. I resolve to help him as much as possible during our journey.

"I'll be along in a minute." Sonia's words are nearly slurred with exhaustion.

She slides to the ground and cradles her head in her arms, resting them on the rock. She is asleep before I have walked five feet.

Making my way to Edmund, I seek a task, any task, that will keep me busy and in motion. He is happy to oblige and hands me some potatoes and a small knife, though I have never prepared so much as a piece of toast. Every potato I have seen up close has been baked, boiled, or mashed. I finally decide they will not prepare themselves and begin peeling and cutting. It turns out that even something as simple as cutting a potato requires a measure of skill, and after three near misses with the knife, I begin to get a handle on the process.

A few hours later, I have learned to cook over a campfire and have even attempted to wash the dinner dishes with a tired, quiet Luisa in the river a short distance from our camp. My own near-drowning and Henry's death have instilled in me an almost primitive fear of moving water, and I stay near the bank despite the river's meandering current.

It is dark and late, though I have no sure way of knowing the time, when Sonia and Luisa head to our shared tent to change for bed. Warming myself by the fire next to Edmund, I feel peaceful and safe, and I know his presence is a good portion of the reason. I turn to him, watching the firelight flicker over his face.

"Thank you, Edmund." My voice sounds louder than usual among the quiet of the trees.

He looks over at me, his face younger in the glow of the fire. "For what, Miss?"

I shrug. "For coming. For watching over me."

He nods. "In times like these..." He hesitates, looking into the darkness of the forest as if he can see clearly the danger that lies ahead. "In times like these you must have those most trusted at your side." He looks back at me. "I like to think I am at the top of that list."

I smile at him. "That is most true. You are family, Edmund, as much a part of me as Aunt Virginia and, well..." I cannot bear to speak Henry's name to Edmund. To Edmund who loved and cared for him as his own son. Who bore his loss with silent tears and gave me none of the recrimination I deserved after Henry's death.

His eyes glaze over as he continues to stare into the night, remembering the thing neither of us wishes to remember. "The loss of Henry nearly undid me. After, when you left...well, it seemed there was almost no cause to go on living." He meets my eyes. I see the pain there as fresh as if I were looking at him the day after Henry's funeral when he took me to say goodbye to James. "It was Alice who made me come with Virginia to London."

"Alice?" I cannot imagine my sister sending help my way.

He nods slowly. "She retreated after you left. I didn't see her for days, and when I finally did, I knew she was lost. Lost to the Otherworlds."

"And then?" I prompt.

"When I saw the look of her, her soul becoming blacker by the day, I knew you would need every possible ally. She may be an ocean away, but make no mistake about it." He pauses and looks into my eyes. "She may as well be standing here with us now. And she is every bit the threat she was when you were under the same roof. Probably more given her desperation."

I allow the words to settle between us, instinctively running my fingers over the raised mark on my wrist as I try to fathom a world in which my sister, my twin, has grown more evil in my absence. Was it not enough that she pushed Henry into the river? That she exposed me to the Souls and their power by reversing Mother's spell of protection? But even these thoughts, these thoughts I hardly have the will to contemplate, do not prepare me for what Edmund says next.

"And then there is the matter of James Douglas," Edmund says.

My head snaps up. "James? What of him?"

Edmund inspects his hands as if he has never seen them before, and I know he does not want to say the thing he will say next. "Alice has been . . . friendly with Mr. Douglas in your absence."

"Friendly?" I can hardly choke out the word. "What do you mean?"

"She calls on him at the bookstore . . . invites him to tea."

"And he welcomes her attention?" I cannot bear the idea, though I have already resigned myself to the futility in clinging to thoughts of James when the prophecy is still no closer to an end.

Edmund sighs. "That might be reading too much into it." His voice is kind. "Mr. Douglas was shocked by your sudden departure. I think he's quite lonely, and Alice . . . well, Alice looks like you. She's your twin. Perhaps James only seeks to remind himself of you in your absence."

My heart beats too quickly in my chest. I am half surprised that Edmund doesn't hear it in the quiet of the woods. I stand up, feeling as if I may be ill. "I . . . I believe I'll go to bed now, Edmund."

He looks up at me, blinking in the dim flickering light. "Have I upset you?"

I shake my head, willing my voice steady. "Not at all. I am too far away to stake any claim on James."

Edmund nods, his face creased with worry. "Your father and I were always honest with each other, and though you are a member of the fairer sex, I somehow imagine that you expect the very same thing."

"It is fine. *I* am fine. I couldn't agree more; we must be honest, even when it is painful." I put a hand on his shoulder. "I'm glad you're here. Good night, Edmund."

His words find me as I turn to leave. "Good night."

I do not look back. And as I make my way to the tent, it is not the prophecy or my sister I see but the fathomless blue of James Douglas's eyes.

I do not expect to travel the Plane our first night in the woods. I am tired. Exhausted, really. I have no desire for anything but the dreamless sleep that becomes ever rarer as I am drawn deeper into the prophecy.

Yet travel I do, awakening to the now familiar sensation of being in a dream that is more than a dream.

I do not have the sense of being summoned, exactly. That is something I have come to *feel* when it happens—a calling of sorts that tells me someone is waiting in the Otherworlds just for me.

This is different.

I know there is a reason I am in the Otherworlds. I know there is something I am meant to see or realize, but my destination and purpose seems controlled by something other than a simple

being. At times like these, it seems that the universe itself draws me across the realm of the Otherworlds toward a revelation that is no less urgent for my ignorance of its purpose.

I am in the world most closely linked to ours. The one in which everything looks the same. The one in which I can sometimes see those I know and love, can sometimes see my world as it exists but with the finest of veils between the physical version and the mystical one that exists in the Otherworlds of the Plane.

I am flying over a wood I know instinctually to be the one in which my body lies sleeping—the one in which we have traveled on horseback. It is dense with trees, and I fly fast enough over the verdant foliage that it appears as a soft, green carpet beneath my body.

At first, I see nothing under the thick canopy of leaves between the sky in which I fly and the ground beneath the trees, but soon, something moves beneath me, first one direction and then another. It is ethereal. An apparition flitting among the trees. I think it an animal, but it travels so fast I cannot imagine how a simple forest creature could seem to occupy every corner of the wood all at once.

Then I hear the breathing.

It is heavy, very nearly labored save for the fact that it does not sound human. It closes in from every direction, and though I cannot name the thing that gives chase, the fact that it appears beneath me does nothing to ease my fear. I know well that the laws of the Otherworlds do not follow our own. I know just as well that my fear is not to be ignored. It has saved me more than once.

The creature draws closer, its breath coming from nowhere and everywhere all at once. There are no landmarks in the forest underneath my flying body. Only mile after mile of trees broken by the occasional small clearing. Even still, I know I am close to safety. I feel the pull of the astral cord. It whispers, *You are almost there*. If I fly just a little longer, I am certain I will return to the body that is mine.

It is not long before I see the clearing ahead, a faint curl of smoke drifting upward from the cooling campfire, our two tents side by side and not far from the horses tied to the trees near the edge of the campsite. I head for the larger tent, knowing it is mine and that Sonia and Luisa are probably sleeping soundly within the shelter of its thin walls. The threatening breathing is still there, but I do not think the creature will catch me. It is not the capture of my soul that has called me to the Plane this night.

Not an imminent threat, but a warning.

I drop into my body effortlessly, without the harsh surprise that accompanied my first travels, and awaken immediately. It takes me a while to settle the racing of my heart, but even then, I cannot sleep. I do not know whether it is my imagination or simply a result of my return from the Plane, but I believe I hear things moving about the trees outside the tent. A rustling, a shifting, a careful stepping over the leafy forest floor.

I look at Sonia and Luisa, still sleeping peacefully, and think I must be going mad.

8

When I emerge from the tent the next morning, sleepy-eyed and groggy, it is to a murky haze that blankets every inch of the campsite. The air is heavy with mist, and it is impossible to see more than a foot away. The horses can be heard whinnying and my friends can be heard speaking to one another, but it all comes as if beneath a thick layer of wool. I feel very alone, though I know the others are not as far away as they sound.

We manage a hasty breakfast and begin breaking camp. Having helped Edmund pack the food and cooking supplies, I head to the tent to help Sonia and Luisa with the blankets. When I get there, Luisa is stuffing articles of clothing into the satchel lying on the ground.

She looks up as I approach. "We will be lucky to see one another in this fog, to say nothing of finding our way through the forest."

I hear an undercurrent of tension in her words, though her face remains impassive.

"We can only hope it doesn't rain." I refuse to ponder the unpleasantness of crossing the forest through not only heavy fog but torrential rain. "Where is Sonia?"

Luisa waves her hand in the direction of the woods without looking up from the satchel. "Attending to personal matters."

"I thought we agreed to accompany one another when we had to leave the camp."

"I offered to go with her, even insisted, but she said she had an excellent sense of direction and would return well before we departed." She pauses, and her next words are spoken with sarcasm under her breath. "Though I imagine if *you* had offered she would have accepted without hesitation."

I tip my head. "Whatever do you mean?"

She continues packing with fervor, avoiding my eyes. "I *mean* you and Sonia have been together for months while I have been stuck in New York with the ninnies at Wycliffe."

Jealousy is evident in her voice, and my heart softens. I drop next to her on the ground, touching her arm. "Luisa."

She continues as if she doesn't hear me. "It's natural that you and she should become close."

"Luisa." This time my voice is more forceful, and she stops her constant motion, finally meeting my eyes. "I'm sorry you could not be here with Sonia and me. We would have liked nothing more. Things are never the same without you. But you must know that eight months apart could not change

the friendship we share. The friendship we *all* share. Nothing could ever change that."

She looks at me in silence a moment before leaning in to embrace me. "I'm sorry, Lia. I'm being foolish, aren't I? I suppose I've let this worry me far too long."

I feel a moment's sadness for all that Luisa has missed. She is right. While Sonia and I have been in London unsupervised, riding horses and attending events with those of the Society, she has been trapped amid the same intolerance and small-minded thinking I once longed to escape.

I pull back and smile at her. "Now, let me help you pack."

She favors me with a brilliant smile, the kind that is all Luisa, and hands me some of the things lying on the ground.

With both of us at work, packing the tent and its contents goes quickly. And still, Sonia has not returned. A seed of worry takes root in my stomach, and I vow to go looking for her if she is not back by the time the horses are ready to leave. While we wait, Luisa and I carry the tents and packs to Edmund. We give him everything except my bow and knapsack. These I plan to keep with me every day until we arrive safely at Altus.

He straps everything else to the animals and has just loaded the last of the packs onto Sonia's horse when she finally stumbles through the trees at the edge of the campsite.

"Oh, I'm sorry to be so late!" She brushes leaves and twigs from her hair and breeches. "I suppose my navigational skills are not what I imagined! Have you been waiting long?"

I lift myself onto the back of my horse, stifling a wave of

irritation. "Not long, though I do think we should stick together while in the wood, don't you?"

Sonia nods. "Of course. I'm sorry if I've caused you worry." She makes her way to her horse.

Luisa is already atop her mount. She says nothing, whether out of annoyance or the impatience to embark, I do not know.

We follow Edmund out of the clearing that was our first campsite. No one speaks for a long while. The mist is suffocating. I feel nearly claustrophobic as it wraps its arms around us, and I have to stuff down occasional moments of panic. Moments when I feel as if I am being swallowed whole by something oppressive and all-encompassing.

My mind is oddly blank. I do not think about Alice. I do not even think about Edmund's confirmation that James and Alice have become friendly. I think of nothing except the backs of those who ride in front of me and my effort not to lose them in the fog.

By the time we break for lunch, I have become used to the long stretches of quiet. We move about, settling into scattered positions near a small stream as we fill our canteens with fresh water and chew bread that is already becoming stale. But we do it all in silence. And in the end, it is no matter, for there is nothing to see or speak of anyway.

Edmund feeds and waters the horses while Sonia, Luisa, and I enjoy the break from riding. Sonia lies on her back amid the grass near the stream, and Luisa, eyes closed and her face serene, leans against the trunk of a tree. I watch them both, feeling as if I am looking for something—something other than the missing pages.

But I do not have long to dwell on my feelings. Edmund soon gives the signal that it is time to get moving, and move we do, mounting our horses and making our way deeper into the forest.

"Lia? Do you think Luisa is all right?"

We have finally retired after a long day of riding, and Sonia's voice drifts to me from her side of the tent. Luisa is still sitting by the campfire—or she was when Sonia and I decided to go to bed.

I think back to the conversation Luisa and I had in the tent that morning and am not entirely certain she would like me to repeat her earlier jealousy. "Why do you ask?"

Sonia's brow furrows as she tries to find the right words. "It seems she has something on her mind. Don't you sense it?"

Hesitating, I try to think of a way to honor Luisa's confidence. "Perhaps, but we are on horseback all day long, and it is ever so hard to carry on a conversation while riding, especially in this infernal fog. Also..."

"Yes?" she prods.

"Well, you and I have been together for a year now, Sonia. Don't you think it possible that Luisa feels a bit left out?"

She chews her lower lip. I recognize the gesture as one she employs when pondering a question of significance and

choosing her reply carefully. "I suppose, but I wonder if it isn't something more."

"Such as?"

Sonia looks at the ceiling of the tent before turning her eyes to me in the darkness of the tent. "You don't think . . . well . . ."

"What? What is it?"

She sighs heavily. "I was just thinking about how Virginia once said the Souls would stop at nothing to get to you, to cause dissension among us."

She does not have to finish. I know what she means to imply. "Sonia." I say her name to give me time. "I know the Souls are out there. I do. But we cannot make anything of a distraction we all feel traveling through this gray and misty wood."

Her eyes find mine across the tent.

"All right?" I say again.

She nods. "All right, Lia."

Some time later, long after Sonia has gone quiet, Luisa returns to the tent. She moves about quietly, easing into her blankets without a sound. It would be simple to ask the questions brought to mind by Sonia's worry, and yet I say nothing. I do not want to give credence to Sonia's fear by voicing it aloud.

"We'll be making the changeover today." Edmund makes the declaration calmly from atop his horse as we depart the campsite.

"What changeover would that be?" Luisa asks.

Edmund stares into the mist, still as heavy as the woolen cloak about my shoulders. "The changeover to the world between ours and the Otherworlds. The world in which Altus lies."

I nod as if I understand precisely what he means. I do not, but that is not to say I dismiss his words, for I have felt change in the wind as well. I felt it as we journeyed on horseback deeper and deeper into the forest. I felt it as I awoke from my fitful slumber, still hearing the eerie, many-footed creatures as they stalked our tent in my dream. And I feel it as Edmund leads the way once again into the dense foliage of the forest.

The day wears on, and Sonia makes nervous conversation while Luisa remains mostly silent. Edmund finally locates a place to break for lunch and refill our canteens. As has become our habit, Edmund takes care of the horses while I pull food from the packs for an easy meal. We are eating in companionable silence when I hear it. No. That is not quite right. I *think* I hear it, but it is more a feeling, a whispered intuition that something is coming. At first, I think it is my imagination.

But then I look around.

Edmund, still as a statue, gazes into the trees with single-minded concentration. Even Sonia and Luisa are silent, eyes turned in the same direction.

I watch them and know that they, too, sense the creatures moving toward us through the forest. And this time, it is not a dream.

9

"Get up, mount your horses, and follow me. Do it now." Edmund speaks the words slowly through nearly clenched lips. "And do not stop for any reason until I say the word."

He is on his horse in an instant, his eyes remaining on the woods behind us as we follow suit. We are significantly slower and louder than Edmund in preparing to ride, though I have never thought of myself as particularly ponderous or loud.

When we are ready, Edmund turns his horse in the direction we have been traveling and takes off like a shot, without a word to his horse. Our own horses jump forward without prodding, a kind of secret communication telling them that time is of the essence even though none of us gives so much as a command.

We race through the forest at lightning speed. I have no idea which direction we travel or if we are still on course for

Altus, but Edmund does not hesitate as he leads us through the forest. It is difficult to say if it is because he is certain we are heading in the right direction or if it is because he so fears the thing stalking us that he no longer cares if we run astray.

We travel so quickly through the forest that I am forced to hunch low over Sargent's neck, and still, twigs catch in my hair and branches claw at my skin. I feel it all with a sort of detached observation. I know I am racing through the forest with only a bow and my mother's dagger for protection. Likely I am running for my life. But somehow I cannot feel the fear I know must be lurking somewhere beneath my skin.

I hear the river before I see it. It is a sound I will never forget. When it is, at last, in plain sight, I am relieved that Edmund pulls tightly on the reins, bringing his horse, and our assemblage, to a quick stop at the edge of the water.

He stares out over the river, and I bring my horse next to his, following his gaze.

"What do you think, Edmund? Will we be able to cross it?" I ask.

His chest rapidly rises and falls, the only indication of his exertion. "I think so."

"You think so?" My voice comes out louder and more shrill than I intend.

He shrugs. "There is no guarantee, but I think we can manage it. It's a pity, though."

His words are cryptic and make me feel that I have missed an important part of our conversation. "What's a pity?"

"That the river isn't deeper."

I shake my head. "Yes, but if it were too deep, we might not be able to cross it."

"True enough." He gathers the reins in his hand, preparing to urge his mount into the water. "But if we had trouble crossing it, so, too, might our pursuers. And if they are what I think they are, we should pray for the deepest body of water we can find."

Crossing the river is not as difficult as I fear. I do have a moment's anxiety as we reach the deepest portion, the water nearly reaching my knees, but Sargent surges forward against the current with a minimum of trouble.

I do not have time to speak further with Edmund about the thing giving chase through the woods. We travel nearly full speed for the rest of the day after crossing the river. There are no stops for food, water, or rest until the sun descends so far that it is difficult to see one another. It is clear that Edmund would like to continue, but no one asks whether we should keep going. The safety of our party must come first. It will do no good if one of us is injured along the way.

We work together to prepare food, care for the horses, and set up the tents. For the first time, Sonia and Luisa help as well, and I wonder if they, too, feel their nerves wound tight with fear. I assist Edmund with supper, fill a bucket of water for the horses from the nearby stream, and feed them each a few apples. And all the while, I listen. All the while, my eyes stray to the trees surrounding our campsite. All the while, I wait for

the creatures that chased us through the forest to burst into the clearing.

Sonia and Luisa sit silently by the fire after dinner. Their new silence with each other makes me uneasy, but there are more important concerns at the forefront of my mind. I wander over to Edmund, who is brushing down one of the horses where it is tied to the trees.

He nods as I approach and pick up an extra brush from the ground. I run it through the coarse gray fur of Sonia's horse and try to order the many questions running through my mind. It is not difficult to choose the one at the forefront.

"What is it, Edmund? The thing that follows us?"

He doesn't answer right away. He doesn't even look at me, and I am wondering whether he heard the question at all when he finally speaks, though not to answer my question. "I have not traveled these woods, have not been in this in-between world, in a very long time."

I stop brushing and tip my head at him. "Edmund. I would trust your suspicion over another's certainty in a matter such as this one."

He nods slowly, lifting his eyes to mine. "All right, then. I believe we are being followed by the Hellhounds, Samael's own demonic wolf pack."

I spend a moment trying to connect my knowledge of the mythological hellhounds with the possibility that they could be following us. "But... the Hellhounds aren't real, Edmund."

"Even so," he says, raising his eyebrows, "there are those

who would deny the existence of alternate worlds, demonic souls, and shape-shifters as well."

He is right, of course. If the measure of reality is based only on things in which the rest of the world believes, there is no Samael, no Lost Souls, no prophecy. Yet we know them to be real. It only makes sense, then, to accept the reality in which we find ourselves, however far that reality may be from everyone else's.

"What do they want?" I ask.

He places the brush gently on the ground before rising to stroke the horse's mane. "I can only guess that they want you. The Hellhounds are chosen disciples of Samael's army. Disciples who have made their way here beyond past Sisters. Past Gates. Samael knows that with every step through this wood, we draw closer to Altus. And drawing closer to Altus means drawing closer to the missing pages of the book that may help close his door to our world for all of eternity."

His explanation doesn't shock me as much as it should. It is not that I am unafraid, exactly, for even now I feel the blood race faster through my veins at the thought of meeting my death at the mercy of the Hellhounds. But I know that in order to get to the end of a thing, one must start at the beginning.

"All right. So how do we escape the Hounds? How do we beat them?"

He sighs. "I've never encountered them myself, but I have heard stories. I suppose that is all we have to go on." He pauses before continuing. "They are bigger and stronger than any

wolf in our world, you can be sure of that. Even so, they do occupy a living body, and that body is vulnerable to death just like any other. It takes more to kill one of the Hounds than it would take to kill something found in our world, but it can be done. The thing is…" He rubs the stubble that has sprouted on his cheeks in recent days. I hear it scratch the flat of his palm.

"Yes? What is it?"

"We don't know how many of them there are. If they travel in a large pack, well…we only have one rifle. I'm a good enough shot, but I'd rather not bet on me against a whole pack of demon hounds. I'd prefer to bet on another weakness."

"What sort of weakness?"

He looks around as if afraid to be overheard, though I cannot imagine who would be about other than those in our party. When he speaks, it is with a lowered voice. "I've heard it said that there is one thing in particular that gives the Hounds pause."

I remember Edmund's words just before we crossed the river: *If they are what I think they are, we should pray for the deepest body of water we can find.*

I meet his eyes as realization dawns. "Water. They are afraid of water."

He nods. "That's right. Well, I believe it is, though I'm not sure *afraid* is the right word. I'm not sure the Hounds are truly afraid of anything, but it is said that deep, swiftly moving water gives them pause. It is the death they most fear, and I have heard it said that when confronted with a dangerous

body of water, they are more likely to turn heel than to give chase."

Death by drowning, I think before remembering something else.

"But can they not shift into another form, say...a fish or a bird or something else that can better navigate the water? At least until they are out of harm?" It was Madame Berrier in New York who informed me of the Souls' ability to change shape. I have not been able to look at a crowd in the same way since.

Edmund shakes his head. "The Hounds, unlike those Souls who shift from shape to shape, live and die in their form. They are honored to sacrifice themselves to such a role, for there is only one appointment more coveted than that of the Hounds."

"Which appointment is that?"

Edmund reaches into his pocket for an old apple to feed the great gray horse. "Assignment to the Guard, Samael's personal contingent of Souls in the physical world. The Hounds secure only this in-between place on the way to Altus while the members of the Guard walk freely among our people and can shift at will in order to do Samael's bidding in our world. Though you should fear any Soul in human form, those of the Guard should be feared above all others. They are carefully chosen for their viciousness."

"But how will I know them? I already distrust any stranger, any animal, even, for fear it is one of the Souls in disguise. How am I to watch even more carefully for members of the Guard?" I can hardly fathom this new fear, this new threat.

"They have a mark. One that is present when they are in any human form." He studies the ground, avoiding my eyes.

"What kind of mark?"

He waves in the direction of my wrist though it is covered by the sleeve of my jacket. "A snake, like yours. Around their neck."

We stand in the darkness, each lost in our own thoughts. I have stopped petting the horse, and he nuzzles my hand to remind me of his presence. I stroke his face, trying not to picture something as horrifying as a particularly cruel legion of Souls with the hated mark branding them about their necks.

"How much time do you think we have?" I finally ask, turning my attention back to the Hounds.

"We rode hard today. Hard and fast. I tried to keep us on course for Altus while also winding us through the woods in a way that might throw them, even for awhile. And then there was the river... True enough it was not very deep, but even a river such as that could be intimidating for the Hounds. We can hope, at least, that they stopped to think before crossing it."

I try not to let my frustration and fear get the better of me. "How long?"

His shoulders sag. "A couple of days at most. And an extra one if we ride just as hard tomorrow and are very, very fortunate."

Before bed, I break the news of the Hounds to Sonia and Luisa. It is a testament to our strange situation that they do not seem surprised to hear about the threat to our safety, and we are all moody and quiet as we prepare for sleep. Edmund has insisted on guarding the camp, shotgun in hand, while Sonia, Luisa, and I sleep. I feel guilty as I lay in the relative comfort of our tent, but I know I cannot offer to help Edmund keep watch.

This night my greatest concern lies not with the Hellhounds but with my sister.

I have given much thought to meeting her on the Plane in the Otherworlds. In truth, the thought has lurked in the corners of my mind ever since Edmund told me about her and James. Meeting her would be dangerous, but so is the game she plays with James. And I've no doubt that it *is* a game.

All of Alice's actions revolve around her desire to bring Samael into our world so that she can assume the position of power she believes is rightfully hers. It is impossible not to be hurt by the news that she and James have grown close in my absence, but I cannot find an ounce of anger in the knowledge. Only fear for James and, if I am honest with myself, more than a twinge of jealousy.

And so I must meet Alice. There is no other way, really, to take the measure of her intentions. I might hear of it from Aunt Virginia or Edmund, but I am her twin. The Gate to her Guardian, however twisted our roles have become.

Traveling the Plane has always felt private, and I wait until I know Sonia and Luisa are asleep, their breath slowing into the steady rhythm that only accompanies deep slumber.

It does not take me as long as it once did, nor as much effort, to fall into the eerie half-sleep required for my soul to rise out of my body and enter the Plane. It is hard to remember a time when leaving my body felt frightening. Now, traveling the winding road through the Otherworlds, I feel only free.

I fly over the fields surrounding Birchwood, my feet nearly, but not quite, touching the ground. I am still grounded in the physical world and as such am far more vulnerable when flying the Plane. But the flying itself cannot be helped, for it is the swiftest way to travel. My surest guarantee of safety — though it is anything but sure — is to stay close to the ground, finish my business in the Otherworlds, and return to my own world with haste.

I follow the river past the house and toward the stables. The water rushes below, and it takes effort to avoid thinking of Henry. I have not seen him in the Otherworlds since his death, though I have not seen my parents there either since shortly before it. I have not attempted to contact them on the Plane. I know well the risk they face.

My mother and father have been running from the Souls since their respective deaths, refusing to cross into the Final World in case I should need their help. I can only hope that whichever world my parents occupy, it is one in which they are together with my brother.

There is a lake some distance past the stables, and it is here that I touch my feet to the wild grass surrounding the water. It has become more and more difficult to find locations near my childhood home that do not hold some horrifying memory, but this is still one place in which nothing bad has happened. Even on the Plane, I can feel the grass, green and springy, beneath my feet. It reminds me of the many times Alice and I stood barefoot in this very spot, taking turns throwing stones into the water to see who could throw them the farthest.

I gaze across the field in the direction of the house and am not surprised to see her coming. I learned long ago the power of thought on the Plane. One need only think of the person one wishes to see, and that person or being will feel the call.

Alice walks toward me from the direction of the stables, and I know even this small thing, the choice to walk rather

than fly, is no accident. It is Alice's way of reminding me that here in the Otherworlds, I am on her territory. That with the protection of the Souls, she may move at leisure while I must hurry and hide.

I watch my sister approach, taking note of her figure, slighter now than when I left. She still walks with characteristic confidence, that lift of chin and straightening of the back that has always been my sister's way of carrying herself, but when she stops in front of me, I am truly taken aback.

Her skin is as pale as the sheets that covered the furniture in the Dark Room after our mother's death. I would think Alice sickly if not for the hum of tension in her body. I feel it speeding just under her skin, as real as if it were crackling under my own. Her cheekbones jut harshly from her face, an echo to the gauntness of her figure, once feminine and now so slender that her clothes hang loosely from her frame.

But it is her eyes that make my stomach twist with fear and loss. The vibrant glimmer that was always uniquely Alice has been replaced with an unnatural shine. It speaks of the ancient prophecy that has us in its grip and to the evil of the Souls and their hold on my sister. It tells me she is lost.

She looks at me carefully, as if by looking closely enough she might see the changes in me and my newfound power. After a few moments, she smiles, and it is this that turns the sadness in my heart into something I almost cannot bear, for it is the old Alice smile, the one she used to save just for me. The one in which I can glimpse the sorrow lurking beneath her

nearly manic charm. It is disturbing to see my sister's shadow prowling beneath the lines of harsh cheekbones and hollow eyes.

I swallow hard and push away the memories. When I say her name, it feels foreign on my tongue. "Alice."

"Hello, Lia." Her voice is just as I remember. If not for the fact that we are standing in the Otherworlds, in a place few recognize as real and fewer still can occupy, I might think we are meeting for tea. "I felt you calling."

I nod. "I wanted to see you." It is the simple truth, though the reasons are far from simple.

She tips her head. "Why would you want to see me? I imagine you are quite busy at the moment." There is patronizing humor in her voice, as if my trip to Altus is an imaginary adventure crafted by a child.

"As are you, from what I hear."

Her eyes grow flinty with suppressed anger. "I suppose Aunt Virginia has been speaking of me, then?"

"Only giving me news of my sister. And even then, not telling me anything I cannot see for myself." I wonder if she will deny crossing into the physical world so that I could see her prowling the halls of Milthorpe Manor, but she does not.

"Ah, you must be speaking of my visit a few nights ago." She actually looks amused.

"Alice, the veil between the worlds is sacred. You are breaking the laws of the Plane, laws set by the Grigori. I have never doubted your power, your ability to see and do things

far beyond that which most Sisters can, but using the Plane to transport yourself to another place in the physical world is forbidden."

She laughs, and the sound travels through the fields of the Otherworldly Plane. "Forbidden? Well, you know what they say: like mother like daughter." The bitterness in her voice is palpable. I feel the heat of it on my face.

"Mother knew she wouldn't be here to suffer the consequences of her actions." It is harder now to speak of my mother. I know firsthand the horror of being enslaved by the prophecy, and it is difficult to blame her for escaping it, however horrifying her methods. "She did what she did only to protect her child, as any mother would. Surely you see the difference between her motivation and yours?"

Alice's face hardens further. "Mother's actions, whatever her motivation, were also a violation of the Grigori's laws. She altered the course of the prophecy by casting the spell of protection around you. I can hardly congratulate her for violating an ancient law just before killing herself to avoid the consequences."

It is not easy to keep my temper in hand, but talk of our mother will get us nowhere. There are more immediate things with which I must concern myself.

"Edmund tells me you have been seeing James."

The smile, sinister and sly, creeps to the corners of her mouth. "Well, the Douglases *are* dear friends of the family. And James has always taken an interest in Father's library, as you well know."

"Don't toy with me, Alice. Edmund says you have become friendly, that you spend time with James...invite him to tea."

She shrugs. "What of it? James was saddened by your departure. Isn't it only right to offer him friendship in the wake of his loss? Or is only one Milthorpe sister good enough for James Douglas?"

I have to swallow hard before answering. Even now, it is impossible to imagine James with anyone but me.

"Alice...You know well my feelings for James. Even in the prophecy, there are things...sacred things that must not be trifled with. Henry was one of those things." I choke out the words feeling as if they cut my throat to pieces. "James is another. An innocent. He has done nothing to harm you—or to harm anyone. I would ask you as one sister to another to leave him alone."

Her face grows impassive. It takes on a familiar stillness, and I remember a time when I could watch Alice for what seemed like hours and never see a flicker of emotion pass over her fine features. For one naive moment I believe she might consider my appeal. But just as quickly I see the anger darken her eyes. Worse than anger, worse than ambivalence, I see the pleasure she takes in holding the power to harm another.

I see it and know my request will have no effect. It will instead be taken as a challenge, a gauntlet Alice will not be able to ignore. I see it all in an instant and know I have done far more harm to James than if I had never spoken of

him at all. When Alice finally speaks, her words come as no surprise.

"I don't think James is any of your concern, Lia. In fact, I think it is safe to say you gave up the right to comment on his life when you abandoned him and fled to London with hardly a word."

I steady myself against her words, for she is right, of course. I did leave James, and I did so with no more than a letter, a passing mention of our love before boarding the train that would take me away from Birchwood.

Away from Birchwood and away from James.

And so there is nothing more to say. Alice will use any and all of her power to see that Samael can cross into our world, and she will do so with as little thought as she gives to making James a pawn in the game of the prophecy.

"Is that all, Lia?" Alice asks. "Because frankly, I'm growing tired of these conversations. Conversations in which you ask the same questions over and over again. Silly questions, really, with the simplest of answers: Because I want to. Because I can." She smiles, and it so pure and so without guile that I believe for a moment that I may actually be going mad. "Is there anything else?"

"No." I want it to sound strong, but it is just a whisper. "There is nothing else. You needn't worry. I will not seek you again. Not for a purpose such as this. Not to ask a simple question. The next time I seek you it will be to finish this once and for all."

She narrows her eyes, studying me closely, and this time there can be no mistake that it is she who attempts to take the measure of *my* power. "Just be certain you want to bring this to its conclusion," she says. "Because when you do, when it's all over for good, one of us will be dead."

She turns and walks away without another word. I stare after her until she is but a speck in the distance.

11

When I awaken the next morning, it is so dark that I think it is still night. But when I look around the tent, I see that Luisa is gone. Sonia is asleep, so I ease from beneath my blankets and make my way from the tent, trying to figure out the time. It is the sky that tells me it is morning, for though it is a deep midnight overhead, the color gradually lightens, becoming the palest of blues near the sunrise in the distance.

Even still, I know it must be very early. Edmund is awake, still at his post at the edge of camp. I approach him without trying to be quiet. I shouldn't like to have the shotgun pointed my way. I speak his name when I am still some distance away.

"Edmund?"

He turns his head without alarm. "It's early yet. What are you doing up?"

I stop in front of him, lowering myself to a neighboring boulder so that we are eye to eye. "I don't know. I woke up and saw that Luisa wasn't in the tent. Have you seen her?"

He shakes his head, genuine puzzlement in his eyes. "No. I haven't heard a thing."

I gaze out into the darkness of the forest. It is quite possible Luisa had personal needs that required attending. I say nothing to Edmund for fear of embarrassing us both, though I am confounded by the idea that Luisa would go into the woods alone after our discussion about Sonia doing the very same thing.

"Were there any problems last night?" I ask.

He shakes his head. "Not really. I heard some rustling, but whatever it was didn't sound large and didn't sound fast. Probably just the animals that make their home here."

"What are our chances, really, of escaping the Hounds?"

He does not respond right away, and I know he will not give me the answer I want, but one true and based on thought and calculation. "About fifty-fifty, I'd say, mostly because we're in the woods, and we're growing closer and closer to the sea. Smaller creeks and streams are already becoming bigger rivers. Our chances of hitting a large body of water are getting better by the day. There are only a couple of things that worry me."

I push down my panic at the thought of crossing a deep and swiftly moving river. "Such as?"

"If Samael has sent the Hounds after us, there are other

things he could send along the way. The Hounds may not be our only obstacle."

I prod him to continue. "All right. You said 'a couple of things.' What is the other one?"

He stares down at the ground before meeting my eyes. "A large body of water would be a blessing and a curse. Anything big enough to prevent the Hounds from crossing might well be big enough to keep us from crossing as well. But that is not really the worst of it, if you know what I'm getting at."

I nod. "If we find a river, we'll have no choice but to try and cross it to lose the Hounds. But we might not know if it's even possible until we are halfway across."

"That's right."

"It is not as if we have a choice, is it?" I continue without waiting for an answer. "We will just have to keep moving and brave the water when the time comes. Time and fortune have been on our side so far. We have to hope it will continue to be so."

"I suppose you're right." But he does not sound too sure.

I stand up and brush myself off. "I still have not heard Luisa return, but I think I know where she may be. I will see if I can find her. It's not far at all."

He nods. "I'll start breakfast. We should leave soon." I am already halfway to the tree line when his voice finds me. "Don't go too far. I'm fast, but if you run into trouble, it would be best if you were close."

He doesn't need to tell me. I know it is dangerous to leave his line of sight. I also know I could wait. Luisa will likely

return on her own at any moment. But the truth is that I am curious. Sonia's fears over Luisa's loyalty echo in my heart, however much I wish to discount them. Luisa's behavior of late *has* made me uneasy, and though I do not like to think of myself as spying, I feel a sense of responsibility to consider every possible scenario.

Even one in which Luisa is used by the Souls to sabotage our mission.

It grows darker as I leave the campsite. Even the dying fire and the moonlight in the clearing offered some illumination, but now I am surrounded on every side by trees. They rise far above my head, reaching toward the sky, dusky with the approaching morning.

It is easy to find the small path Sonia and I sought immediately upon arrival the night before. For obvious reasons, it has become habit to seek a private spot near every new site while Edmund makes camp. The path is surrounded by trees that provide shelter for the necessities that arise while making a journey such as ours. It leads to a small stream, and I hear the water rushing well before I arrive at its bank.

I do not want to announce my arrival, so I walk carefully along the path to the river, keeping an eye out for Luisa as I go. I do not see her along the way. In fact, I almost do not see her at all, even when I arrive at the clearing leading to the water.

It takes a moment for my eyes to adjust to the additional light afforded by the clearing, but when they do, Luisa becomes visible, bent over something near the river's edge. I tell myself she could simply be washing in preparation for the day ahead, but somehow I know that is not at all what she is doing.

I do not want to walk through the clearing where she will see me before I am able to observe her, so I creep along the tree line, trying to keep myself hidden as I make my way to the riverbank. It is my good fortune that the river rushes so loudly. The sound of it muffles my clumsy steps and the snapping of dried twigs as I make my way to the water's edge. Once there I have a better view of Luisa and see clearly what it is that she is doing.

Luisa gazes into one of the tin bowls we use to take meals. I see the water glimmer inside it, though not much else from where I am standing, and I understand immediately that she is scrying. It is not such an important revelation, really. It is true that we all made a pact long ago not to use our powers unless necessary to our goal of bringing an end to the prophecy, but it is very possible Luisa decided to scry in an effort to see the progress of the Hounds or to see any additional obstacles we might overcome.

It seems harmless. At first.

It is only as I stand there contemplating Luisa's actions further that I get the sense that something is not quite right. It takes me a moment to place it, and when I do I realize why it disturbs me so.

The simple truth is that we have not made, *do* not make, decisions with regard to the prophecy—our part in it and our powers—without consulting one another. Yet Luisa is scrying

in the night, having left our tent to brave the forest on her own even as the Hounds give chase. And she has done so without a word to any of us, which can only prompt the question: What is she hiding?

Our moods are as gray as the sky above while we pack our things for another day on horseback.

I woke Sonia after creeping back to the tent, and Luisa returned shortly afterward. I was not surprised when she used the excuse of tending to personal matters and not wanting to wake us as reason for her absence. Even when she left the tent to eat breakfast, I did not speak to Sonia of my morning excursion to spy on Luisa. I cannot say why, for of all the strange things that have happened in the past year, the newfound secretiveness between Sonia, Luisa, and me is the most disturbing of all.

Edmund rushes us through the breaking of camp. I sense the undercurrent of concern in his unusually terse orders, but when he grabs the shotgun, I begin to truly worry.

"Stay here," he says, turning without another word and disappearing into the woods.

We stand in shocked silence, staring after him. We have not been traveling long, but even in so few days we have established a kind of routine—a routine that involves waking in the morning, dressing and preparing for the day as quickly as possible, packing our individual supplies, and eating a quick

meal before mounting our horses and beginning the day's journey. Nowhere in that routine has Edmund ever departed for the forest with a shotgun in hand.

"What is he doing?" Sonia asks.

I shake my head. "I have no idea, but whatever it is, I'm certain it's entirely necessary."

Sonia and Luisa stand stock-still, eyes trained on the place where Edmund disappeared into the forest. As usual, I have patience for neither sitting nor standing, and I pace the clearing of our campsite, worrying about what Edmund is doing and wondering how long we should wait before going to look for him. Thankfully, I don't have to answer that question, for Edmund reenters the clearing a short time later. This time he is in a hurry.

"Mount up. Do it now." He walks directly to his horse without a glance at any of us. He is astride and ready to ride in seconds.

I do not question him. Edmund would not move so quickly nor bid us to do so if there was not cause. But Luisa is not as pliant.

"What is it, Edmund? Is something wrong?" she asks.

He speaks through gritted teeth. "With all due respect, Miss Torelli, there will be time enough for questions later. Now is the time to mount your horse."

Luisa places her hands on her hips. "I believe I have a right to know why there is a sudden rush to break camp."

Edmund sighs, rubbing a hand over his face. "The fact of

the matter is, the Hounds are close, and there is something else out there, as well."

My head whips up almost of its own volition. "What do you mean? What is it?"

"I don't know." He turns his horse toward the forest. "But whatever it is—*whoever* it is—is on horseback. And tracking us."

12

It is a long morning, silent save for the horses' hooves cutting a path across the forest floor. We speed through the trees, often so tightly packed there hardly seems to be a way through. I stay low, gripping Sargent's neck as the wind whips his fine black mane into my face and my own hair is ensnarled several times by low-hanging twigs.

There is little to do but think during the morning's journey. And there is much to think about: my sister and our meeting on the Plane, my fear for James, Sonia and Luisa and the distance that seems to be growing between us, our journey toward Altus, and the demonic Hounds giving chase.

But it is Luisa to whom my thoughts return again and again.

I want to deny the conclusion taking shape in my mind, but

the images replaying there make it more and more difficult. I see Luisa's face, set in the unfamiliar, almost angry expression she has worn almost every day since we departed London. I see her reentering the tent after her frequent and ill-explained disappearances. I see her crouching in the early morning light by the river, scrying in secret.

I've known, of course, that this was possible—that the Souls could, and likely would, seek to divide us. But I suppose I simply did not realize that it could happen like this. That it could be so insidious, a gradual separating of the bond that I have come to view as sacred, the bond between Sonia and Luisa and me—between two of the keys and myself, the Gate. Clearly, I have been naive.

The time will come for me to address Luisa's betrayal, however unwilling her part in it may be, but in this moment, as we race through the wood leading us closer and closer to Altus, I cannot afford the distraction. For now, I shall have to assume that anything Luisa knows, the Souls may know as well. And that means keeping as much as possible from her.

We stop only once to feed and water the horses. The distrust in the air is a palpable thing, a living, breathing entity. I pace the ground while Edmund sees to the horses and Sonia and Luisa rest against two trees near the stream. There is no conversation as we wait for the horses to cool down enough to continue. There are no questions about our plans for the day or our proximity to the ocean that will mean we are close to Altus.

My nerves are pulled taut with a building anxiety I began to

feel sometime during the morning's ride. It is an anxiety that has little to do with Luisa and everything to do with the thing chasing us through the wood. I have learned not to discount such feelings, on the Plane or in our world. They are usually informed by my newly heightened gifts and senses. I know the nagging, incessant plucking at my nerves for what it is—a warning of the swiftly approaching Hounds. In some dark corner of my mind I am certain I can hear their breathing as they approach.

When Edmund finally strides toward his horse and bids us to do the same, I cannot mount quickly enough. I pull up next to him and lower my voice so that the others, busy situating themselves, cannot hear.

"They are going to catch us, aren't they?"

He takes a deep breath and nods. "Today, if we don't find a river."

"And will we?" I ask the question quickly, aware that we only have so much time before the others are ready to ride.

He looks around, making certain of our privacy before lowering his voice to continue. "I have a map of sorts. It is an old one, but I don't believe this forest has changed in the past hundred years."

I am surprised. Edmund has not made mention of a map before now. "Is that how you have been guiding us?"

He nods. "My memory is not what it used to be, you see. I didn't want to tell anyone..." He looks around again in the direction of Sonia and Luisa. "I didn't want someone else to get ahold of it. The location of Altus has always been held in

the highest confidence. Very few know of its existence at all, and fewer still know how to reach it. Your father left me the map before his death to ensure that I could get you there if you ever needed safe haven. There are other... safeguards in place to keep out unwanted visitors, but nonetheless, I would hate to lead an enemy to its door."

I am hardly in a position to pass judgment on Edmund and his secret. I have more than a few of my own.

I nod. "All right, then. What of this map?"

"At first, I was leading you to Altus by the quickest way possible, but when I realized the Hounds were following, I started taking a more circuitous route."

"But... if the Hounds are following shouldn't we try to get to Altus *faster* rather than slower?"

He nods. "That is one way of looking at it, but even if we make good time, there is always the possibility that they will catch up to us. But the map... the map shows a large body of water, a river very wide, that may just help us lose them entirely. It is only slightly off our original course and is not far from the ocean where we are to meet the boat to Altus. If we can lose the Hounds at the river and make straight for the sea, we may be out of danger entirely. At least where the Hounds are concerned."

"Is it deep enough?"

He sighs and begins turning his horse, looking at me over his shoulder. "That's just the thing. We won't know until we get there, but it appears large on the map."

He shouts instructions to the rest of the group as I make for

my usual position in the line. I try not to think too hard about Edmund's revelation. It is impossible to know if we can outrun the Hounds, just as it is impossible to know if the river will be deep enough to leave them behind and just as it is impossible to know who follows on horseback somewhere in the dark woods behind us. It only makes sense to conserve my energy, mental and otherwise, for things in which I have a hand.

For now, all I can do is ride.

I would like to think we will outrun them, that the Hounds are far enough behind that their catching us is only a distant possibility, but it is not true. I know they grow closer and closer still, though we travel so swiftly that I cannot imagine how fast the Hounds must be that they are able to move even faster.

I know that Edmund feels it, too, for just a short time after leaving our resting place, he urges his horse on even faster. I hear him scream at the animal, and I hunch even lower over Sargent's neck, silently begging him to move faster though I know from his labored breathing that he has already been pushed too hard.

I did not have time to look at Edmund's map. I did not even have time to ask him how far we are from the river that he is counting on to be our saving grace. But as we ride farther and farther through the trees, as the sky grows duskier with the coming evening, I hope fervently that it is near and utter muttered pleas of assistance to any who might be listening—God, the Sisters, the Grigori.

But it is not enough. It is only seconds later, only seconds

after my hurried prayers, that I hear them coming in the trees right behind us. What moves through the forest is no simple animal. I hear howling screams and know immediately that a wolf or a dog would be a blessing compared to what follows us. It is not the growl of an animal but something much, much more terrifying.

Something inhuman.

Then there is the crashing. The beasts on our tail do not give chase with the light-footed grace of a forest animal. Instead, they beat ferociously through the foliage with pure power and strength. Limbs snap off trees as the creatures barrel toward us. Their footfalls are the sound of the sky itself splitting in two.

Luisa and Sonia do not look back but keep Edmund's pace with single-minded concentration. I focus on their backs and am running through the painfully short list of escape possibilities when I hear the unmistakable rushing of water. The path ahead brightens, first a little at a time and then all at once, and I know we are nearing the river.

"Don't stop. Please, don't stop," I whisper in Sargent's ear. A river like the one Edmund described would give any horse pause, and pausing is something we cannot afford.

We burst through a clearing, and I see it, a green jewel shimmering in the fading sunlight. Even as we break free of the trees and head for the water, the Hounds are so close I can smell them, a strange mixture of fur, sweat, and something like rot.

Luisa's horse runs into the river without hesitation followed by Luisa's, but Sonia's horse slows, coming to a stop near the edge of the water. I hear her urging the animal forward, pleading as if he can understand every word. It does no good. The great, gray beast stands stubbornly still.

There is only a moment—one moment in which everything moves both too slowly and too quickly—to decide what to do. It is an easy decision if only because there are so few options left.

Pulling my horse to a stop, I turn to face the Hounds.

At first, the clearing in front of me is empty. But I hear them coming, and I use the time to reach behind me, pulling the bow from across my back and grabbing an arrow from inside my knapsack. Threading the arrow and pulling it back in preparation for the Hounds is second nature, though all my practice at Whitney Grove could not prepare me for the beast that first crashes through the trees.

It is not what I expect. The creature is not black with red eyes as I imagined a Hound would be. No. Only its ears glow crimson, its fur glimmering white with the brilliance of fine cut glass. It is an eerie contrast, seeing such a beast—and a beast it is, standing nearly as tall as Sargent—covered with such virgin fur. I would almost be willing to brave my fear to stroke that shimmering fur if not for its emerald eyes. Eyes like mine. Like my mother's and my sister's. They call to me, a terrifying reminder that, though we may be on opposing sides, we are inexorably connected through the prophecy that binds us all.

I can hear the other beasts howling in the forest behind the Hound in front. I don't know how many will follow, but it is all I can do to try to eliminate as many as possible and hope to allow my friends more time to cross the river.

It is not easy to take aim. They are faster than any beast I have ever seen and their nearly translucent fur blends seamlessly into the surrounding mist. It is only the glow of their ears and those magnetic eyes that keep me from losing them in the fog completely.

Aiming carefully for the area I hope is the beast's chest, I try to find the pattern in his gait. Then I pull the bow tighter and let the arrow fly. It sails through the air, arcing gracefully over the clearing and hitting the Hound so suddenly that I am almost surprised to see him go down.

I am pulling the string back for another shot when something moves out of the corner of my eye and another pristine beast breaks through the tree line on my right. It veers into the clearing in front of me as my mind works at light speed, trying to figure my odds of hitting one more. Holding fast, I focus on the Hound in front of me. I am certain I can take him before he reaches me when yet another Hound turns into the clearing from the left.

And still many, many more can be heard howling in the woods behind these two.

My arms begin to shake as I hold my position... thinking, thinking... trying to decide what to do. A sudden crack sounds behind me to the left, and the Hound entering the clearing falls in an instant. Gunpowder scents the air, and I know without taking my eyes off the clearing that Edmund is covering me with his rifle.

"Lia! There isn't time! Get to the river *now.*"

Edmund's voice shakes my certainty. Still gripping my bow, I wheel Sargent to face the river, making a break for the water with as much speed as I can manage while clutching my bow. Edmund zips past me, heading for the middle of the river, but Sonia's horse still stalls at the bank. She struggles with the reins, trying to coax him into the water to no avail. He high-steps around the rocky ground, lifting and turning his head in response to Sonia's commands.

I do not have time to think. Not really. Racing toward the water, I stretch out a hand as I come up behind Sonia's horse. When I reach his flank, I slap with all my might.

At first, I don't know if it has worked, for my own horse speeds past Sonia and heads straight into the water. His hooves splash across the river bottom, but it is more a sensation than a sound for I cannot hear anything but the Hounds. Their howl is so close I believe I feel the heat of their breath on my back. I push Sargent farther into the river, praying he will not stop or turn around and head back to the bank.

But it is not Sargent that should worry me. He is willing and able to continue to the middle of the river. It is my own fear that rises suddenly within, starting at my feet, completely submerged in the river, and continuing up my legs and into my chest until my heart beats so madly I can no longer hear even the Hounds. My breath comes fast and shallow, but I do not feel the urge to flee. Instead, I pull hard on the reins, forcing Sargent to a stop so hard and fast that he nearly rears out of the water as Sonia whips past us into the river.

But I am rooted to Sargent, and Sargent, at my behest, is rooted to the riverbed. I am terrified into a kind of apathetic stillness, and in this moment, I would rather die at the hands of the Hounds than brave the river.

"It's time to go."

I turn toward the sound of the voice. When I do, Edmund is back at my side. I both wish he had continued to the other side of the river and love him for staying.

I have time to meet his gaze for only a second before a sound on the riverbank gets my attention. It is not the Hounds, but something else. Some*one* else, just beyond them. A caped figure astride a black horse positioned behind the Hounds, as if they are no more than hunting dogs.

This alone would be mystifying enough. But when the figure pushes back the hood of his cape, I am left with only more questions.

13

I try to register too many things at once: the Hounds entering the water though they are clearly hesitant, Edmund standing to my side and refusing to continue with the others, and Dimitri Markov calmly mounted atop his horse behind the Hounds at the riverbank.

None of it does anything to spur me forward.

"It is time to go, Lia." Edmund's voice is soft but firm, and even through my fear I register that he has used my given name for the first time in all the years I have known him. "They feel your fear. They're coming for you. There are too many for the rifle, and you're not close enough to the other side to hold them at bay."

His words make sense in some distant corner of my mind, but I still do not move. The Hounds splash carefully into the water, wetting first their paws and then continuing, albeit slowly, until they are submerged up to their bellies and standing only a few feet away from Edmund and me.

And still, I cannot move, cannot will myself to prompt Sargent forward though his muscles tense with the urge to flee. I know he feels the danger in the air every bit as much as I.

It is only as Dimitri makes a move toward the river, toward me, that I shake loose from my stupor, though still not enough to cause me to move. I am not the only one who pauses to watch his progress. The Hounds turn as well, their impressive snowy heads swiveling to face this new player in our drama. Dimitri stares them down, and for a moment I am sure there is some manner of unspoken communication between them.

The Hounds tense as Dimitri's sleek horse splashes through the shallowest water toward us. Their heads swing from side to side, alternately watching me and keeping track of Dimitri's progress without moving from their position. It is as if they know him, as if they are deferring to him out of some bizarre brand of respect. I can see the need in their eyes when they look at me, the desire to close the gap between us and take me while they can.

But theirs is a thirst that goes unquenched. They simply watch as Dimitri brings his horse alongside mine. The current becomes stronger as the sky darkens toward night, and I feel Sargent trying to keep a foothold on the rocky riverbed as Dimitri reaches out to take the reins from my freezing hands. He looks into my eyes, and I feel that we have known each other forever.

"It's all right. Just trust me, and I'll get you across." There is tenderness in his voice, as if something unspeakably intimate has passed between us since our meeting at the Society, though we have not seen each other once from that moment to this.

"I'm . . . I'm afraid." The words are out of my mouth before I have time to check them, and I hope that they are softer than I imagine. That perhaps Dimitri hasn't heard my cowardice over the roar of the river.

He nods. "I know." His eyes burn into mine. In them is a promise. "But I won't let anything happen to you."

I swallow hard, and somehow, I know that he will die before he sees me come to harm, though I cannot say why that should be when we don't know each other at all. Still, I nod without speaking and grab hold of the saddle.

Dimitri places one hand on my bow. "Here, let me help you with this."

I am surprised to see the bow still in my hands. Holding on to it is a habit. My fingers are so cold Dimitri can barely pry it from my hand, but after a moment, he finally manages to free it from my stiff fingers. He lifts it over my head, positioning it gently against my back.

"There you are. Now hold on tight." He presses my hand to the front of the saddle until my fingers grip the leather of their own volition.

In this one instance, I do not mind being spoken to as a child.

Dimitri meets Edmund's eyes and Edmund nods as if to

prompt us forward in front of him, but Dimitri shakes his head.

"You must go in front. You will not be under my protection otherwise." Edmund hesitates and Dimitri continues. "You have my word that nothing will happen to Lia."

Hearing Dimitri speak my name, Edmund nods, urging his horse forward into the deeper water as Dimitri gathers Sargent's reins, drawing my horse closer to his own mount.

"Hold on." It is the last thing he says to me before following Edmund farther into the river.

At first, Sargent must be pulled forward by Dimitri's strong hands, but as the horse finds it more and more difficult to maintain stability against the power of the current, he finally eases forward after Dimitri. I sense the animal's trepidation as he seeks to gain his footing by stepping carefully along the rocks at the bottom of the river.

I cling to the saddle with all my might. My fingers cramp, but I hardly notice. I try to focus on Edmund in front of us, and when I look beyond him, I see Sonia and Luisa astride their horses on the opposite bank of the river. My spirits lift as I realize they have made it.

If they have made it, so can we.

But I do not have time to hope. All at once, Sargent falters, slipping and struggling to regain a foothold on the slippery river bottom. Panic surges through me as I slide off his back, the water closing in around my thighs as I hold desperately to the saddle. It is not the water itself that gives rise to terror, but the sound of it that threatens my last vestige of sanity.

That mad roar, that frenzied race of water over rocks. It is the sound of my brother's death. The sound of my own near death trying in vain to save him.

I fight the urge to scream, but when I look at Dimitri, his eyes are as steely as the sky above us. He is not afraid, and in his steadfast belief that we will make it across the river, I find my own belief.

I hold on tighter. "Come on, Sargent. We're almost there. Don't give up on me now."

He doesn't. He seems to understand, for his legs straighten and he lifts himself farther out of the water, plodding forward after Dimitri and his horse as if there was never any question of his doing so. It is only seconds later that the water level begins to drop, revealing first my sodden thighs, encased in the wet wool of my breeches, and then my calves. Soon enough, we are rising out of the depths of the river, and my feet are out of the water completely as Dimitri leads Sargent to the others waiting a few feet beyond the bank.

"Oh, my goodness, Lia!" Luisa dismounts and is on the ground in an instant. She rushes toward me, her shirt and pants as wet as those clinging to my own body. "Are you all right? I was so frightened!"

Sonia brings her horse over to mine, reaching over for one of my icy hands. "I didn't know if you were going to make it!"

For a moment, all the suspicion of previous days drops away. For a moment, we are three friends as we have been since the prophecy first shrouded us in its murky secrets.

Edmund leads his horse over to us at a trot. He eyes Dimitri

with something like admiration. "I didn't expect you for two days yet, but I must say I'm glad you were early."

My brain is fuzzy about the edges, and I only dimly register Edmund's words and the fact that he knows Dimitri and was somehow expecting him. A clattering rises out of the quiet. I do not realize at first that it is coming from my mouth, but soon my teeth chatter together so noisily that I can hear them even above the river.

"She's cold and in shock," Dimitri says.

"Let's get off this riverbank then." Edmund's eyes drift to the Hounds, still standing in the water as if they might make a run at us any moment. "I don't like the look of them."

Dimitri follows Edmund's gaze to the Hounds before turning back to us. "They will not follow us, but that doesn't mean we are free from danger. It would be wise to make camp for the night and regroup."

Edmund turns and heads back to the front of the group. We fall into line out of habit, though Dimitri still leads Sargent by the reins. I do not have the energy to insist that I can manage fine on my own. In all honesty, I am relieved to let someone else take the lead for a while.

The forest begins again not far from the bank of the river. As we enter the darkness of the woods, I dare to glance back. I can see the Hounds over Edmund's shoulder, still standing in the water where we left them. Their green eyes find mine even across the expanse of rushing water, even through the smoky twilight. They are the last things I see before we disappear into the woods once again.

“Drink this.” Dimitri holds a tin cup toward me and keeps me company while the others change out of their wet clothes.

I reach a hand out of the blanket wrapped around my shoulders to take the cup from him. “Thank you.”

It is bad tea, both leafy and weak. I have become used to it over the previous days, and after the cold of the river and the shock of the Hounds, I hardly notice its bitter heat. I hold the cup with both hands, sipping from it as I try to transfer its warmth to my still-cold hands.

Dimitri settles onto the log next to me, stretching his hands toward the fire Edmund built just after choosing this as our camp for the night.

“Are you all right, Lia?” My name sounds natural and right coming off his tongue.

“I think so. Just very cold.” I swallow hard, trying and failing to block from my mind my panic at the river. “I don’t know what happened back there. I just . . . I couldn’t move.”

“Lia.”

I do not want to turn at the sound of my name, but my eyes are drawn inexorably to his. His voice is a command I cannot ignore, though it is as gentle as the mist that hangs in the woods as night descends.

“I know what happened,” he continues, “and I don’t blame you.”

There is understanding in his eyes. It confuses and, yes, even

angers me. I put the cup in the dirt next to me. "What, exactly, do you know about me? And how have you come to know it?"

His expression softens. "I know about your brother. I know he died in the river, and I know you were there."

Tears sting my eyes, and I jump to my feet, walking somewhat unsteadily to the edge of the campsite to compose myself. When I think I can speak without a shaking voice, I stalk back to Dimitri, letting all the anger and frustration of the past weeks, no, the past months, flow through every crevice of my body.

"What can *you* know of my brother? What can you know of his death and my place in it?" I am unable to keep the bitterness from pouring out of my mouth. I have lost track of my own questions, but getting answers is no longer the point. "You know nothing of me. Nothing! And you have no right! No right to speak of my brother."

My own mention of Henry dissolves my anger in an instant, and I am suddenly back to fighting the sadness, the overwhelming, all-consuming despair that nearly caused me to fling myself from the cliff near Birchwood before coming to London. All at once, I can do little more than stand in front of Dimitri, still clutching the blanket around my shoulders as my breath comes hard and fast on the heels of my tirade.

He stands and walks over to me, stopping only when he is very close. Too close.

His words, when they come, are colored with tenderness. "I know more than you think. About the prophecy. About your life before London. About you, Lia."

For a moment, I think I will become lost in his eyes. I think I will drown and drown in the sea of them until I no longer wish to find my way home. But then his words drift back to me: *I know more than you think. About the prophecy*...

The prophecy. He knows about the prophecy.

"Wait a minute." I step back. I am breathing hard, though this time from something far more complex than anger. "How can you know about the prophecy? Who, exactly, *are* you?"

14

Dimitri runs his fingers through his dark hair, and for a moment, he looks almost a boy. His face is grim as he gestures to the log near our feet. "You should probably sit down."

"I would like to know who you are before I sit down, if you don't mind." I fold my arms across my chest.

He chuckles, and I throw him a look meant to stop his laughter in its tracks. It does not quite do its job. Not at first.

He sighs. "If I assure you that I am on your side, that I am here only to protect you, will you sit and let me explain?"

I try to find malice or dishonesty in his face, his eyes, but there is only truth.

I nod and sit. He did, after all, save me from the Hounds. And although I have not had the opportunity to speak to Edmund, it's clear that he and Dimitri are somehow acquainted.

Dimitri lowers himself next to me. He spends a moment

staring into the fire before speaking. "I am not supposed to be here at all," he says. "I have... crossed boundaries to be here. Sacred boundaries that are not meant to be crossed."

I am cold and tired, but I try to quell my frustration. "Why don't you tell me everything?"

He looks up, meeting my eyes. "I am a member of the Grigori."

"The Grigori? But I thought the Grigori's purpose is to create and enforce the laws of the Otherworlds."

"It is," he says simply.

I shrug, not understanding. "Then why are you here?"

"I was sent to keep watch over you as you seek the missing pages and the other keys to the prophecy."

"To keep watch over me? You mean to protect me?"

He takes a deep breath. "Not exactly."

Now I am worried. "Why don't you explain *exactly* what you were sent to do?"

"I was sent to ensure that you were not using prohibited magic in your quest to end the prophecy." He says it all at once, and it only takes me a moment to realize why it took him so long to say such a simple thing.

"You were sent to *spy* on me?"

He does, at least, have the grace to look chagrined. "Lia, you must understand. The prophecy has been unfolding for centuries, but never has someone come so close to finding its end. Never have so many in the Otherworlds believed that the end may really be near. That Samael may finally end his rule in that world and, potentially, in this one.

"The Grigori wish more than anyone to see the prophecy brought to its end, to see peace in the Otherworlds. But things have gotten out of hand. And someone must try to keep them *in* hand as much as possible. That has always been the task of the Grigori."

My fury boils over as I think of my sister. "And while I am under your supervision, what of Alice? Who is watching her while she runs roughshod over the laws of the Grigori?"

"We have tried watching Alice." I hear the defeat in his voice. "It has done no good. Where even the Souls acknowledge the power of the Grigori, at least outwardly, Alice does not. She does not care for the laws of the Otherworlds, nor does she recognize our authority. Worse, she is powerful enough that she may travel the Plane at will while avoiding detection. Though I hate to admit it, she is beyond our control. I believe even the Souls are challenged to manage her."

"Then why do they work in concert with her? Why do they ally themselves with her at all?"

He raises his palms in a gesture of resignation. "Because they cannot have you. Alice is their most powerful ally in the physical world, even more powerful than the many Souls who are waiting here for Samael's arrival, because she is connected to you. Through her, they hold out hope of reaching you."

I shake my head. "But... Alice holds no sway over me. We are, for all intents and purposes, enemies."

He tips his head. "Yet isn't it true that you come if she summons you? That *she* comes if you summon her? Isn't it true that you see her spirit form in the night when she travels the

Plane? That she has seen you in the night as well, though you are thousands of miles apart?"

"Yes, but that was not my intention. I did not seek to show myself to Alice, to cross the boundaries of the Otherworlds. I was as surprised as anyone when she looked up from her ritual and saw me there."

"I know. We all know. It is Alice who defies the laws of the Otherworlds by using her powers as a Spellcaster. But that is not the point, is it? At least not in this conversation?" He reaches out to take one of my hands. "The point is, you *are* connected, Lia. You share the inextricable bond of sisters, twins, and are further linked through the prophecy.

"The Souls know this. They cannot know for certain that Alice will give them any advantage in their quest to see Samael enter the physical world through the Gate. Through *you*, Lia. But neither can they afford to do away with her. She has been a great help to them so far. She has been their eyes and ears in the physical world. And then there is the matter of the missing pages."

I have been lulled into a state of near tranquility through nothing more than the warmth of the fire and the gentle pressure of Dimitri's hand over mine. But his mention of the missing pages causes me to shake the fog from my mind.

"The pages? What have they to do with Alice, beyond her not wanting me to find them, I mean?"

He looks surprised. "Well, I mean...No one knows for certain what they entail. They were hidden long ago for safe-

keeping. We know they provide details about ending the prophecy, and one can only assume that whatever details they provide involve both the Guardian *and* the Gate. I assume the Souls would rather keep Alice, even in her current unbridled state, than risk relinquishing their hold and needing her later."

I turn my gaze to the fire, mulling over Dimitri's words in the ensuing silence. There are questions. I feel them gliding like wraiths through my consciousness, but the shock of the Hounds and the river, together with what Dimitri has said, makes everything difficult to grasp. There is only one thing that stands out in my mind. One thing that fights its way up from the depths of my twisted thoughts.

"You said you have crossed boundaries to be here. *Boundaries that shouldn't be crossed.* What did you mean?"

He sighs. When I look over at him, his face is turned to the fire. I suppose it is his turn to try to find answers within its flames. He looks down at his hands as he begins talking.

"It is not the place of the Grigori to become involved in either side of the prophecy. I was only supposed to observe you from afar, and I was able to do that for some time using the Plane. Only..."

"Yes?" I prompt.

He looks up from his hands, turning his dark eyes on me. They glitter like polished ebony in the night. "I could not stop myself from intervening. From the first moment I saw you, I felt... something."

I raise my eyebrows, finding a moment's humor in his choice of words. "*Something?*"

A smile touches the corners of his mouth. "I am drawn to you, Lia. I'm not sure why, but I could not leave you to face the Hounds without assistance."

My heart beats giddily inside my chest. "That is very kind. But what consequences will you face for defying the laws of the Grigori? Or are your laws only for mortals and those of the Otherworlds?"

His face grows serious again. "The laws are for everyone, myself included. In fact, even more so for me." I do not have time to question him on the point before he continues. "I *will* face consequences, but whatever they are, they will be less difficult for me to bear than the thought of leaving you to traverse this wood without safe escort."

He offers the declaration simply, as if there is nothing unusual in feeling such concern after so short a time. But the oddest thing of all is my own acceptance, for even as he says it, it seems somehow natural that we should be together in the woods leading to Altus. As if, like Edmund, I was waiting for Dimitri to arrive all along.

❦

The two hours before bed are spent eating, cleaning up, and caring for the horses, though I am not permitted to help in any way. As we eat, Dimitri provides the group with an abbreviated explanation of his presence. As far as Sonia and

Luisa know, Dimitri is a member of the Grigori sent to aid Edmund in escorting us to Altus. He does not expand upon his feelings for me or the possible consequences he will face for assisting us.

When I enter the tent after saying good night to Edmund and Dimitri, the air is unusually heavy with tension. I have become used to the strained silences between Luisa and Sonia—between all of us—but this time I can almost feel the weight of words that were either spoken in my absence or are weightier for having not been spoken at all.

Yet even our newfound awkwardness with one another cannot stifle the curiosity over Dimitri's sudden appearance.

Sonia's whisper is none too quiet. "That is the gentleman from the Society!"

"Yes." My preparations for bed make it easy to avoid her eyes.

"Wait just a moment," Luisa breaks in. "Do you mean to say that you were acquainted with Dimitri before today?"

There is an edge to her voice and I wonder whether she is jealous that Sonia and I have shared yet another experience. My heart softens, but it does not last long. There is no room for tenderness when Luisa is a traitor for the Souls, however unwilling her complicity.

I begin pulling the pins from my hair. "*Acquainted* is not really accurate. Sonia and I met him at a gathering in London, that is all."

"Did you know who he was even then?" Sonia asks.

I drop my hands, my hair still half pinned, as I turn to look at her. The accusation in her voice is tinged with anger.

"Of course not! I would have told you had I known."

"Would you, Lia? Would you really?" Her eyes are alight with a fury I do not understand.

I tip my head, unable to believe what I am hearing. "Sonia... Of course I would. How could you think otherwise?"

She narrows her eyes as if she is not sure whether or not to believe me, and we stand that way a moment in uncomfortable silence before Sonia's shoulders finally relax and the air escapes her mouth in a rush.

"I'm sorry." She rubs her temples, wincing as if in pain. "I am so tired. So very tired of the horses and the woods and the endless fear of the Hounds and the Souls."

"We are all tired. But I promise you that I knew nothing of Dimitri until just a while ago." Sighing, I try to keep hold of my own frustration. My own exhaustion. "I cannot do this any longer. I am going to bed. We'll no doubt have another long day tomorrow."

I do not wait to see if they agree before turning to change. It doesn't matter if they want to keep talking or not, for if we do, if I am forced to listen to their complaining and petty resentments a moment more, I fear I will scream. Tomorrow I will speak to Sonia about Luisa's betrayal. It is not a conversation to which I look forward.

Later, as I settle into the blankets in the silence of our tent, I think I will be awake for a long time reliving the danger of

the previous hours. But they have taken their toll, and I am asleep almost as soon as my head hits the ground.

I have the sense that I have been deeply asleep for some time when I awaken within a dream. I am certain that I am not traveling, though my dream feels very real. In it, I am standing in a circle, my hands clasped with faceless individuals on either side. A great fire burns before me, and across the licking flames I see others enshrouded in robes and clasping hands in the same manner.

An eerie chant arises from the center of the group, and I am surprised to feel my own mouth move, to hear words, at once foreign and familiar, emerging from my lips in time with the others. I feel myself falling into a trancelike state, and I have almost given myself over to it, have almost stopped asking questions within my own mind, when a terrific crack tears straight through my body. I cry out, my own eerie chant suspended even as the others continue as if nothing is wrong at all. As if I am not, at that very moment, being torn in two by some invisible intruder.

I pull away by instinct, stumbling toward the fire as the hands that once held mine close together, trapping me within the circle of robed figures. Stumbling farther forward, I fall to the ground in a heap as the pain rips through me again. Even in my dream, I smell the grass, sweet and musky, under my body, and I use my hands to try to push myself off the ground. To get my feet underneath me once again.

But it is not my fall nor my effort to stand up that jolts me

out of my dream. No. It is my hand braced against the hard earth. Or not my hand, exactly. My wrist and the medallion that encircles it.

The medallion that has rested safely on Sonia's wrist since we left New York a year ago.

Until now.

15

I am comforted by the sight of Sonia's face so near to mine when I awaken from my dream. Despite the recent tension, hers has been the face of friendship since the dawn of our quest to end the prophecy.

I sit upright, my hand clasped to my chest as if to quell the runaway beating. "Oh! Oh, my goodness!"

Sonia places a hand on my arm. "Shh. Hush, Lia. I know. I know." She presses me back against the pillow, and there is something sweetly sinister in her voice. Something all the more frightening for its innocence. "Just rest, Lia. It does not have to be so hard."

I am at first confused. Her words seem a bunch of gibberish that I don't have the coherence to decode. But in the end, there is no need for words. In the end, it is the medallion, clasped around my wrist just as in my dream, that tells me all I need to know.

"What . . . what is this? Why is the medallion on my wrist, Sonia?" I do not take the time to find the clasp in the dark. Instead, I rip at the velvet ribbon by which the medallion hangs until it forcibly breaks loose of its clasp and falls to the floor of the tent.

Sonia scrambles in the darkness, digging through the blankets that line the floor of the tent. I begin to understand even before she finds it, but when she does, when she crawls back to my side, the medallion in hand, I know for certain.

"Wear it, Lia. Just for a while. It is for the good of everyone, not the least of which is you." Her eyes shine in the darkness, and in that moment, I know horror far beyond anything felt when facing the Souls, the medallion, even Samael himself. In that moment, seeing Sonia's angelic eyes glittering with madness is the worst punishment of all.

I do not know how long I stare into the blue of her eyes trying to reconcile the Sonia I know with the girl in front of me, the girl attempting to use me as the Gate through which evil itself might pass. But when I finally come to my senses, I scoot back toward the wall of the tent.

And then I scream and scream and scream.

"I thought it was you." My words are directed at Luisa, who sits near me by the fire.

We are alone for the time being, bundled in blankets against

the cold while Edmund and Dimitri subdue Sonia in the other tent. I have not seen either of them since they pulled her kicking and screaming away from me.

Luisa looks surprised. "Me? Why?"

I shrug. "You were acting strangely—disappearing at odd times, seeming . . . angry and withdrawn."

She moves closer to me, taking one of my hands. "I knew, Lia. I knew something was wrong with Sonia. I asked her about it, but she only became defensive."

"But . . . I saw you. Scrying by the river." Even under the circumstances, I am embarrassed to admit that I was spying.

But Luisa seems not to care. "I *was* scrying. I was trying to see something that would tell me about Sonia. Something that would help me convince you."

"Why didn't you simply tell me, Luisa? Warn me?"

She sighs, dropping my hand as a look of regret passes over her exotic features. "You would not have believed me if I came to you with only suspicion. Not about Sonia. I was waiting until I had proof." Absent from her voice is the bitterness to which I have become accustomed over my closeness with Sonia. Now she sounds only sorry.

A wry laugh erupts from my mouth into the night. "Well, we have proof now, don't we?"

It is not a question that requires an answer, and we both know it. I do not know what to say about Sonia, and Luisa clearly feels the same way, for we sit in the almost-silence of the crackling fire without speaking. I can hear murmured voices coming from the tent, but I do not attempt to decipher the words spoken among Edmund, Dimitri, and Sonia. They are simply a backdrop to my own convoluted thoughts.

The sound of boots crunching across hard ground announces Dimitri approaching from the darkness outside the light of the fire. When I turn my head, he is there.

"She's quiet for now," he says, and I know he is referring to Sonia. "Are you all right?"

"I'm fine." I do not have the words to tell him that I am *not* fine. That I am shaken to the very core by the realization that the Souls may turn even my most trusted ally against me. That the medallion no longer has a safe place to reside until we find the missing pages.

Dimitri sits on my other side, and Luisa leans over to look at him. "How is she, Mr. Markov?"

"If I'm going to speak to you of such matters, I insist you call me Dimitri," he says.

I shrug when she glances at me for approval.

"All right, then. Dimitri," she says. "How is Sonia?"

"She is . . . distraught and not in her right mind."

"What do you mean?" Luisa asks. "Does she realize what she tried to do? Does she remember it?"

"Oh, she remembers it well and without apology. She was ranting about why Lia should wear the medallion . . . about why she was doing the right thing in placing it on Lia's wrist while she slept. We tried to talk sense into her, but it seems the Souls have her well in their grasp."

"It cannot be." I shake my head. "Sonia is so strong."

"Even the most gifted among us would struggle to keep the

Souls at bay." Dimitri's eyes are sympathetic as he explains. "They must have known she had the medallion, just as they must know she is your friend and confidant. None of us should be surprised, really, that it has come to this."

But I am surprised. Sonia has always seemed stronger than the rest of us. Better, somehow, and surer of her gifts and her place in the prophecy. It is almost a sacrilege to imagine her working to the good of the Souls. I do not say it aloud, though. It will only make me sound naive.

"So what do we do?" Luisa asks Dimitri. "About Sonia? About Lia and the medallion?"

"We have to keep Sonia away from Lia for the rest of the journey. And we have to try and keep her calm."

"How do you propose doing either given her state of mind?" Remembering Sonia's fevered pleas, her shrieks as Dimitri pulled her out of our tent, the task seems anything but simple.

"I've ground mistletoe into her tea. It will render her complacent enough, I think, at least for a while," Dimitri says.

I remember something I read during one of Father's many lessons in the library at Birchwood. "Isn't mistletoe poisonous?"

Dimitri shakes his head. "Not this variety. It is an ancient plant known to induce calm and found only in these woods and on the isle of Altus. We should be able to locate enough to see Sonia through until we can get her to the Sisters."

Luisa nods. "All right. What about the medallion? Having it on Sonia's wrist is the only thing that has kept it from Lia all this time."

Dimitri drops his gaze to his hands, and I know he is thinking, trying to come up with a way to keep the medallion near enough for safekeeping while also ensuring my own safety from its power to use me as the Gate.

I stand as an idea takes hold and a surge of restless energy begins to work its way through my bones.

"How long do we have until we reach the island?" I direct my question to Dimitri, hoping he is more familiar with the woods than I.

He furrows his brow. "Well, it is difficult to say for certain. It depends how quickly we travel."

Luisa sighs. For as long as I have known her, patience has never been one of her stronger virtues. "An approximation will likely do, Dimitri."

I catch a glimpse of annoyance before he turns to me to answer. "I would guess about three days. Why?"

I do not answer his question right away. Instead, I ask one of my own. "Who has the medallion now?"

"Well . . . I do," he says.

"May I?" I hold out my hand, but asking is a formality. If it belongs to anyone at all, it is to me.

"Are you certain that is a good idea, Lia?" I hear the fear in Luisa's voice. It is an echo of my own, but I know there is no other way.

"I'd like the medallion, please." I want to believe I see admiration in Dimitri's eyes, but perhaps it is only resignation.

In any case, he reaches into his pocket and pulls something

from it. The breath catches in my throat as I glimpse the black velvet ribbon trailing from his hand. I have observed it, of course, on Sonia's wrist. But seeing it safely clasped on the wrist of someone in whom I had infinite trust is different from seeing it unencumbered. There can be no doubt that it seems far more dangerous for its freedom.

Dimitri hands me the medallion, and I shut my eyes as my fingers close around the whispery velvet. That, together with the cold metal of the medallion, is more familiar to me than my own soul. Recognition ripples through me as a mixture of hate and terrifying need slams into my body. It takes effort to open my eyes. To bring myself back to the present and gather my thoughts.

All of that and I have not even clasped it against my skin.

Still, I cannot dwell on that which cannot be changed. What has to be done, however painful, however terrifying, however impossible it may seem.

I wrap the ribbon around my right wrist and lock the gold clasp. The mark is on my other wrist, but I know that is no guarantee of safety. The medallion has found its way back to my wrist in the past through circumstances more far-fetched than this.

When she speaks, Luisa's voice shakes. "But... Lia, you cannot wear the medallion. You know what could happen."

"I know better than anyone, but there is no other way."

"Perhaps you could give it to Edmund or... Dimitri? Anyone but you..."

I do not take offense to her words. I know that she seeks only to protect me, and she knows that I am most vulnerable to the pull of the medallion. My cursed role as Gate has seen to that.

"No, Luisa. I was fortunate to have Sonia look after it for a time, but I cannot put off my responsibility to it forever."

"Yes, but..." She looks from me to Dimitri and back again. "Dimitri?"

He holds my gaze. I do not know what he sees there, what makes him stare straight through me until I feel all the secrets of my soul are laid bare, but whatever it is, he sees it with certainty.

"Lia is right," he says. "She should be the one to secure the medallion. It belongs to her."

He does not flinch, and in this moment, without a shred of doubt in his eyes, I feel the stirrings of something deeper than physical attraction. Deeper even than the strange connection that has bonded us almost since the beginning.

Luisa is flustered. "But how will you keep it from traveling to your other wrist through three days and nights?"

I pull my gaze from Dimitri with effort and turn to Luisa. "I have only ever lost control of it when sleeping."

She looks at me as if I have gone daft. "Yes?"

I shrug. "I simply won't sleep."

"What do you mean, you won't sleep?"

"Just what I said. It is three days to Altus. I'll stay awake until we get there. I am sure once we arrive, the Sisters will have some idea what to do."

Luisa turns to Dimitri. "Will you talk sense into her? Please?"

He walks toward me and takes my hand before smiling at Luisa. "She sounds perfectly sensible to me. It is the best solution we have at the moment. I trust Lia with the medallion over anyone."

She looks at us as if we are equally mad before throwing her hands in the air. "And what of Sonia? Shall we make Lia responsible for her as well?"

Dimitri's eyes darken even in the dim light of the fire. "Of course not. Edmund and I have discussed it. He will ride at the front with Sonia's horse tied to his. You"—he looks at Luisa—"will ride behind them, followed by Lia. I will ride at the back in case anything should go amiss. Should Sonia need to attend to personal matters, you will accompany her. Even in her current state, I cannot imagine her trying to escape." He lifts his head, taking in the darkness that surrounds us beyond the light of the campfire. "There is simply nowhere for her to go."

For a moment, I think Luisa may argue. She opens her mouth as if to say something, but closes it again just as quickly. "Very well," she says, and I hear the grudging admiration in her voice.

Dimitri nods at her. "Lia may not be able to sleep, but you should. She will need us all in the coming days."

Luisa's nod is hesitant, and I know she does not want to leave me to face the sleepless night alone. "Are you certain you'll be all right, Lia?"

I nod. "Of course. I already have half a night's sleep, though tomorrow will be another matter altogether."

"You needn't worry, Luisa." Dimitri puts an arm around my shoulders. "I'll be here all night. Lia won't be alone for a moment."

The relief on her face is impossible to disguise, and with it comes the tiredness that has been lurking at the corners of her eyes. She walks over and wraps me in an embrace. "I'll see you in the morning, then. Give a shout if you need anything, will you?"

I nod, and she turns to make her way back across camp.

"Come." Dimitri pulls me down next to him on the ground near the fire. He leans against the log, drawing me back so that I may lean against his chest. "I'll keep you company until morning."

"That isn't necessary. Really. I'll be fine." At first I fight such intimacy by holding my body a half inch from his. After a few minutes, though, I cannot resist leaning my head back against his strong shoulder. It fits perfectly, as if it was made to nestle into exactly that spot. "You should sleep," I tell him. "Just because I cannot doesn't mean you shouldn't."

His cheek rubs against my hair as he shakes his head. "No," he says. "If you are awake, I'm awake."

And all night, he is.

It is only later that I realize with a touch of shame how very long it has been since I have thought of James.

16

We have only been riding for an hour, but I already know that ignoring Sonia's pleading will be the hardest part. It began as soon as the sun rose on the foggy morning.

I kept my head down as I passed the tent in which Sonia was brought her breakfast, but I could not avoid hearing her voice. And though it came to me in pieces, I did not need the entirety to understand how far she was lost.

"...please, I'm sure if you just tell Lia..."

"She doesn't understand... Samael is her ally..."

"...will only make things worse for her in the end."

The sound of Sonia's voice, the voice that has been my companion in things both wondrous and fearsome over the past year, pleading the case of Samael was almost more than I could bear. As if that was not enough, I was shaken by Dimitri's insistence that I remain at the perimeter of the camp as

Sonia was brought to her horse. I could not tell if he was keeping us so totally apart because he feared my lack of strength or Sonia's power, but for once, I did as I was told.

I am not tired. Not yet, though I know that will come soon enough. For now, I am carried along by my own taut nerves and the awareness of the medallion humming through my body. I have not worn it since leaving New York. Since acknowledging the danger of wearing it with the limited power I possessed at the time.

Now it is only mine.

Its presence on my wrist makes me feel terrifyingly alive, as if every nerve ending is exposed and raw. I feel every sigh of the wind, every rustle of the leaves in the trees overhead, as if they are under my own skin. My very heartbeat pulses with a power that is almost painful for having to be restrained.

I try not to think of it.

All through the long day of riding, I focus in front of me on Luisa's back and Sargent's strong body carrying me through the woods. They stretch into a shady green sameness that I cease noticing after a while. As I ride, I wish for only two things: a quick arrival at the Isle and the ability to stay awake long enough to reach it.

The shadows are long and the air chilly when Edmund finally locates a campsite both near enough to water and sheltered enough to give us some semblance of cover should we need it. I walk Sargent to one side of the camp as Edmund and Dimitri escort Sonia to the other. The mistletoe Dimitri slipped into

her tea at breakfast must be wearing off, for her voice is strong and carries to me on an increasingly cold wind.

"Lia! Lia! Will you speak to me? Just for a moment?"

It hurts me to turn my face from the sound of her voice, but turn it I do.

Tying Sargent to a tree, I drop to the ground, leaning against a neighboring trunk and closing my eyes as if doing so will blot out the sound of Sonia's voice.

"Try not to listen, Lia." Luisa settles next to me on the hard ground. Neither of us cares for comfort at the moment, and besides, even the ground is preferable to more time in the saddle.

I turn my face to look at Luisa and rest my head on my bent knees. "I have done little else but listen to Sonia these past months."

She tips her head in sympathy. "I know. But surely you realize that it is not really Sonia who is calling to you now? Who put the medallion on your wrist in the dark of night?"

"I do. But it doesn't make it any easier. I look at her face and see Sonia, but the words she speaks..." I do not have to finish.

Luisa reaches out and tucks a stray piece of hair behind my ear. "This will pass, Lia. It will. We will get to Altus and the Sisters will help Sonia find herself once more."

"And what of me?" I ask. "I cannot stay awake forever, and yet the medallion will be my burden from this day forward. Where does that leave me?"

"I don't know. But I do know that we have come a very long way already." Luisa smiles. "Let us take one thing at a time. Let us get to Altus, and the rest will come."

I nod, rising up from the ground. "I'm going to help with dinner."

She glances back toward the one completed tent—the tent in which I know Sonia has been placed for safekeeping.

"Do you think it wise? Perhaps we should let the men take care of camp tonight." Compassion is evident in her eyes. "She will not stop, Lia."

"I need to do something. I'll go mad if I sit still any longer."

We make our way toward the fire, just lit by Edmund. I don't know how Sonia knows of my approach when I make such a point not to speak near the tent, but she begins harassing me from within it almost immediately.

Edmund's face softens when I reach the fire. "Are you all right?"

I swallow the sadness that rises like a tide with his inquiry. "I would like to help with dinner, please."

He hesitates, nodding slowly and proffering a knife and a bag of carrots. I take them to the small table we use for food preparation. For a while, I lose myself in cutting and chopping and manage to ignore Sonia, alternately pleading and railing at me from inside her tent.

Or this is what I tell myself as I try to block her voice from my mind.

Dimitri and I sit by the fire as Edmund keeps watch outside Sonia's tent. Luisa has the other tent all to herself. She will likely be the only one sleeping well tonight.

"Are you warm enough?" Dimitri tucks the blanket tighter around my shoulders. He has insisted on keeping me company through another long night, and though I would not admit it aloud, it is nice to feel his sturdy chest behind me as I lean back against him.

"I'm fine, thank you. But you really should sleep. Someone in the group should be coherent, and I'm quite sure it will not be me."

Dimitri's voice comes from near my ear. "I need less sleep than you might imagine. Besides, lately when I sleep, I only dream of you anyway."

I laugh nervously, caught off guard by so bold a declaration, and try to make light of the moment. "Yes, well, let us see if you still feel that way after a couple of days without sleep and me to blame!"

Dimitri twists his head to get a better view of my face. I hear the teasing laughter in his voice. "Do you doubt my ability to stay awake alongside you?" He continues without waiting for my answer. "Why, that sounds like a challenge! And I accept!"

I cannot help laughing, even under the circumstances. "Very well. It's a challenge, then."

He settles himself behind me, nuzzling his face into my

hair, and I cannot help but wonder at my ease in his presence. Perhaps it is the mystical wood that makes it seem we are in another world entirely, but I feel as if I have known Dimitri forever. I experience none of the awkwardness I would expect from such close proximity to a gentleman I have known so short a time. My comfort is a distraction in and of itself, and I begin to wonder at my ability to stay awake while kept warm by the fire and his body against mine.

In an effort to stay alert, I propose a game of One Hundred Questions, and we take turns asking one another questions ranging from the absurd to the bittersweet. For a while, the prophecy fades into the background and we are like two normal people simply trying to get to know each other better. We laugh, whisper, and confide, and I feel us growing closer with every moment spent together in the dark. It is only when we become tired of asking and answering questions, well before either of us reaches one hundred, that we become quiet once again.

Dimitri buries his face in my hair, inhaling deeply.

I cannot help but laugh. "Whatever are you doing?"

"Your hair smells lovely," he says in answer, his voice muffled from within my hair.

I slap his arm playfully. "Ugh. It likely does not. A journey such as this does hamper one's efforts at hygiene."

He lifts his head from my hair, pulling it back with one hand so that my neck is exposed. "It *does* smell lovely. It smells of the forest, icy river water... you." He lowers his head to my bare neck, and shivers run up my spine as his lips touch my skin.

My head falls to the side of its own accord. Intellectually, I know it is scandalous to allow a gentleman such free rein, especially one I have known so short a time. But the rest of me, the unthinking part of me, wants his kisses to go on and on. It is this part that reaches back with one arm, entwining my fingers in his thick, dark hair and pulling his head more firmly to my skin.

A muffled groan erupts from his throat. I feel the vibration of it on my neck.

"Lia, Lia... This is not how I should be keeping you awake." I hear the anguish in his voice and know that he, too, is struggling against the tide of desire and the expectations of polite society.

But we are not part of that society at the moment. Here in the forest on our way to Altus, we are on our own.

I twist in his arms until I am kneeling before him, grateful for the ease of movement in my breeches. Taking Dimitri's face in my hands, I look into his bottomless eyes.

"This is not you keeping me awake." I lower my mouth to his, lingering until his lips open under mine before pulling away just enough to speak. "This is us, staying awake together. This is me"—I touch my lips lightly to his—"staying awake with you because I want to."

A rush of air escapes his mouth, and he pulls me down to the hard ground, cushioning my head with the bundled-up blanket. His hands travel the length of my body over my clothes, and it does not feel wrong. It does not feel scandalous or improper.

We shower each other with kisses of every imaginable variety, from the tender to those so passionate they steal my breath and cause Dimitri to pull away to compose himself. Finally, through some unspoken cue, we stop. We are in a state of complete dishevelment, and as I lay with my head on Dimitri's shoulder, I note our skewed clothing and rapid breathing and am grateful Edmund is on the other side of the quiet camp.

I am not tired. In fact, the blood seems to rush with new fervor through my veins, and though I am confident and suddenly ready to take on the prophecy once and for all, I also feel the most tremendous sense of peace. As if, for the first time in over a year, I am exactly where I belong.

17

"Give me the medallion, Lia." Luisa, hand outstretched, stands over me after breakfast. "Please?"

I sigh. "I cannot do that that, Luisa."

"But . . . Lia." She is clearly exasperated with me. "Look at you! You're exhausted!"

I laugh, finding a moment's dry humor in her observation. "I'm certain my appearance is less than endearing, but quite honestly, Luisa, it is the least of my worries." It is true. I do not have the energy to worry about how I look, though it cannot be good. My eyes sting from lack of sleep and I cannot remember the last time I tended to my hair.

Luisa narrows her eyes at me. "You know what I mean. You cannot continue without sleep. It is dangerous for you to ride in your condition."

"Yes, well, Dimitri has insisted I ride with him, so I will not be riding Sargent into a tree, if that's what you're worried about."

"It isn't. You know it isn't." She drops next to me. "I'm worried about *you*. If you'd only give me the medallion for a few hours, you might rest enough to finish the journey. I would do it for you, Lia. I would."

I hardly have the energy for the meager smile I offer her, but I offer it anyway and reach out to take her hand. "I know you would, and I thank you for it, Luisa. But can you honestly promise me that the medallion will be safe? That it will not find its way to my wrist so that Samael may use me as his Gate?"

A small line forms on her brow, and I know she wants to make the promise. Wants to make it and mean it. In the end, though, neither of us is surprised that she doesn't.

"No. I cannot promise, but I can *try*."

"It is not enough, Luisa, though I appreciate the offer of help. Truly." I shake my head. "The medallion is mine. It will not leave my wrist again until this is over. Not voluntarily anyway. I will manage somehow."

She nods, handing me her cup. "You better drink this, then. You are going to need it."

I take it, sipping carefully from the warm cup. The coffee is biting, and I hope the horrifying taste of it will be enough to keep me awake for the first part of our journey today. I gulp it down just in time to hear Edmund round up the horses.

Luisa heads over to the horses as I rise to find Dimitri. I am

halfway to the rest of the group when he trots over atop his magnificent mount.

"Ready?" he asks.

I nod, not trusting my voice. Even as exhausted as I am, Dimitri is ridiculously appealing.

He jumps down, holding on to the saddle horn. "You first, then."

It hasn't occurred to me until now that I have not ridden with someone since I was a child, and then, I rode between my father's legs.

"But... how will I... That is, how will we both fit?" I quell my rising embarrassment, and I know a blush makes its way to my cheeks.

His smile is rakish. "It's simple; you mount the horse at the front of the saddle, and I will ride behind you." He leans in, so close that I can smell the minty tooth powder on his breath. My mouth goes dry. "I hope that you will not object to such an arrangement."

I lift my chin. "Not at all." I shoot him a sly glance as I place my foot in the stirrup. "In fact, it sounds rather pleasant."

I catch his admiring grin as I lift myself into the saddle, and then he is behind me, his thighs bracing mine and his arms holding the reins on either side of me. A thrill runs all the way from the top of my head to the tips of my boots.

As we trot over to the others, Sonia casts me a long glance from her horse tied behind Edmund's. I expect her to call out, to beg, plead, cajole. She doesn't. She is perfectly quiet, which is perhaps why the others do not try to shelter me from her, as they did yesterday. I know I should be relieved by her silence. But if I had to name what I feel as we begin another day, it would not be relief. Any consolation I might find in Sonia's silence is stolen by the memory of her ice-blue eyes and that blank, mocking glare.

As soon as the horses are in order and a last check has been made to ensure we've left nothing behind, we head farther into the forest. We travel slower now that we must lead both my horse and Sonia's, and it does not take me long to wonder at the wisdom of my decision to ride with Dimitri.

It *is* pleasant. That is exactly the problem. Were I on my own horse, I would be forced to stay alert, to pay attention to the group and our direction. As it is, I spend the day drifting in and out of half-consciousness, the mist in the wood growing thicker with every step, eventually becoming an all-encompassing shroud that blocks out nearly every trace of light.

With the sun missing, it is impossible to tell if it is midday or evening or somewhere in between. I do not want to bother Dimitri with such a question. In the end, it doesn't matter. We must keep traveling, whatever the time, until we reach the sea that will take us to Altus. And I must stay awake until we get there.

I feel alert for the first time in hours, and I know it is because of Henry. Standing in the distance, well disguised amid the trees of the forest, I might not see him at all if only he was not

Henry. But of course, he is. He could be hidden by a million leaves of a million branches on a million trees, and somehow I would find my way to him.

I look over at the small river where everyone else is watering the horses. I half expect Henry to be gone when I look back, but he is not. He is standing right where he was a moment ago, but this time, he holds a finger to his mouth, signifying silence. Then he beckons me to him with his hand.

I glance back at the rest of the group, still immersed in caring for the horses and tending to their own personal details before we ride again. They will not miss me if I am only gone a moment, and I cannot let a moment such as this pass. A moment when I might actually speak to my brother for the first time since his death.

I walk toward the tree line at the edge of the small clearing. I do not hesitate when it comes time to step into the leafy shade of the woods. As I do, Henry turns to walk deeper into the forest. I am not surprised to see him walking. Death has freed him of his useless legs and the wheelchair that was both his constant companion and his prison.

His voice drifts to me on the fog. "Lia! Come here, Lia! I must talk to you."

I call out to him softly, not wanting to alert the others to my absence. "I cannot be gone long, Henry. The others are waiting."

He disappears behind one of many trees, but his voice still finds me. "It's all right, Lia. We'll just talk a moment. You'll be back in no time."

I continue into the woods, finally reaching the tree where I last saw him. At first, I think it a trick of my own imagination and tiredness, for he is not there. But then I see him, sitting on a fallen log a little to my left.

"Henry." It is all I can say. I am afraid he will disappear if I speak too carelessly into the silence.

He smiles. "Lia. Come and sit with me, will you?"

He sounds just as he always has, and I am not afraid to see him here among my own world. The gifts of the Otherworlds and the prophecy are vast and not always predictable. It would be difficult to take me by surprise after all I have seen.

I walk over, dropping onto the log next to him. When I look into his eyes, they are as dark and infinite as I remember. They are my father's eyes, rich and warm, and for a moment my grief is so great that I do not think I will be able to draw another breath.

I gather my wits, not knowing how long we will have to speak in private. "It is so good to see you, Henry." I reach up to touch his silken cheek. "I cannot believe you're really here."

He giggles. It travels through the forest like smoke. "Of course I am, silly! I came to see you." His face grows serious, and he reaches over, putting his small arms around me in a childish embrace. "I've missed you, Lia."

I breathe in the scent of him, and it's just as I remember, that complicated scent of boyhood sweat and old books and many, many years of confinement. "I've missed you, too, Henry. More than you know."

We stay that way for a moment before I pull away reluctantly. "Have you seen Mother and Father? Are they well?"

He gazes into my eyes, and this time, he is the one to reach out and touch my cheek. His fingertips are warm. "Yes, they are well, and I have much to tell you. But you look so tired, Lia. *You* do not seem well."

I nod. "I cannot sleep. It is the Souls, you see. They have infiltrated our party. They have contaminated Sonia." I thrust my hand toward him. "Now only I can wear the medallion. And I mustn't sleep, Henry. Not until we reach Altus and Aunt Abigail."

There is pity and compassion in his eyes. "Yes, but you will not be able to fight the Souls when the time comes, nor fight them now, if you do not rest." He scoots closer to me. "Put your head on my shoulder. Just for a bit. Closing your eyes for even a few minutes will help you get through the rest of your journey. I'll watch over you, I promise."

He is right, of course. It is not easy balancing the need to protect myself from the medallion and the need to be prepared for an attack from the Souls. If I rest, I will be better prepared to face whatever they have in store between here and Altus. And who better to trust than my beloved brother, who placed himself at risk to hide the list of keys so that Alice would not use it to her gain?

I lay my head on his shoulder, breathing in the wool of his tweed waistcoat. The forest looks odd from this angle — skewed sideways, it is suddenly something foreign and dark with only

an undertone of familiarity. I let my eyes drift close, falling into the delicious emptiness of sleep, a sensation that feels precious for the simple fact that I have not been able to take it for granted these past nights.

I should like to say I have a moment's peace. That I manage a few stolen minutes of rest, and perhaps I do. But the next thing I know, a fierce wind blows around me. No, that is not right. It blows *through* me, coming from some primeval place that opens up from within.

I have a flash of the sea on the many summers we spent on the island as children. Alice and I learned to swim on that island. We would stand on the beach where the water rushed to meet our feet, marveling at the sea's power to pull so much sand back into her watery depths, leaving us standing in an excavated abyss. That is how it feels. As if something has opened up inside of me and is pulling everything important, everything in me, into some ancient place, leaving only an empty shell still standing on the familiar beach.

"Li-a! Where are you, Lia?" The voices come from afar. I haven't the energy to open my eyes and find them. Besides, Henry's shoulder is so comforting, so solid under my cheek. I should like to stay here for a very long time.

But I am not permitted the luxury of slumber. Of ignorance. Instead, I am awoken with a ferocious shaking and then, shockingly, a harsh slap to the face.

"Lia! Whatever are you doing?" It is Luisa's face, her tawny eyes into which I look.

"I'm only resting. With Henry." My words sound slurred, nearly incoherent, even to my own ears.

"Lia... Lia. Listen to me," Luisa says as Dimitri and Edmund run up behind her, breathing heavily as if they have been running. "Henry is not here. You have been lured into the forest!"

Indignation swims to the surface of my stupor. "He *is* here. He's watching out for me while I sleep, and then he will tell me all the things we need to know to get to Altus safely."

But when I try to look for Henry, I realize I am not sitting on the fallen log as I was when I first sat down. I am lying on the ground amid the dead, crackly leaves. I look past Luisa, past Dimitri and Edmund. Henry is not there. "He *was* here. Just a moment ago."

I scramble to rise from the ground, and Dimitri rushes forward to put an arm under one of mine. It takes me a moment to gain my balance. When I do, I turn in a slow circle, scanning the woods for any sign of my brother. But somehow I know he is not there. Was never there. I bury my face in my hands.

Dimitri pulls my hands away. He holds them in his. "Look at me, Lia."

But I am ashamed. I, of all people, have allowed myself to be lured into sleep. Have allowed the Souls to use my love for my brother. I shake my head.

"Look at me." He releases one of my hands and tips my chin so that I have no choice but to look into his inky eyes. "This is not your fault. It isn't. You're stronger than any of us, Lia. But

you're human. It's a wonder you have not fallen under their spell sooner."

I wrench my hand from his and turn, walking away. It only takes a few steps for the fury to find me, and I spin to face Dimitri. "They used *my brother*! Of all the things... of all the sacred things they might use, why him?" Though my question begins with rage, it ends with a whimper.

Dimitri closes the distance between us in two long strides. He puts a hand on either side of my head and stares into my eyes. "Because they will use everything in their power, Lia. *Nothing* is sacred to them. Nothing save the power and authority they crave. If you know nothing else, remember nothing else, you must know and remember this. You must."

18

By the time we make camp for the night, I am in a state of hyperawareness. I feel as if I could not sleep even if given the opportunity, though I have never been so physically exhausted in my life. Once Luisa and Sonia are ensconced in separate tents and everyone else has settled into quiet, I become convinced that it is only constant movement together with constant thought that keeps me awake.

I begin circling the diameter of the campsite while Edmund and Dimitri settle the horses in for the night. Later, Edmund will sit outside Sonia's tent to keep watch, as has been his custom these past nights. I still do not know if he watches her continually to protect me from her or to protect her from herself. I have been too tired to ask.

While I pace, I think. I try to project myself forward,

through the last leg of our journey, to the time when I will see Aunt Abigail at Altus, and forward still to the journey after that—the one that will take me to the missing pages. It is good to occupy my mind, and it has the added benefit of providing me with a glimpse of possible obstacles where I might still design a way around them.

"Would you like some company?" The voice is at my shoulder and causes me to jump, so deep am I in thought and tiredness.

I do not stop walking, but when I turn my head, Dimitri is keeping pace on my right.

I shake my head. "It's not necessary, Dimitri. You should sleep. I'm fine."

He chuckles. "I feel quite well, actually. More alert than usual, in fact."

I smile at him. "Even still, I am counting on you to see me safely to Altus. If you become overtired, the both of us might end up on a different island entirely!"

He reaches down and grabs my hand. "I assure you, I am as alert as the day I met you with the Hounds. I told you; I don't need sleep the way you do."

I tip my head to look at him as we walk. "And how is that, exactly? Are you not... mortal?"

He tips his head back and laughs at the indigo sky. "Of course I'm mortal! What do you think me, a beast?" He bares his teeth and growls playfully.

I roll my eyes. "Very funny. Do you blame me for asking? How else can it be that you do not need sleep?"

"I never said that I don't need sleep at all. Just that I can go considerably longer without it than you."

I give him a sly glance. "I think you are avoiding the subject. Come now, surely we do not have secrets at this juncture!" I am enjoying the mischievous banter. It makes me feel less odd. As if we might be walking in one of London's many parks on a beautiful summer day.

He sighs. When he looks back at me, his smile is a little sad. "I am mortal just as you are, but I am descended on one side from one of the oldest lines in the Grigori and on the other from one of the oldest in the Sisterhood. In fact, every one of my ancestors dating back to the Watchers has formed a union with a member of the Sisterhood. Because of this, my...gifts are extraordinary. Or so I'm told."

"What do you mean, exactly? To what gifts do you refer?" I cannot help feeling that he has kept something significant from me.

He squeezes my hand. "The same gifts you have—the ability to travel the Plane, to scry, to speak to the dead...The more closely we are descended from the original Watchers and Grigori, the more of that power we retain."

I stare into the night, trying to put a finger on what gave me pause. When I find it, I turn back to him.

"You said 'we.'"

"Yes."

"What did you mean?" I ask.

He looks at me with a small smile. "You, too, are descended from an old line. A pure line. Didn't you know?"

I shake my head, though there is a realization, something hidden in the murk of my lethargic mind, fighting its way to the surface. "I only found out recently that my father was a member of the Grigori at all. There hasn't been time to ask questions about his lineage."

Dimitri stops walking, tugging on my hand until I stop beside him. "He was as powerful a member of the Grigori as your mother was a Sister, Lia. You, too, are descended from a long line of unions between the Sisters and the Grigori. It is why you are so powerful."

I shake my head and begin walking, so fast now that he has to trot to catch up. I don't want to find the connections that I am already beginning to find, though I cannot put a reason to it.

"Lia... What is it? This is nothing... Well, this is nothing that should upset you. If anything, you have a better chance of ending the prophecy than anyone before you because of your lineage. It is the reason your Aunt Abigail was so powerful and your mother, too."

I nod. "Yes, but it also means that Alice is probably more powerful than I imagined, and I already imagined her very powerful. Plus..."

"Plus?"

I feel his gaze but do not meet it right away. I keep walking, trying to put words to the sadness I suddenly feel. Finally I stop walking once again. "Plus, I am beginning to understand that I never really knew my father at all. That he must have

felt very alone and did not believe he could share his worries with me."

"He was trying to protect you, Lia. That's all. It is all any of us in the Grigori endeavor to do for the Sisters."

I can do nothing but nod. Nod and walk.

We do not speak again, but Dimitri does not once leave my side. We walk the whole night through, sometimes in silence and sometimes in murmured conversation, pacing circles around the camp as the sky fades from midnight blue to lilac to the palest orange in the distance. We walk until it is time, once again, to ride.

An hour into our ride the next morning, I smell the sea. Knowing it is so close makes it possible to fight the insidious call of sleep, though I have given up the notion of dignity and do not ride erect in the saddle, but slumped against Dimitri's chest. I do not even know if Sonia glances my way or pays me any attention at all. I long ago stopped expending my precious energy worrying about her attention. For the moment, she is quiet, and that is good enough for me.

The forest passes in a blurry haze, and every moment I desire only to close my eyes. Only to sleep and sleep and sleep. But the briny smell of the ocean gives me cause to hope that the end is near.

The wood fades a little at a time, the trees at first becoming only slightly less dense, eventually thinning to the point

where it seems we are no longer in a forest at all. Finally we cross some invisible threshold and are on the beach.

The horses stop all at once, and the sea stretches, moody and gray, into the infinite distance. We stare at it in silence.

Luisa is the first to dismount, dropping to the ground with characteristic grace and unlacing her boots. She pulls them off, followed by her stockings. When her feet are at last bare, she wiggles her toes in the sand, watching them before looking up at me.

"You're not too tired to dip your toes in the sea, are you, Lia?"

There was a time when her mischievous grin would have been catching, when I would have jumped to join her. Now her words come from very far away. They take a long time to reach me, and when they do, they barely make a dent in my consciousness.

"Lia?" Dimitri's voice is husky in my ear, his chest hard against my back. "Why don't you go with Luisa? The cold water will do you good." The air is chilly on my back when he dismounts. Once on the ground, he holds up a hand. "Come."

I take his hand out of instinct and swing one leg over the horse's back, stumbling a little as I hit the ground. Luisa kneels, reaching for one of my feet. "Here. Let me get this." She taps the side of my boot, and I obediently lift my leg, bracing myself against Dimitri's horse.

She proceeds to remove first one boot and stocking and then the other. When the sand, gritty and cold, is at last against my bare feet, Luisa rises. She takes my hand, pulling me toward the water without a word.

I have not lost all my faculties. Even as I stagger to the water behind Luisa I am wondering how we will get to Altus, what is next in our journey. But I do not have the motivation to ask or even to wonder for very long. I allow Luisa to pull me toward the rushing waves until they swallow my feet. The water is frigid, and I get a jolt of something like pain mixed with euphoria as my toes are enveloped by the slippery slickness of it.

Luisa's laugh is carried on the wind, all the way out to sea, it seems. She lets go of my hand and wades farther out, scooping handfuls of water and spraying it in every direction like a child. Even now, I feel the loss of Sonia, for she should be in the water, laughing and rejoicing at how far we have come together... how close we are to Altus. Instead, she is a virtual prisoner, carefully watched by Edmund and Dimitri behind us. Sadness and resentment war within me. It is a losing battle no matter the outcome.

"Wait a minute..." Luisa has stopped playing in the waves. She stands a few feet in front of me, gazing through the mist in the distance. I follow her gaze but see nothing. The fog stretches on and on, blending together with the gray of the sea and the nothingness of the sky.

But Luisa does see something. She continues staring before turning back to Edmund and the others.

"Edmund? Is that—" She does not finish her sentence, but turns back to the water.

When I turn to look at the rest of the group, Edmund is walking slowly toward us and peering into the same distance.

He walks right into the water, unmindful of his wet boots, stopping right next to me.

"Why, yes, Miss Torelli. I do believe you're right." And though he addresses Luisa by name, he seems to be talking to everyone and no one in particular.

I turn to him. "Right about what?" My tongue feels fuzzy in my mouth.

"Right about what she sees," he says. "There."

I look in the direction of his stare and, yes, there is something dark making its way toward us in the water. Perhaps it is my lack of sleep, but I feel suddenly frightened as the object comes closer and closer. It is monstrous. A large, hulking thing all the more frightening for the utter soundlessness of its approach. I feel an irrational, hysterical scream building in my throat as the object breaks through the last of the mist hanging over the sea.

Luisa turns to us with a grin. "See?" She bows dramatically, rising to hold an arm out toward the thing now bobbing silently in the water. "Your chariot awaits."

And then I understand.

As we rise and fall with the waves, I do not remember why I believed the ocean would be an improvement over the horses. We have been at sea for some time, though it is impossible to tell how long; the sky is the same gray it has been all day. No lighter and no darker. From that, I can only guess that we have not yet passed another night.

I do not even try to keep track of our progress. My tiredness is too deep-seated to allow clear thought, and, in any case, the fog soon swallows the shore. I settle for a vague belief that we are traveling north. I am carried so close to sleep by the rhythmic rocking of the water that I feel an irrational urge to jump into the water, to escape the hypnotic swaying of the boat in any way possible.

We boarded the boat soon after it arrived on the beach. Edmund and Dimitri took it in stride, as if it is perfectly natural for a boat to appear suddenly out of the mist and whisk us, without a word, to an island not shown on any map in the civilized world. But I wonder how it knew we were there.

I also wonder what will become of Sargent and the other horses, though Edmund assured me they would be "taken care of." I wonder about the robed figures standing at either side of the boat, propelling us almost noiselessly through the water. They have no distinguishing characteristics—I cannot even tell if they are male or female—and have said nothing. And though I have many questions, I ask them silently, for I've not the soundness of mind to form the inquiries aloud.

Sonia is at the front of the boat while I am at the back. The longer we are at sea, the more subdued she becomes. Eventually, she stops looking over her shoulder to shoot me angry glares, choosing instead to stare into the mist. Edmund is never far from her side, while Dimitri is never far from mine. I take comfort in his presence, however silent. I lean against him, trailing my fingers through the water as Luisa dozes, head in hand near the middle of the boat.

The water is unusually still. There is the rocking, but it is the slow, gentle glide of the boat through water, for the sea is as smooth as the looking glass that used to hang over the mantel in my chamber at Birchwood. I wonder, as I stare into the water, if the mirror is still there. If my room is just as I left it, or if it has been stripped of everything that made it home to me for so many years.

At first, there is nothing to see. The sky is so gray that I cannot even find my reflection and the water is not clear enough to decipher anything below its surface. But as I continue running my fingers through it, something bumps up against my hand. I wonder if it is a dolphin or a shark, and I pull my hand back into the boat, knowing it could be any number of strange creatures I have seen in Father's many books on the sea.

I tip my head a little further over the boat and am rewarded with a glimpse of an eye. It is rather like an alligator or a crocodile, the way it emerges from the water, peering at me with the rest of its body still beneath the surface. But of course, it can be no such thing. Not in the ocean. I tear my eyes from the creature for a quick moment, looking back to my companions in the boat to see if anyone has noticed.

For the first time since we have been traveling, Dimitri is dozing next to me. A quick look around the boat tells me that the journey has caught up with everyone else as well. Sonia and Luisa are as deeply asleep as babes in the nighttime, while Edmund gazes trancelike over the prow of the boat.

I glance back at the water, wondering if I have imagined the sea creature. But no. It is still there, moving effortlessly

alongside the boat and seeming to survey me with its sympathetic eye. It blinks, and the creature rises slightly out of the water. It is very like a horse, though when its scaly tail slips quietly out of and then back into the water, I realize it is not like any horse I have ever seen.

It is the eye that draws me. Though I can't explain it, there is understanding there. Understanding of all I have endured. The creature's mane flows like kelp behind its sizable head, and I reach farther out of the boat, straining to reach the powerful neck moving beneath the surface of the water. It is at once feathery and slippery, and I am hypnotized by that infinite gaze together with the curious feel of its skin. I stroke the creature's neck, and its eye closes momentarily as if in pleasure. When it opens again, I realize my mistake.

I cannot remove my hand.

It is stuck to the creature's body. The great eye blinks once, and then sinks lower into the water, taking me with it. I am at first too shocked to say or do anything, but as my body is pulled overboard, I begin to kick and flail. The commotion causes everyone in the boat to jump to attention.

But it is too late. The creature is stronger and more powerful than I imagined, and I am over the side of the boat and into the water in no time at all. The last things I see are not Dimitri's eyes, frightened and confused as they are, but the faceless figures who still man the front and back of the boat. They make no move amid the chaos that has broken out on the boat.

I manage a deep breath before I am pulled entirely under

the water. At first, I fight. I try and try to pull my hand from the thing's neck, but it does not take me long to realize the futility of it. The creature does not bolt toward the bottom of the sea, though it is surely capable. It swims downward languidly, as if it has all the time in the world. Its pace is tortuous, for my end does not come quickly. No. I have time to contemplate my death.

The water is a murky underworld of shadowy shapes and slippery objects that bump up against me, and soon, too soon, I am filled with the apathy that I know accompanies drowning. My body floats behind the creature's massive body, but my hand is as irrevocably attached to its neck as it was in the moment before it pulled me into the sea. My will to fight leaves in one big rush, and I allow myself to be pulled, farther and farther into the watery depths, without struggle. The truth is that I am tired. So very tired. This is the second time the water has vied for my life.

Perhaps it is fate. Perhaps it is meant to claim my soul.

It is my last conscious thought.

19

Despite everything that has happened, I am fairly certain it is the choking that will kill me.

I awake in the bottom of the boat, spitting up water and coughing until my throat is raw. I see the shadows of other figures in the periphery, but it is Dimitri's face, worried and desolate, that is at the forefront of my vision. He leans over me, bracing one of my shoulders while I cough up the never-ending stream of seawater that seems to have filled every pore, every crevice, every vein in my body.

Finally the coughing ceases, at least for the moment, and Dimitri gathers me in his arms and pulls me to his wet chest.

"I'm sorry," I say. There is no question that I am to blame. I do not remember everything, but the bizarre creature that pulled me into the water and my own naiveté are things I will not soon forget.

He shakes his head, and when he speaks, his voice is hoarse and gruff. "I should have been watching...should have been paying more attention."

I am too drained to argue. I wrap my arms around him and press my wet body to his.

Luisa kneels next to me, her face as worried as I have ever seen it. "Are you all right, Lia? One moment I was sound asleep, and the next thing I knew, your feet were disappearing into the sea!"

"It was a kelpie." Dimitri says it as if it is the most realistic thing in the world instead of a creature found in books on ancient mythology. "Probably doing the Souls' bidding just as the Hounds did in the wood. They want to stop you from reaching Altus and the missing pages."

Luisa begins pulling objects from her bag. "You're both shivering! You'll catch your death!"

Even in my current state, I manage to find irony in her exclamation, but I am grateful for the blankets she produces first from her knapsack and then from Edmund's. Dimitri wraps me in one, putting the other around his own shoulders before leaning back against the side of the boat and pulling me against him.

Luisa, satisfied that we are, at least for the moment, safe and well, moves back to her original seat. Edmund takes up his position next to Sonia, who looks as if she hasn't moved during the entire episode. It is only then that I really see him. His face does not look right. It is as if he has aged ten years in

the time since I last saw him, his features twisted by fear and anguish and desolation. I know immediately why it is so, and my heart wrenches with guilt.

Edmund has already lost one child to the water. Henry may not have been Edmund's own in the traditional sense, but there can be no doubt that he loved my brother as a son. Losing him nearly ruined Edmund, and now I have brought him back to that place...that terrifying place where anything, no matter how precious, can be taken without notice or apology.

I know I should say something. Make amends for the worry I have caused. But I cannot find the words, and my throat closes with regret. I meet his eyes and hope he knows.

"It was you, wasn't it? You are the one who saved me?"

I am leaning against Dimitri's chest. Even with the blankets and the warmth from Dimitri's body, I am so cold that I no longer fear falling asleep. I do not think my body could relax enough to drift into slumber even if it were possible.

He does not answer right away, and I know he is trying to decide how much to tell me. Those moments under the sea are lost to me. I have only vague remembrances of infinite darkness, shadowy figures, and finally, a strange light that illuminated the blackness in the moment before I thought I was dead.

But it *was* Dimitri. That much is clear from his soaking

wet clothing and hair. I want to understand it. To understand *him*.

His chest rises behind me as he gathers breath to answer. "Yes. I exercised my authority over the creature as one of the Grigori."

"You have such authority?"

"I do." He pauses. "But I am not supposed to use it."

I twist in his arms to look at his face. "What do you mean?"

He sighs. "I am not supposed to intervene in the path of the prophecy. I am not supposed to aid you at all, actually. I've been walking a fine line, and doing it within the boundaries of the Grigori's law, I believe, by helping you stay awake, by acting as an escort to Altus. Even with the Hounds I did not, technically, intervene. They stepped aside of their own accord when they saw that I was with you."

I hear something unspoken in his hesitation. "But there is more, isn't there?"

"It's nothing for you to fret about, Lia. I don't want you to worry over a decision I made and would make again if given the opportunity. Not coming after you was simply not an option. Would never be an option."

I touch his face. His skin is cold under my fingertips. "But we are in this together, aren't we? Now more than ever."

He hesitates before nodding.

"Whatever you face because of your intervention, you will not face it alone if I can help it."

"I crossed a very real line by going after you. I used magic... magic that is forbidden in the physical world, to

render the kelpie powerless. Its strength, while greater than that of a mortal, is still considerably less than that of the Grigori. And many of the Sisters as well. In fact, you would have been able to escape yourself if you had undergone a bit more training. Your powers are considerable as well, though still undeveloped."

I know that it has little to do with the subject at hand, but I cannot help feeling indignant. I have, after all, been refining my power for months.

"I am not as well versed in the use of my gifts as you, but I think I have done fairly well developing my skills these past months."

He tips his head. "But you have not developed them on your own. Not really. Have you?"

I do not understand the point he is making at first, but when I do, when the realization dawns, it is with true horror. "Sonia. I have been training with Sonia." I shake my head, as if my protestation will render his claim invalid. "But she was fine. She was fine until we entered the wood."

He tucks a piece of my hair, ropey and stiff with salt, behind my ear. "Was she?" He takes a deep breath. "Lia, the Souls did not gain control over Sonia in one night. It was probably a progression of sorts."

I turn so that my back is once again against his chest. I do not want him to see the mixture of sadness and anger and disbelief that I know is reflected in my face. "You think Sonia has been under the influence of the Souls for some time."

It is not a question, but he answers anyway. "I think it is

more likely than the alternative, don't you? That perhaps her alliance with the Souls began by subtle suggestion, maybe even disguised as someone other than who they are?"

"But... that would mean..." I cannot finish.

Dimitri does it for me. "It would mean that perhaps Sonia did not help you fully tap the power that is yours, either by accident or by choice." He shrugs. "For instance, did you know that you are a Spellcaster like your sister? It will take time to develop your power, but it is there. You can be sure of it. And I imagine Sonia knew it was there as well."

I cannot meet his eyes, though I am not surprised by the revelation. I don't know why I should feel ashamed, for it is Sonia who has betrayed our cause. It is Sonia who has betrayed me. I only know that I feel terribly naive.

And now everything falls into place, however much I wish it would not.

Sonia, under the influence of the Souls, has been aiding me in developing my power *just enough.* Just enough so that I would believe I was getting stronger. Would believe I had a fighting chance. Just enough so that I would not seek more. Would not believe there *was* more. Her insistence that we travel the Plane together in the name of my safety was in fact a desire to know every move I made on behalf of the prophecy. Her worry over pushing myself too hard was instead simply concern over the too-swift development of my power.

When I remember her mad insistence that I wear the medallion, it hardly matters whether her betrayal began by choice or by deception. It is very clear how it ended.

I begin to tremble. Not with fear. Not with sadness. No. With pure, unbridled fury. I cannot even look at Sonia's slumped figure at the front of the boat, for fear I will lunge at her and knock her over the side.

My anger, no, my *rage*, frightens me. At the same time, I thrill in its power, though I don't dare analyze what that says about how much I have changed. Never have I felt such wrath. Not even for my sister. Perhaps it is because I have always feared Alice. Have always known I could not fully trust her, though it took many years to admit that, even to myself.

But Sonia . . . Sonia was different. Her purity, her innocence, made me believe in goodness. It made me believe there was hope. Somehow, the destruction of that hope angers me more than any other betrayal.

Dimitri rubs my shoulders with his hands. "It is not her, Lia. Not really. You know that."

I can only nod.

We sit in the silence of the all-consuming mist. It has grown thicker yet since I was pulled from the water. Even the others in the boat are little more than shadows, just smudges in the fog. Then, all at once, the boat stops its effortless glide.

I sit up. "Why aren't we moving?"

"Because we are here," Dimitri says behind me.

I move to sit on one of the planks that act as a seat inside the boat, and try to make out any sort of shape in the distance. But it is no use. The fog is too all-encompassing.

"Why are we stopping, Mr. Markov?" Luisa's voice is groggy from the middle of the boat.

"We've arrived at Altus," he says.

She looks around as if he is mad. "You must be seeing things. There is nothing within a mile of here save this bloody fog!"

Either I am punchy from lack of sleep or I am actually feeling more like myself, because her bad language causes me to laugh out loud.

Dimitri rubs one palm over his face in a gesture that illustrates either his tiredness or his frustration with Luisa's excitability. "Trust me, it's here. If you will only wait a moment, you'll see what I mean."

Luisa crosses her arms over her bosom in a gesture of impatience, but Edmund follows Dimitri's gaze out over the water. The activity does nothing to move Sonia. She is as listless as ever and seems to have no interest at all in whether or not we have arrived at Altus.

Noticing movement near the front of the boat, I look over to see one of the robed figures turn outward to face the water. I catch a glimpse of long, slender fingers reaching up, and then the hood of the robe is lowered to reveal a cascade of hair so blond it is nearly platinum. It shimmers down the back of the girl at the front of the boat, and I see now that it *is* a girl, or more accurately, a young woman.

I am spellbound as she lifts her arms, the flowing sleeves of her robe falling back to reveal creamy white skin. A strange hush descends over us. The water does not lap against the side of the boat, and it seems as if we collectively hold our breath, waiting for what is next.

When it happens, it is worth the wait.

The girl begins to mutter something in a language I have never heard before. It sounds almost like Latin, but I know that it is not. Her voice winds its way through the fog. It winds its way around us and then flows out and over the water. I hear the words traveling long after they leave her mouth, though not as an echo. It is something else. A remembrance. It flows outward until the mist begins to lift, not all at once, but still quickly enough for me to know it is not nature alone at play.

The water glistens in sunlight that was not there only moments before. The sky, once dull gray when visible at all, glimmers above our heads, and I am reminded of the autumn sky in New York, a deep blue richer than at any other time of year.

But all of this is not the thing that takes my breath.

No. That claim belongs to the lush island before us.

It shimmers in the water, a mirage of beauty and serenity. A small harbor lies not far from the boat, and from its banks the island rises in a gentle slope. Toward the top of the island and in the distance, I can make out a smattering of buildings, but they are too far away to decipher clearly.

Most beautiful of all, though, are the trees. Even from the water, I see that the island is dotted with apple trees, the crimson fruit a flurry of exclamation points amid the lavish green of the trees and grass that seems to cover the island.

"Oh... It's lovely!" It seems too small a word to describe what is in front of me, but it is all I have in this moment.

Dimitri smiles down at me. "It is, isn't it?" He looks back at it. "I never stop being awed by it."

I look up at him. "Is it real?"

He chuckles. "It is not on any conventional map, if that's what you mean. But it is here, hidden by the mists and present to those among the Sisterhood, the Grigori, and those who serve them."

"Well, I should like to see it up close," Luisa says.

Edmund nods. "Miss Milthorpe needs sleep and Miss Sorrensen needs . . . well, Miss Sorrensen needs assistance." We all look at Sonia, now staring almost angrily at Altus. Edmund looks back to Dimitri. "The sooner the better."

Dimitri tips his head at the robed woman who made Altus appear. She moves back to her position at the front of the boat and picks up her oars as the woman at the rear does the same.

I take my seat, watching the water as it moves beneath the boat. As it takes me closer and closer to the island that harbors answers to the questions I am still learning to ask.

20

I am surprised to find several figures waiting when we disembark from the boat. Like our traveling companions, they are robed in deepest purple and lined up on the dock. I know from their fine features that they are all women. They seem to be waiting for us with some ceremony.

Edmund steps off with Sonia first, followed by Luisa. I wait with Dimitri, disembarking before him. When he introduces me as Amalia Milthorpe, Lady Abigail's great-niece, the women bow formally in my direction, but naked suspicion and perhaps even resentment is evident in their eyes.

Once the rest of our party is properly introduced, Dimitri goes to the women, greeting each of them personally in low murmurs. Finally he reaches the woman at the head of the line. She is older, perhaps even older than Aunt Virginia, but when she pulls back the hood of her robe to kiss Dimitri's cheeks, it is to reveal ebony hair without a touch of gray. It is twisted into such an elaborate knot that I think it must reach the floor when unbound. He says something to her quietly, and then looks my way. The woman nods and moves toward me, her gaze piercing mine. I feel suddenly violated.

Her voice is soft and smooth. It belies the fear she instills in me. "Amalia, welcome to Altus. We have long awaited your arrival. Brother Markov tells me you are quite tired and require protection and shelter. Please allow us the privilege of providing you with both."

She does not wait for my answer, nor does she wait for me. She simply turns and begins walking up a stone pathway that seems to wind to the very top of the island. Dimitri reaches for my hand and takes my bag, leading me forward. The others fall into line, the robed women at the back of our strange group.

About halfway to the top of the hill, I begin to think I will not make it. My exhaustion, held at bay by the terrifying and frigid plummet through the ocean, resurfaces as we make our way on the peaceful island. It is a riot of color and sensation—the brilliant red of the apples on the trees that seem to grow wild everywhere I look, the many robed and half-hidden faces that are alternately mysterious and fearsome, the rich green of the grass along the side of the pathway, and the soft, sweet scent that reminds me of my mother. It is all there, but in an amalgam that is at once overwhelming and surreal.

Luisa's voice, when I hear it, seems to come from within my own head. It is both louder and more muffled than usual.

"Goodness!" she says. "Are there not carriages or horses? Any mode of transport that does not involve us trudging up this neverending mountain would suffice."

"The Sisters believe that walking is good for the soul," Dimitri says, and even in my current state I think I hear the humor in his voice.

Luisa is not amused. "Nothing is as good for the soul as comfort, in my opinion." She stops to wipe her brow with the back of her sleeve.

I try to keep walking. To put one foot in front of the other. I think if I can do only that, if I can only keep *moving*, I will reach the end of the path. But my body has something else in mind. It stops working altogether until I am standing perfectly still in the middle of the path.

"Lia? Are you all right?" Dimitri stands in front of me. I feel his arm on mine. See his concerned face.

I want to reassure him. To tell him that, of course, I am perfectly fine. That I shall just walk and walk and walk until such a time when I might finally lay down and rest with dignity. A time when I might rest without fear of the Souls taking charge of the medallion that is, even now, heavy on my wrist and my mind.

None of that is what I say. In fact, I don't say anything at all, because the words that sound so reasonable in my head will not form on my lips. Worse, my legs are no longer willing to support my body. The ground rushes toward me with alarming speed until something lifts me above it.

And then there is nothing at all.

It is the pulsing on my chest that draws me out of the blackness.

I feel it there for what seems a long time before I have the energy to swim my way out of the lethargy that weighs down my limbs as well as my will. When I finally open my eyes, it is to a young woman with eyes as green as my own, her hair a brilliant white halo against the candlelight reaching to me from the recesses of the room. Her face is kind, her forehead creased with worry as she looks down at me.

"Shhh," she says. "You must sleep."

"What... What..." I will my hands to reach for the thing I feel on my chest. It takes me some time to make my arms obey, but when they do, I grasp at a smooth, hard oval attached to a string around my neck. The object is hot to my touch and throbs with an energy I can almost hear. "What *is* this?" I finally manage to ask.

She smiles gently. "It is only an adder stone, though a powerful one, to be sure. It is to protect you. From the Souls." She takes my hands and tucks them under the thick blankets that cover my body. "Sleep now, Sister Amalia."

"What about... what about Dimitri? And Luisa? And Sonia and Edmund?"

"They're quite all right, I promise. Everything is well in hand. Altus is off-limits to the Souls, and the adder stone will protect you while you sleep. You've nothing to fear."

She gets up from the bed, disappearing into the dim room,

lit only with candles, behind her. I want to stay awake. I want to formulate the many, many questions clamoring for attention, but it is no use, and I slip back into the nothingness before I can put up a fight.

"Are you awake now? Well and truly?"

This time it is a different girl who hovers over me. She is younger than the shadowy woman who told me about the adder stone and cared for me during the time I floated in and out of consciousness. This girl looks at me not with worry but with open curiosity.

I fumble beneath the sheets for my wrist, breathing a sigh of relief as my fingers touch the cool disc of the medallion, the whispery velvet of the ribbon. It is still there along with the familiar mixture of relief and resentment that accompanies its presence.

The voice of the other woman drifts to me in the haze of memory: *It is only an adder stone, though a powerful one, to be sure. It is to protect you. From the Souls.*

My hand feels leaden as I lift it to my chest, fumbling for the stone around my neck. When my fingers close around it, I am baffled to find it smooth and with a heat that should burn my skin and somehow does not. I resolve to ask more about it later and drop my hand back to the coverlet.

"May I..." My throat is so dry I can hardly speak. "May I have some water, please?"

The girl giggles. "You could ask for the moon right now and

the Sisters will see to it that it arrives prettily wrapped on your doorstep."

I don't know what she means, but she reaches for the table at the side of the bed and pours water into a heavy ceramic mug, lifting it to my lips so that I can drink. The water is icy and pure in a way that is almost sweet.

"Thank you." I let my head fall back onto the pillow. "How long have I been asleep?"

"Two days or so, off and on."

I nod. I have vague memories of waking to the darkened room, the flickering candles casting shadows on the wall as graceful figures moved about in the half-light.

"Where is the other girl? The one who cared for me before?" I ask.

She purses her lips as she ponders my question. "Did she have very white hair and green eyes? Or was her hair dark, like yours?"

"I... I think it was light."

"That would be Una. She has cared for you the most."

"Why is that?"

She shrugs. "Don't you want to know my name?" She is petulant now, and I see that she is probably no more than twelve.

"Of course. I was just going to ask. You have such pretty hair." I reach up and touch a shimmering lock. It glows gold even in the faint light of the candles, and I try not to feel the pain near my heart. "It reminds me of a dear friend of mine."

"Not the one they have in hiding?" She seems angry at the comparison.

"I don't know where they have her. I only know that she is as dear to me as a sister." I decide to change the subject. "So? What *is* your name?"

"Astrid." She says it with the satisfaction of one who finds her own name pleasing.

I smile at her, though it feels more like a grimace. "It's a beautiful name."

My mind, sufficiently warmed up with talk of hair and names, is finally moving. I try to rise onto my elbows, hoping to dress and find Dimitri and the others, but my arms wobble underneath me until I fall back onto the pillow.

But that is not the worst of it.

The worst of it is the sheet, which falls to my waist as I attempt to rise, revealing my shockingly bare upper body. I grasp for the edge of the sheet, raising it quickly to my neck and realizing with true horror how soft and crisp the sheets are against my entire body. Or more accurately, against my entirely *bare* body.

It takes me a moment to formulate the words. When I do, they come out more a sputter than a question. "Where are my clothes?"

Astrid giggles again. "You would have preferred sleeping in your traveling attire?"

"No, but... surely someone could have found me a dressing gown of some kind... a shift... anything at all? Or do you not

have clothes here on Altus?" I regret the bite of my words but am filled with mortifying visions of a stranger stripping me bare as a babe.

Astrid eyes me with blatant curiosity, as if I am an exotic animal on display. "Certainly we have clothing, but why would you want to wear it while you sleep? Wouldn't it be uncomfortable?"

"Of course not!" I snap. "One is supposed to sleep in nightclothes!"

It is a ridiculous conversation, like trying to describe color to someone who cannot see, and I ignore the devilish voice in my head that sees reason in her argument and cannot help noticing the cool slide of the sheets against my naked skin.

"If you say so." Astrid's smile is sly, as if she sees straight through my argument and knows exactly what I am thinking.

I lift my chin, trying to reclaim some of my dignity. "Yes, well . . . I'll need help locating my clothing, please."

She tips her head playfully. "I should think you'll need to eat and rest a bit before resuming normal activity."

"I have things to which I must attend. People I need to see."

She shakes her head. "I'm afraid not. I have strict instructions to see that you rest and eat. Besides, you see how it is; you are too weak to be about just yet."

I am suddenly weary of Astrid's sly giggles and knowing glances.

"I'd like to see Una, please." I wonder if she will be offended, but she rises with only a sigh.

"Very well. I shall ask her to come to you. Is there anything I can get you while you wait?"

I shake my head, wondering if a gag for her condescending mouth would be too much to ask.

She leaves the room without another word, and I wait in a silence so total I wonder if there is a world outside the room at all. I do not hear voices or footsteps or the clank of silver on porcelain. Nothing to indicate that people are living, eating, or breathing outside of my room.

I look around, clutching the sheet to my chest, until the faint sound of graceful footsteps approaches the door. It swings open without a sound, and I marvel that such a door—it looks as if it was carved out of a giant oak—can move without a creak.

Una closes it quietly behind her. I do not know her at all, and yet I am happy to see her as she approaches the bed. She emanates goodness and serenity, something I somehow remember even from my addled, half-awake state the last time we spoke.

"Hello," she says, smiling. "I'm so happy you're awake."

I see in her eyes that she is, and I return her smile. "Thank you for coming. I..." I throw a glance at the door. "You were very good to me while I slept."

She laughs and it travels all the way to her eyes in a sparkle. "Astrid can be a bit much, can she not? I had something else I needed to attend to, and I didn't want to leave you alone. Was she a terrible pest?"

"Well...not *terrible*."

She grins. "Hmmm, I see. That bad, was she?" She looks at the water cup on the bedside table. "At least she had the good sense to give you water. You must be dying of thirst and very hungry besides!"

I have not thought of food until this moment, but the second Una mentions it, my stomach twists with emptiness.

"I'm starving!" I tell her.

"It is no wonder!" she says, rising. "You have been asleep for nearly two days." She moves to a wardrobe at the far side of the room, talking as she goes. "I'll set you out some clothes and fetch you food and drink. We will have you right as rain in no time."

I try again to rise on my elbows, and this time I manage it. It is the first time I have gotten a glimpse of the whole room. From this angle, it does not seem as enormous as it did when the shadows hid its far corners. It is sparsely furnished, with only the wardrobe, a small chest of drawers, and a simple writing table and chair in addition to the bed and night table. A heavily draperied window rises from the floor all the way to the ceiling high overhead. The walls are stone. I can smell them, cool and musty, now that I am coherent, and I somehow know that they have sheltered the Sisters for centuries. The thought brings me to the reason for our journey.

"How is my Aunt Abigail?" I ask Una from across the room.

She turns a little so that I can see her face. Her brow creases with worry. "Not well, I'm afraid. The Elders are doing all they

can, but…" She shrugs. "It is the way of things, is it not?" It makes sense, of course, for Aunt Abigail must be quite old, but even Una sounds sad.

"May I see her?" I ask.

She closes the doors to the wardrobe and walks back toward the bed with a garment draped over her arm. "She's sleeping. She has been asking for you for days. Was unable to sleep, if the truth is told, until she knew you had arrived safely. Now that she is finally comfortable, it would be kindest to let her rest. You have my word, though, that you will be summoned the moment she awakens."

I nod. "Thank you."

"No. Thank *you*." She meets my eyes with a smile that I return as she lays the garments at the end of the bed. "There, now. Put these on while I get you something to eat. There is water for washing on the bureau."

"Yes, but…" I do not want to be rude in the face of her hospitality. "What of my own clothes?"

"They're being laundered," she says. "Besides, I think you'll find these decidedly more comfortable." There is a twinkle in her eye, and I catch the slightest air of Astrid, minus the hint of malice I thought I recognized in the other girl's eyes.

I nod. "All right, then. Thank you."

She smiles in answer and turns to leave, closing the door quietly behind her.

I wait a moment before daring to leave my bed. Already I feel weak, and I have done nothing more than rise to a half-sitting position and speak to Una. I have a vague recollection of falling on the stone pathway leading to the top of the island in the moments before I lost consciousness. I am mortified at the memory and fervently hope that I will not collapse on the floor of my room.

I begin by throwing back the covers and swinging my legs over the side of the bed. The room is surprisingly warm, even in my state of nakedness. The rush of cold air I expect without the covers does not come, and when I manage to place my feet on the stone floor it, too, is warm.

Holding on to the bedside table, I lift myself ever so carefully to a standing position. A wave of dizziness hits me, but it only last a few seconds. When it passes, I shuffle to the end of the bed on limbs stiff from lack of use, the adder stone resting wantonly between my naked breasts. Even alone as I am, I cannot help but feel self-conscious, but when I reach the clothes that Una has laid out for me, I become certain that there must be some mistake.

Either that, or someone is having a good laugh at my expense.

21

"You didn't leave me everything! I'm missing...all kinds of things!"

Una puts a tray laden with bread, cheeses, and fruit on the night table and makes her way to where I sit on the bed. Her soft lilac robe, identical to the one I am wearing, swirls around her feet and against her body. I catch an outline of the womanly figure underneath along with my first hint that there has not, after all, been a mistake.

She looks me up and down. "It doesn't look like you are missing anything."

I feel embarrassment tint my cheeks. "But there's not enough of it!"

She tips her head with a smile. "There are undergarments and a robe. What else do you require?"

I stand up, wobbling a little until my remaining dizziness

passes. "Oh, I don't know...some trousers? A gown? And how about some shoes and stockings? Or am I supposed to go barefoot?"

"Lia..." I startle at the use of my name. "Oh, may I call you Lia? It's so much less stuffy than Amalia."

I nod and she continues.

"I will provide you with sandals when we leave the room, but while you are here at the Sanctuary, you don't need anything else. Besides," she says, raising her eyebrows, "I took your clothes to the laundry, and there *are* quite a lot of them! Is it not uncomfortable to be so encumbered all the time?"

I cannot help feeling a bit indignant. Here I have thought myself an independent young woman, ever freer since my days at Wycliffe, yet Una has turned that notion on its ear.

Ignoring her question, I straighten my back and try not to sound like I am sulking. "Very well. But I would like my own clothing back in case I should require it."

She heads for the door. "I'll fetch it while you take breakfast."

I call out just before she closes the door behind her. "I'll have you know I wear breeches instead of skirts when I ride!"

I catch her knowing smile as she shuts the door and have the distinct feeling that she is quite amused with my puritan ideals.

"Luisa will be happy to see you," Una says. "As will your guide, Edmund, though he is attending to business, as I understand it."

We are walking the length of a long stone hallway exposed to the elements save for a roof. It reminds me of the palazzi I saw when traveling in Italy with Father.

I notice that Una has not mentioned Sonia, and though I imagine she is trying to be tactful, it is Sonia who weighs most on my mind.

"What of my other friend?" I turn my head to her as we walk, hoping to catch a nuance in her expression that will tell me something her words do not.

She sighs, appraising me with her eyes. I wonder if she will be honest or gentle. "She is not well, Lia, but I will save the details for Brother Markov. His position is such that he will likely know more than I would anyway."

Brother Markov. I wonder about the title and the veiled reference to Dimitri's position, but Sonia is foremost in my mind.

"May I see her?"

Una shakes her head. "Not today."

There is such finality in her tone that I do not bother arguing. I shall ask Dimitri instead.

Una looks up as a gentleman, full-lipped and sporting a devilish grin, approaches us on the walkway. His breeches are snug, his white tunic fitted through the shoulders.

"Good morning, Una."

"Good morning, Fenris," Una answers. It is quite obvious she is flirting.

Once we are a safe distance from the retreating gentleman, I turn to look at her. "Who was *that?*"

"One of the Brothers. One of the more... notorious among their rank, actually. I have no intention of seeing him, but he has such a reputation that I quite like giving him a taste of his own medicine."

"Really? I'm impressed!" I laugh. "And who are the Brothers?"

"The Brothers are exactly that—our Brothers."

"Fenris is your brother?"

She laughs. "Not *my* brother. A Brother. That is, he was born to one of the Sisters and has not yet decided if he will leave to make his way in your world or stay and serve the cause of the Sisterhood."

"I'm afraid I don't understand."

Una stops walking, placing a hand on my arm so that I stop as well. "The Sisters are not bound to Altus. We may make a life in your world, as your mother and aunt did, if we choose. But even staying on the island does not mean our lives cease moving forward. We still fall in love, marry, and have children, and those children must also choose their own paths when they come of age."

I still do not understand where a gentleman such as Fenris enters into the equation. "But who are they? The Brothers?"

She raises her brows. "You do not imagine the Sisters give birth only to females, do you?"

I think of Henry and know that they do not. "The Brothers are the male offspring of the Sisters who choose to have children."

It is not a question, but she nods in answer anyway. "And the male descendants of the Grigori who, if they remain on

Altus, are only permitted to marry from the Sisterhood. They are all our Brothers, really, and they may stay to serve the Sisterhood or even the Grigori, if they are so chosen."

I am still standing in one place, contemplating her answer, when I realize she has started moving again and is now a few steps ahead. I have to walk quickly to catch up and feel myself tiring though I have been out of bed for less than an hour.

A few minutes later I grasp the question at the back of my mind. "Una?"

"Hmmm?"

"Do the Brothers live here on the island with you?"

"Of course." She does not seem surprised by my question. "They live in Sanctuary, where we all reside."

"Under the same roof?"

She smiles as she looks over at me. "It is only in your world, Lia, that it is uncommon for men and women to live together in mutual respect and honor. That it is unnatural for men and women to express feelings for one another outside of marriage."

"Well, yes... but we do so after marriage, of course."

She tips her head as her eyes grow serious. "Why is marriage a requirement for mutual respect and honor?"

She does not seem to require an answer, and it is a good thing. Her questions crowd my already overwhelmed thoughts until I am forced to push them aside.

Una turns down a wide hallway and places her hand on the knob of a door to our right. When she opens it, waving me in before her, I feel at home instantly.

The room is a library, and though the walls, like the rest of those at Altus, are crafted of stone, they are lined with books just like those in Father's library at Birchwood. And if the atmosphere is not enough to put me at ease, the company certainly is, for Luisa looks up from one of the tables near the back of the room. Her face lights up when she sees me.

She rushes over. "Lia! I thought you would never wake up!" She squeezes me tightly and then draws back to look at me, her lips tightening in an expression of worry.

"What?" I ask. "I'm fine. I simply needed to sleep, that is all."

"You do not look fine! I have never seen you so pale. Are you certain you should be up and about?"

"Quite. I've been asleep for nearly two days, Luisa! I simply need to walk in the sun a bit and my color will be back to normal in no time."

I smile to reassure her, not wanting to tell her that I am, in fact, still quite tired. That I do still feel very weak despite having eaten, washed, and dressed.

"Yes, well. It is lovely here." She is breathless with excitement and looks healthy and well-rested in her own light purple robe. "I cannot wait to show you the grounds! Rhys has shown me so many amazing things!"

I raise my eyebrows. "Rhys?"

Luisa shrugs, trying to seem casual while she flushes crimson. "He is one of the Brothers who has been showing me the island. He has been very helpful."

I grin, feeling a little like my old self. "I'm quite certain he has!"

"Oh, you!" She slaps my arm playfully, followed by another quick embrace. "Goodness! I *have* missed you, Lia!"

I laugh. "I should like to say I've missed you as well, but since I have spent the past two days in the deepest sleep of my life, I'm afraid I did not miss much!"

"Not even Dimitri?" she asks with a sly smile.

"Not even Dimitri." I am happy to have surprised her, if only for a moment. "Until the moment I awoke, of course. Now I miss him terribly!"

She laughs, and it carries through the room like a strong wind just as I remember. I suddenly notice Una standing at my side and feel terribly rude.

"Oh, I *am* sorry! I haven't introduced you!"

Puzzlement crosses Luisa's face. She follows my gaze to Una and breaks into a smile. "Una? We met days ago, Lia. She has been keeping me company and assuring me of your good health."

"Wonderful," I say. "Then we are all acquainted."

I am about to ask Luisa about Edmund when the door opens behind me. Turning to the sound, the sunlight is so blinding from the half-open door that the figure standing within its frame is at first only a golden burst of light. When the door closes and the room is once more shrouded in semidarkness, I cannot stop myself from running across the room in greeting.

I throw myself into Dimitri's arms in a terribly unladylike manner. I don't care. Not for a moment. It feels like forever since his dark eyes have stared into mine.

He laughs into my hair. "I'm happy to see I am not the only one who has suffered."

"You suffered?" I ask against his neck.

He laughs. "Every second you've been asleep." Leaning back to get a better look at me, he kisses me on the lips without seeming to mind that Luisa and Una are right there in front of us. "Are you all right? How are you feeling?"

"A little weak, maybe, and still a little tired. But I will be fine with a bit more time and rest."

"Altus is the perfect place for both. Come, let me show you some of the island. It will do you good to get out of doors."

I look at Una. "Is it all right?"

I don't know why I ask her permission, but it seems an odd thing to go wandering about the island when I am meant to find the location of the missing pages.

"Of course." She waves away my question, answering as if she can read my mind. "There is time yet for you to speak to Lady Abigail about the purpose for your visit, and she is still sleeping, in any case."

I turn to Luisa. "Do you mind?"

She grins. "Not at all. I have plans of my own."

Dimitri leads me to the door, and I resolve to ask Luisa later about the seductive new purr in her voice.

"Does it ever rain here?"

Despite the fact that I have been coherent less than twenty-four hours, it seems impossible that the weather on Altus could be anything but warm and gentle.

"We wouldn't have so many trees if it didn't."

He smiles down at me as we make our way farther up the stone path, and I see him as if for the first time. His skin glows with good health against the same brown trousers and fitted white tunic Fenris wore when Una and I passed him in the outer hallway. The white is brilliant against Dimitri's dark hair, and it is impossible not to notice the taut pull of fabric across his shoulders. When I meet his gaze, a slow smile spreads from his eyes to his mouth and he raises his eyebrows as if he knows exactly what I am thinking.

I smile into his eyes, oddly unembarrassed.

Glancing back the way we came, I get my first real look at the building in which I have spent the last two days sleeping. Seeing it from the outside is considerably more impressive than seeing it from within, though it is not at all tall or imposing. Crafted entirely of a bluish gray stone, it sits low and long on the top of the hill I attempted to climb the day we arrived. The roof appears to be copper and has mellowed to a mossy green that stands in subtle contrast to the sprawling lawns and deeper emerald of the leafy apple trees.

It is beautiful, though that hardly seems an adequate description. As I look at the ocean stretched below, the building they call the Sanctuary, and the smaller structures surrounding it, I feel the greatest sense of belonging. The greatest sense of peace. I wish I had known sooner that I was a part of the Sisterhood. Of Altus. It is as if I have been missing a piece of myself for a very long time—a piece whose loss I did not feel fully until reclaiming it.

We pass several people on the path, and Dimitri says hello to each of them by name. He smiles with characteristic charm, though they seem strangely immune to his friendly nature. He reaches down to take my hand as we pass a lovely older woman who glares openly in answer to his greeting. I imagine she is simply aged and cranky, but I can no longer stay silent when a young woman responds angrily to Dimitri's greeting by saying, "You should be ashamed!"

I stop walking and stare after her retreating back.

"How rude! What is the matter with everyone?" I turn to look at him in bewilderment.

Dimitri hangs his head. "Yes, well . . . not everyone is as supportive of our journey as we would like."

"Whatever do you mean? How can they not be supportive? We seek only to find the missing pages in order to end the prophecy. Is that not what the Sisters want?" He doesn't answer, and I begin to understand that I am not seeing the whole picture. "Dimitri?"

"They don't know you as I do." His face colors either with shame or embarrassment, and I feel how hard it was for him to say aloud.

It is so simple, really, that I cannot believe the possibility has eluded me until now.

"It's because of me." I stare at the ground for a minute before looking up at Dimitri. "Isn't it?"

He puts his hands on my shoulders and looks into my eyes. "It doesn't matter, Lia." I cannot hold his gaze, but he touches

my chin with his fingers and turns my face to his so that it is impossible to avoid his eyes. "It doesn't matter."

"Yes, it does." I don't mean for it to sound harsh, but it does. I turn away from him and continue on the path, this time avoiding the eyes of any who pass.

It takes only seconds for Dimitri to catch up to me. He does not speak right away, and when he finally does, I get the sense that he is treading very carefully.

"I am not defending them, but try and understand," he says.

I do not want to hear opinions that others have formed in their ignorance without even knowing me. But Dimitri needs to say it, and so I will hear it.

"I'm listening." I say it without looking at him and try to keep my focus on the path ahead.

He sighs. "You are the only Gate to ever come to Altus. To ever be *welcomed* at Altus. It is just... well, it is just not done. Has not been done in the past. Until now, the Gate has always been an enemy. An enemy of the Sisters, though one of them, as well. Perhaps *more* an enemy because she was one of them. Your mother and father escaped judgment, at least the open judgment of those on the island, by residing elsewhere."

"Is it not proof enough that I'm here? That I have risked my life and the lives of those dear to me to make this journey?" I am aware of a building anger. It is not the fury I felt when learning of Sonia's betrayal, but a slow simmer that threatens to build and build until it has nowhere to go but out.

"Lia... Until you find the missing pages and use them to

end the prophecy, the Sisters have no way of knowing if that is truly your intent. Your mother—"

I stop walking, glaring at him. "I am *not* my mother. I love her, but I am not her."

The breath seems to leave his body in a rush of defeat. "I know that. But they don't. All they have on which to base their judgment, their hope, is the past. And your mother tried to fight the Souls. Wanted to fight them. But in the end, she was not able to hold them at bay. *That* is what the Sisters of Altus know and what they fear."

I start walking again, this time more slowly. He follows, and for a time, we walk without speaking. It takes me a while to form the words I know I must say. To ask the question I fear most. When I finally do, I find I must steady my voice.

"And you are shunned because of your... involvement with me?" He doesn't answer right away, and I know he is trying to soften his response. "Just answer, Dimitri. What do we have together if we cannot speak plainly?"

"*Shunned* is a bit harsh," he says softly. "They don't understand. I have already been summoned to the High Court for saving you from the kelpie. That is scandal enough for someone of my..."

"Station?" I finish for him.

He nods. "I suppose. And now there is the matter of my romantic involvement with a Sister clearly designated as Gate, and not just any Gate, but the one with the power to finally bring about the return of Samael."

"You sound as if you're defending them." I cannot keep the bitterness from my voice.

"No. I am simply trying to understand them, and to be fair in my own judgment even when they are not."

It is impossible to be angry. With every word Dimitri says, I know he speaks the truth. Most importantly, I learn more about him and become more certain that he is a good man. How can I fault him for such qualities?

This time I reach for his hand. It feels so large in mine, and yet I have the strongest urge to offer him the same protection he has offered me. I don't know how effective I would be in shielding him from anything significant, but I suddenly know that I would do anything to try to keep him from harm.

"It seems there is only one thing to do then."

"What is it?"

"Prove them wrong."

And in this moment, as I smile into his eyes, I am certain that I will.

22

We walk hand in hand toward the other side of the island. The path slopes downward toward a grove of some kind, and I realize we have not come upon anyone else for quite some time. I am astounded at the absolute quiet.

"Come," Dimitri says. "I want to show you something."

He pulls me off the path and toward the grove. I have to run to keep up, and I try not to trip on the field of grass and wildflowers.

"What are you doing?" I laugh. "Where are you taking me?"

"You'll see," he calls out.

We wind our way through the trees, and it becomes clear that it is an orange grove. I remember my mother's scent. Oranges and jasmine. I am aware of the adder stone, pulsing and hot, beneath my robe.

The grove seems neverending. I would be frightened of

becoming lost were it not for Dimitri, for the trees grow in a strange order that only nature seems to understand. Dimitri knows exactly where he is going, though, and I follow him without question.

We break through the trees and the sky unfolds before us. The sea, glistening below, churns white as waves crash on the jagged cliff that descends steeply from the grove to the water.

"I used to come here as a boy," Dimitri says from my side. "It was my secret spot, though I imagine my mother knew right where it was. Not much is a secret on Altus."

I smile as I try to imagine Dimitri a dark-haired boy with an impish grin. "What was it like, growing up here?"

He wanders back to a nearby tree, reaching up and pulling a small orange from its branches.

"It was . . . idyllic. Though I didn't know it at the time."

"What of your parents? Do they live on the island?"

"My father does." A shadow passes over his face, and when he continues I understand why. "My mother is dead."

"Oh . . . I'm . . . I'm sorry, Dimitri." I tip my head, smiling sadly at him. "I suppose that is yet another thing we have in common."

He nods slowly, walking back toward me and gesturing to the grass near the edge of the cliff.

"Come. Sit."

I drop to the ground, and Dimitri follows suit. He continues without mention of his parents, and I understand that the subject is closed.

"Altus is like a very small town, only with a considerably more open mind." He rolls the orange in his palms as he talks. "In many ways it was not very different from your own upbringing, I suppose. There were marriages, births, deaths."

"And everyone, men and women, living in close proximity." I am still getting my head around the fact and cannot resist bringing it up.

"Ah, you've been talking to Una. Good. Does it shock you?"

I shrug. "A little. It is... different than what I'm used to, I suppose."

He nods. "It will take some time to become accustomed to our ways, Lia. I know that. But you should try not to think of them as new or foreign. Really, they are older than time itself."

I gaze out over the water, pondering his words. I don't know if I am ready to contemplate them now. They ring of a reality I could not have envisioned just a few weeks ago, despite having been oddly unchaperoned in London.

"Tell me about Sonia," I ask, in part to change the subject, and in part because I am finally feeling strong enough to hear the truth about my friend.

Dimitri begins peeling the orange, trying to keep the peel in one piece. "Sonia is still... not herself. The Elders have her cloistered."

"Cloistered?" I am confused, feeling one moment as if I have landed in a hedonistic commune and another as if I am in a nunnery.

He nods. "In seclusion. Very few of the Sisters are trusted

and powerful enough—your aunt would have been one of them were she not so ill—to perform such rites. Only they can see Sonia while she is recovering."

I cannot help but be alarmed. "Rites? They aren't hurting her, are they?"

He reaches out to touch my hand. "Of course not. It is the Souls who have hurt her, Lia. The Sisters have to vanquish the Souls' hold on Sonia so that she might come back to herself." He pulls his hand away and finishes peeling the orange. "Releasing Sonia from the Souls' authority may take some time, and only the Elders can see it done."

"When can I see her?"

"Tomorrow, perhaps." And in his tone, the knowledge of another closed subject.

I pull a few tufts of grass. "And Edmund? Where is he?"

He breaks the orange in half, and I have the sudden urge to smell his hands. "He is here on the island. The first day, he sat outside your room until he fell asleep on the floor. We had to move him, still asleep, to a room of his own."

I cannot help smiling at the mention of Edmund, and suddenly I cannot wait to see him again.

"You care for Edmund very much, don't you?" Dimitri asks.

I nod. "Next to Aunt Virginia, he is the closest thing I have left to family. He has seen me through..." I take a deep breath, remembering. "Well, through many horrible things. His strength makes me believe that I don't have to be strong all of the time. That it's okay to lean on someone else just for a while."

I am embarrassed to have said aloud what I have so often thought, but Dimitri smiles softly, and I know just what he is thinking.

His gaze is hot on my face. I feel so many things in it. So many things that one should not be able to feel through a simple look—power, confidence, honor, loyalty, and, yes, perhaps even love.

He pulls his eyes from my face and tears off a section of the orange. When he lifts his arm, I think he will hand it to me, but instead, he holds it toward my lips. Of course, in New York or London, it would be highly improper to allow a man to feed me.

But I am not in New York or London.

Leaning forward, I take the orange from his hand with my mouth, my lips brushing his fingertips as I draw the fruit between my teeth. When I bite into it, I realize how small it is. The section is only slightly more than a bite, and sweeter than the oranges I have had occasion to eat elsewhere. Dimitri's eyes linger on my mouth while I chew.

I look at the rest of the orange, still sitting in his open palm. "Aren't you going to taste it?"

He licks his lips, and when he speaks, his voice is hoarse. "Yes."

He moves toward me and his mouth is on mine before I have time to think. His kiss brings forth the remnant of another Lia. One who has never had to wear a corset and stockings. One who is not ashamed when her body thrills at the feel of his urgent lips on hers and the touch of his fingers through the

delicate fabric of her robe. This Lia lives by the rules of the island rather than the laws of London society.

His mouth still on mine, he pushes me back onto the soft grass and we lose ourselves in the wind and the sea and the feel of each other. When he finally pulls away, his breath comes fast and heavy.

I lace my fingers together behind his neck and try to pull him to me once again. He groans, but only graces my cheeks and eyelids with tender kisses.

"We come from different places, Lia, and in many ways, different times as well. But now, here, I want you to know that I honor the laws of your place and time."

I know what he means and try not to blush. "What if I don't want you to?" The words are out of my mouth before I have the chance to think them through.

He props himself on one elbow, fingering a length of my robe. "You are lovely in lilac," he murmurs.

"Are you changing the subject?"

He smiles. "Perhaps." He leans down and kisses the tip of my nose. "In order to have honor of my own, I must respect the laws of your world as long as you're a part of it. Should you decide to become a part of mine... well, then, we may honor those laws together."

I sit up, folding my legs underneath my robe. "You want me to stay on Altus with you?"

He plucks a small wild daisy from the grass and tucks it behind my ear. "Not now, of course. We must find the missing pages and banish the Souls. But afterward... Nothing would

make me happier than to build a life with you on Altus. And don't you feel it? A connection to this place?"

I cannot lie, and so I nod. I am overcome, at once flattered beyond measure and frightened out of my mind at what the future, once as sure and certain as the rising sun, might now hold.

"What if I don't want to leave my world?" I have to ask.

He leans over and kisses me softly, lingering over my lips before pulling away just an inch so that I can almost feel his lips move when he speaks. "Then I will join you in yours."

He kisses me again, but when I close my eyes, it is not Dimitri's proclamations of love that ring through the halls of my mind, but those of another man, spoken long ago.

❦

I jump as Luisa storms into the room, slamming the door behind her.

"This is ridiculous, Lia! Utterly ridiculous!" She holds her arms out, the deep purple sleeves of her new robe fluttering around her slender arms. It is a few shades deeper than our day robe and identical to the one Una left for me. "Una tells me we must wear *robes* to dinner!"

I laugh at Luisa's tone, as if robes are rats. "Yes, robes are what the Sisters wear on Altus." I try not to sound as if I am speaking to a five-year-old.

"Don't be patronizing," she says. "You know what I mean: how are we to go to our first big dinner on Altus in noth-

ing but...but..." She gestures at her silk-clad body before continuing. "*This?*"

I shake my head. "What did you do while I was asleep all those nights? What did you wear then?"

"I ate in my room, mostly, so it didn't matter what I wore. I think they were waiting for you to have some sort of celebration."

The breath hitches in my lungs. I am not ready to meet the whole of the island. "What sort of celebration?"

She wanders to the bed, flinging herself backward onto it and speaking to the ceiling. "I don't know. But I don't believe it will be too formal. I overheard one of the younger girls saying something about how it would be 'inappropriate' to have too merry a feast."

I think of Aunt Abigail, fighting for her life at this very moment, and find that I agree with the unnamed Sister.

Luisa sits up. "Even still, Lia...I should like to have something nice to wear, wouldn't you? Don't you miss your lovely gowns?"

I shrug, fingering the lush folds of violet that spill around my legs. "I'm becoming used to the robes, and they *are* comfortable, aren't they?"

I move to the looking glass to pin my hair and almost do not recognize the person staring back at me. This is the first time I have bothered to view my reflection since we left London. I suppose in many ways I am a different person, and I wonder if perhaps the changes have been for the better. I turn

from the glass, deciding on a whim to leave my hair unbound and curling around my shoulders.

"I would sacrifice comfort for fashion on *any* occasion, and tonight especially," Luisa says from across the room, and her baleful expression causes me a moment's pity.

I make my way to the bed and sit next to her. "And why should tonight be special?"

She shrugs, but the knowing smile working its way to her mouth gives her away. "No reason."

"Mhm. So it wouldn't have anything to do with...oh, I don't know...a certain Brother who happens to reside here on the Island?"

She laughs. "Oh, all right! I *would* like to look my best for Rhys! Is that so wrong?"

"Of course not." I stand. "But look at it this way; there is every possibility that, were you to appear at dinner in a gown, Rhys would simply think you an over-trussed goose."

I know that I am making headway when Luisa chews her lower lip, a thoughtful expression replacing her high color of a moment ago. "Really, Luisa. I think the silk robe's rather exotic. Rather...sensual."

She thinks a moment longer before standing in a huff. "Oh, fine! I shall wear the infernal robe. Besides, it's not as if I have a choice unless I should like to attend naked!"

"That is true." I link my arm with hers as we head for the door. "But who knows? Perhaps Rhys would like that even better!"

Luisa turns to me, her mouth open in shock. "Lia! You've become absolutely scandalous!"

I suppose I have, and as we make our way to the dining hall I remember Dimitri's offer at the grove and wonder if the choice between one life and the other is truly mine to make. Perhaps I will not be capable of returning to the person I once was and the life I once lived.

I remember Henry's words from long ago and think them as appropriate as ever.

Only time will tell.

23

As we enter the dining hall, I am startled at the quiet that descends among the crowd. I try to ignore it as I make my way across the room with Luisa.

The hall is cavernous, filled with robed women and dashing men dressed head to toe in black. The massive chandelier, lit with a thousand candles, casts a warm glow over the center of the room. I wonder how someone was able to reach high enough to set the candles alight, for the chandelier hangs by a heavy chain that stretches so far upward I cannot even see its end.

"What do we do?" Luisa whispers.

"I don't know. I suppose we should look for Dimitri or Una."

"Or Rhys," she says.

I roll my eyes. "Yes. Or Rhys."

I step farther into the room, trying to keep my head high and a smile—generous enough to seem friendly but not so generous as to make me seem mad—plastered on my face.

It is times like these when I miss Sonia terribly. In truth, it was often for her that I would pull back my shoulders and find a brave smile, even when I was cowering inside. I have always been stronger for her support and companionship, and I feel the loss of it as powerfully as if I had only lost her to the Souls today.

"Thank goodness," Luisa breathes. "There is Dimitri."

I follow her gaze and see him making his way toward us. I do not think it is my imagination that his smile is private and meant only for me. He stops in front of us, taking both of my hands.

"There you are." He says it simply, as if he has been searching for me forever only to find me in a most unexpected place.

He has traded his daytime trousers for tighter-fitting black ones and wears a matching black tunic in place of his white one. The black makes him seem dangerous, and in the glow of the candles hanging from the chandelier and those placed at the periphery of the room, he is more handsome and thrilling than ever.

When he leans in, I think he means to kiss my cheeks, but instead his lips find my mouth. The kiss is lingering but not unseemly. I sneak a glance around the room, noticing that those in attendance look either chagrined or surprised, and I know Dimitri has made a declaration. He has told them that he is with me, whatever they may say. I do not think it possible, but my heart opens to him even further.

"Hello," I say. My voice is not as bold as I would like it to be, but I am caught off guard both by the mood of the others in the hall and by Dimitri's gesture.

He grins, seeming more like the private Dimitri I have come to know. "Well, hello."

And now my smile is real, for somehow when I am with him, it does not seem to matter what the rest of the world thinks or says.

He links one arm with mine and one with Luisa's and escorts us toward a table at the center of the room. It is a cue of sorts, and the crowd begins talking again, first in low murmurs and soon enough in voices so loud it is as if the awkwardness of the past moments was only a dream.

"I'm sorry you had to make your way to the dining hall alone." He has to speak loudly to be heard over the din. "I thought Una was bringing you, or I would have come for you myself."

"She was going to," I say. "But she wanted to check on Aunt Abigail. It seems she is still not awake."

He nods gravely, and I see from the concern on his face that I am not the only one who is worried about Aunt Abigail.

We stop at a long table directly underneath the chandelier. It is already mostly occupied, though there are three seats remaining, reserved, it seems, for us. I worry for a moment that Luisa will not be permitted to sit with her new beau, but when her face breaks into a beatific smile I follow her stare

and realize Rhys is already seated at our table. I shall have to ask Dimitri later if it is by chance or design.

An older woman with raven hair rises first. She bows a little in greeting, her steely eyes meeting mine, and I realize she is the Sister who led us up the path just before I fell unconscious.

"Welcome to Altus, Amalia, daughter of Adelaide." Her voice is lower than I remember.

It is strange to hear my mother's given name spoken aloud. I don't think I have heard anyone speak it since before her death. It takes me a moment to gather my wits.

I return her bow. "Thank you."

Dimitri turns to me and bows formally, fulfilling his part in some kind of ritual I do not understand. "Amalia, Lady Ursula and the Sisterhood welcome you."

I return his bow, feeling suddenly shy.

Dimitri repeats the small ceremony with Luisa, and introductions are made around the table. Everything happens so quickly that I forget most of the names as soon as they are spoken, but I know I will not soon forget Rhys's piercing eyes and the way they seem to see only Luisa. He is as dark as Dimitri, but quieter and less able or willing to make conversation. I should like to ask Luisa what they speak about when they are together, but I believe speaking may not be among their most favored activities. She is, even now, sitting so close to him that I see their thighs touch under the table.

As soon as we sit, the others in the hall take their places at tables across the massive dining hall. Food is brought in short order, and I can hardly keep pace with the dizzying array of

fruits, vegetables, crusty bread, and sweet wine, though I do notice that there is no meat.

As we are served I catch my dinner companions casting curious glances my way. I cannot blame them, I suppose. Using Dimitri's earlier argument, I imagine they have many questions that politeness begs they not ask.

It is immediately clear that Ursula holds stature, but I do not have a private moment during dinner to ask Dimitri for the details of her title. She takes full advantage of her position, though, whatever it may be. The server has not yet stepped away from our table when the first question is fired.

"Dimitri tells me you endured quite a journey to find us, Amalia." She sips from her goblet of wine.

I finish chewing the fig in my mouth. "Yes. It was...grueling."

She nods. "It seems you are not one to shy away from tasks both difficult and dangerous."

The words themselves sound like a compliment, but something in her tone tells me they are not. I want to be witty, to see the question behind the question, but my brain is still recovering from the extraordinary lack of sleep. I decide to take her statement at face value.

"The prophecy has taught me well that some things must be done however much we wish to avoid them."

She raises her eyebrows. "Do you? Wish to avoid them?"

I look at my hands, folded together in my lap. "I think anyone would wish to avoid some of the things I have experienced this past year."

Ursula tips her head, contemplating something before she

speaks again. "And what of your sister, Alice? What does she wish to avoid?"

My head jerks up at the unexpected mention of my sister, as if Alice's name might conjure her presence. I wonder why Ursula would be interested in my sister when it is a well-known fact that Alice is in violation of the Grigori and their laws.

I try to keep my voice level. "My sister rejects her role as Guardian. In your great knowledge and wisdom, I imagine this is something of which you are aware." I bow my head, hoping it passes for respect when in fact I am only trying to hide my growing disdain.

I do not look up to meet her eyes, but I feel her gaze harden. When she finally answers, I know it is because she must, because staying silent any longer will make her look weak. The concession brings me a bizarre sense of victory. "What I am *aware* of is that the future of Altus, of the very world, is at stake. Surely you understand that your role is one of privilege, do you not? Especially given the nature of your *rightful* role in the prophecy."

I hear the danger in Ursula's low, leisurely voice. It is far too easy to think it is that of a cat when it is in fact that of a lion. But I am too new to the ways and people at play in the prophecy to alienate a possible friend or foe. For I see now that it is a game, best played three or four moves ahead.

I look up and meet Ursula's eyes while the other eyes at the table are all trained on me. "Privilege speaks to something that implies fortune." I pause. "What have I to gain compared to all I have lost to the prophecy? A sister, a brother, a mother, a father..." I think of James and our lost future, and the melancholy hits me, even as I privately acknowledge my feelings for Dimitri. "Forgive me, but in my experience, the prophecy has been more a burden than a privilege, though that doesn't mean I will not honor it."

It may well be my imagination, but it seems the rest of the hall has grown quieter, as if everyone is listening with half an ear to the conversation at our table.

Ursula taps her fingers against the thick wooden tabletop as she considers her move. She tips her head. "Perhaps you should leave it to others better suited, more willing, to accept its *burden*."

I consider her words, but they do not make sense under the circumstances. "It is not as if I have a choice in the matter, is it? No choice worth contemplating. I would never allow Samael to use me as his Gate."

"Of course not," she murmurs. "But you are forgetting the other option available to you."

I shake my head. "What other option?"

"Do nothing. Allow the responsibility to pass to another Sister."

I look around the table, noting how the others seem to shift nervously in their seats and avert their eyes as if seeing something distasteful. All except for Dimitri and Luisa. Luisa looks as confused as I feel. She meets my eyes and I see the questions there. Questions I cannot answer. Dimitri, on the other hand, shoots daggers at Ursula.

I look back at her. "It could take generations for another Angel to be appointed by the prophecy."

She nods slowly, waving her hand in a gesture of dismissal. "Or it could take no time at all. No one knows what the prophecy dictates."

For a moment, I believe I am going mad. Is a Sister of the prophecy, an Elder no less, suggesting I do nothing? Is she asking me to pass my duty to another even when it might mean waiting centuries for the prophecy to end? Centuries in which Samael's Souls would gather in our world?

Dimitri suddenly speaks, his voice icy with rage. "I beg your pardon, Sister Ursula, but it seems quite clear what the prophecy dictates, does it not? It dictates Lia as more than the Gate—as the Angel, the one Gate with the authority to summon or refuse Samael. As such, Lia may exercise free will to choose either course. In all your wisdom, would you not agree that we owe her a debt of gratitude for choosing the side of right?"

Checkmate, I think. At least for now.

I squeeze Dimitri's hand under the table, for while I do not want to cause him more trouble, I cannot help but be grateful for his intervention.

Around the table, a silence ensues that can only be called awkward. We are saved from attempting to rescue what little remains of our pleasant dinner when Astrid appears, making a small bow at Ursula's elbow.

"Mother? May I sit at your table? I should like to get to know our guests." Her voice is sweet and timid, minus the

condescension that was present when she spoke to me in my room.

Mother? *Mother?* Ursula is Astrid's mother.

Ursula smiles, but not at Astrid. Her eyes remain fixed on me even as she answers her daughter. "Of course you may, my love. Take your seat next to Brother Markov."

Astrid's cheeks flush scarlet, and she bows toward her mother briefly before making her way to the other side of Dimitri. Once seated, she looks up at him, her adoration evident.

"Altus was not the same while you were away," she says demurely.

I think I note impatience in his eyes, but he covers it well. "And I am never the same without Altus." He turns to me and smiles. "How was your dinner?" Leaning in close enough so I can smell the wine on his breath, he whispers, "Aside from the company, of course."

I grin. "Lovely."

We pass the remainder of dinner without incident. Astrid sulks on the other side of Dimitri while Luisa remains thoroughly immersed in Rhys. Before long, a strange sort of music starts up at the front of the hall. Rhys stands and holds a hand out to Luisa. Together, they depart the table to dance, as do many others at our table and those nearby.

Dimitri reaches into a bowl on the table, plucking a luscious red strawberry from its interior and holding it to my mouth. This time I bite the glistening fruit cleanly from the stem without a thought. He smiles, and something secret and warm passes between us.

He dispenses with the stem on his plate, and his expression grows suddenly serious. "I'm sorry, Lia."

I swallow the rest of the strawberry before answering. "For what?"

"For Ursula. For all of it."

I shake my head. "You needn't be. It's not *your* fault."

He looks around the room at the couples swirling across the floor to a slow, sad song in a kaleidoscope of violet and black silk. "These are my people. My family. And you . . . well, you are something even more, Lia, as I'm sure you must know by now." He lifts one of my hands and kisses my palm. "I want them to be kind to you."

I take one of his hands and repeat the gesture.

For a moment, it is as if I am looking into his eyes for the first time. I am lost, and nothing else matters. Then the music abruptly shifts to something merry, and Dimitri stands, pulling me to my feet.

"Do me the honor." It is not a question, and before I know it, we are in the middle of the room among the other couples. I think I catch a glimpse of Luisa, but she disappears into the crowd before I can be sure.

"But . . . I don't know how to dance to music like this!" I say, looking around at the swiftly moving dancers.

He places one of my hands on his shoulder and the other on his waist, doing the same to me. "Not to worry. It's quite simple, I promise. Besides, you cannot call yourself a Sister if you won't dance!"

And then we are off and moving through the crowd in time

to the music. At first, Dimitri more or less drags me around the room. The footwork is every bit as complicated as the dances we learned at Wycliffe, and the music makes it hard to get my bearings. It does not flow the way Strauss and Chopin do. It trills and bounces and lilts.

We bump into more than a few people as I try to familiarize myself with the steps, and Dimitri leads me through the room calling out "Pardon me" and "Very sorry." After a while, though, I begin to feel more confident. Dimitri still leads, but I manage to keep up without stepping on his feet.

I am just starting to have fun when the music shifts. A happy roar erupts from the floor and in a moment, Dimitri is gone. I scan the bodies crowding around me, but before I can find him, another gentleman is on my arm.

"Oh! Hello!" I say.

He wears the same clothes as Dimitri without the same flair. But he is pleasant enough, and he returns my smile. "Hello there, Sister."

Just as I am thinking it will not be so bad to pass the time with this nice gentleman until Dimitri returns, the man disappears into the crowd and is quickly replaced by another. This one is fair, with hair as golden as Sonia's. We do not have time to do more than exchange a smile before he moves smoothly away and is replaced by another.

The pace of the music, and the dancing crowd along with it, grows increasingly frenzied, and I have little choice but to keep up as best I can through a parade of partners. There seems

to be some method to their madness, some order in which everyone changes partners, but I am at a loss to explain it.

I try a couple of times to extricate myself from the dance altogether, but separating myself from my partners and the crowd proves impossible. After a while, I give myself over to it, allowing myself to be spun to and fro until I am dizzy with music and laughter.

I am laughing with giddy abandonment as my new partner, a portly, older gentleman, spins me across the floor, passing me to yet another gentleman.

"Well, I must say, you're looking a right side better than the last time I saw you." The voice is unmistakable, though I nearly did not recognize Edmund for the fresh shave and difference in attire.

I grin up at him as we make our way across the dance floor. "I might say the same of you!" And it is true, for he looks well-rested and wears the same costume as the Brothers, somehow giving the trousers and tunic an elegance befitting a man of his age.

He nods. "The journey to Altus is never an easy one, and this one was worse than most. Especially for you. Are you feeling well?"

"Much better, thank you." I am beginning to feel breathless from all the dancing while Edmund is as relaxed as if he has only been dancing a moment. "And look at you! You're quite the expert. I would venture a guess this is not the first time you've danced on the island!"

His eyes are merry as he favors me with a wink. "I'll never tell."

It is the happiest I have seen Edmund since Henry's death, and a rush of joy and well-being washes over me. I am about to ask him where he has been since we arrived on the island and to what business he has been attending, when he leans in to speak.

"It wouldn't do for me to monopolize the prettiest Sister on Altus. I'll see you soon enough."

And then he is spinning me to yet another partner. I am about to protest that we have only just seen each other again after many days when I realize I have been passed back to Dimitri.

"I'm sorry!" he shouts over the crowd. "I tried to find my way back, but..." He shrugs, whirling me toward the edge of the crowd until we circle right off the area reserved for dancing.

Dimitri keeps us both moving, not pausing for even a moment until I am pressed against the cold stone wall in the shadow of the glowing candles. We stand there for a moment trying to catch our breath. Even Dimitri's cheeks are flushed, and I've no doubt mine are as well.

"Did you have fun?" he asks when his breathing finally slows.

I nod, catching my breath. "It was difficult to keep up at first, but I think I did rather well, all things considered."

He smiles. "It's in your blood."

I bow my head, feeling strangely shy that, in many ways, Dimitri knows more about me than I know about myself.

He tips my chin so that I am forced to meet his eyes. "I didn't want to share you tonight." Touching his lips softly to mine, I feel the urgency build in his kiss until he pulls away with what I feel is effort. "You taste of strawberries."

I am staring at his mouth, wondering how much privacy we can count on in this dark corner of the room, when Astrid comes up behind Dimitri. He does not see her and bends down for another kiss.

"Ahem." I clear my throat, glancing from Dimitri to the space over his shoulder until he turns to see her.

"Astrid," he says. "What can we do for you?"

Her face hardens as she looks from Dimitri to me and back again. I know I am not imagining the anger in her eyes. She seems to be measuring her words, wondering at the merit of releasing her resentment. In the end, she simply narrows her gaze and directs her words to Dimitri as if I am not present at all.

"Una has sent word that Lady Abigail is awake and asking for Sister Amalia."

Dimitri nods. "Very well. Thank you."

Astrid remains in place as if her feet are nailed to the floor.

"I will see Lia to Lady Abigail. You may go."

A lick of white-hot fury rises in her eyes, and I know she is angry to be so dismissed. Dimitri *is* her Elder, though, and it seems clear that a certain level of respect is in order. In the end, she does nothing but turn heel and leave, disappearing into the still-swirling crowd.

Dimitri turns back to me. "I know how worried you are about Lady Abigail. Let us go now, and I'll take you to her."

I don't know why I hesitate, for seeing Aunt Abigail is the culmination of our long journey and a lifetime of questions and confusion. It is the key to my own future. To the end of the prophecy.

Perhaps that is why it takes me a moment to nod. To begin moving.

It has been pleasant to lose myself in food and music. Even my confrontation with Ursula was a welcome distraction compared to what awaits. Still, it was inevitable that it would come to this, and so I follow Dimitri from the dining hall, knowing it is the beginning of the end.

And if I am very, very fortunate, perhaps the herald of a new beginning as well.

24

"I feel I must apologize for Astrid." Dimitri speaks as we make our way to Aunt Abigail's room. "I've known her since she was born, but where I have always seen her as a younger sister, it seems she views our relationship quite differently."

We are walking the long, outdoor hallway I remember from this morning. It seems to wind all the way around the Sanctuary, and I have no idea where we are in relation to anything else.

I look up at him with a teasing smile. "It's all right. I can hardly blame her." I don't know if it is the wine or the dancing or the stars glittering in the black sky, but the silk of my robes lifts and falls against my bare legs and I feel suddenly very alive.

Grinning, Dimitri reaches for my hand. "I do believe the air on Altus is having an effect on you."

"Perhaps." A smile touches my lips as we continue walking, our hands clasped.

I do not know how long we have to speak freely, and my thoughts return to more serious matters. There are things I must understand. "Dimitri?"

"Yes?"

"Why is Ursula so... quick-witted?"

He throws his head back and laughs. "You are far kinder than I would be in your place."

He leads me around a corner, stopping as we come to the entrance of the building. The hallway continues, but it is indoors from here, and I understand that Dimitri desires the small amount of privacy that being outside offers.

"Ursula is the Elder who reigns directly beneath Lady Abigail. Should Lady Abigail pass away, as I am sorry to say may happen soon, Ursula stands to take her place."

"I don't understand what this has to do with me. I wouldn't challenge her right to the position; I'm not even a resident of Altus."

He sighs, and I have the sense that we are having this conversation almost against his will. "Yes, but Lia, there are two other Sisters who hold claim to the position above Ursula." He looks out into the black night before bringing his gaze back to mine. "Your sister, Alice. And you."

For a moment, I cannot make sense of his words. "What do you mean? That's impossible."

He shakes his head. "No, it's not. All the Sisters are products of unions between the original Watchers and earthly women.

But you and Alice are direct descendants of Maari and Katla, the originators of the prophecy. It's why you were chosen as Guardian and Gate. It's the way it has always been."

"And?"

"*And* the Lady of Altus must be as closely related to Maari and Katla as possible. Aunt Abigail was a direct descendant, and other than Virginia, you and Alice are her only living relatives. Her only blood. But Alice is not eligible to take the role because of her current defiance of the Grigori's rules. Ursula is descended from the same line, though not as directly."

I shift from one foot to the other, trying to understand what he is saying. "All right, but what of Virginia? She is older than I. Surely she lays greater claim to the position."

He shrugs. "She doesn't want it. She renounced her claim when she moved away and was likely not powerful enough to rule effectively anyway."

I remember Aunt Virginia once telling me that the gifts of the Sisterhood were bestowed before birth. That some of us are inherently more powerful than others. She did not seem to mind admitting that she was considerably weaker than even her own sister, my mother.

"Well, I don't want it either." I hesitate before continuing. "Though... I don't know enough about Ursula to know if she should have it instead."

Altus and the Sisters, Ursula, Alice, Aunt Abigail dying just down the hall. It is all too much. I lift my fingers to my temples as if doing so will drive it away.

Dimitri takes my hand. "Come. Let's go to Lady Abigail. The rest will wait."

I nod, grateful to be led. We make our way through the door and into the inner hallway. Dimitri is beside me every step of the way, and I can no longer imagine bringing the prophecy to an end without his companionship, his loyalty.

Of course, it is not that simple, but I force from my mind the question that rises again and again in the sea of my consciousness: *Where does that leave James?*

❧

The room is dimly lit, though not because it is closeted by tightly shut or draperied windows as one would expect in a sick room. On the contrary, two sets of double glass doors are left open to the warm night air. The breeze off the water sighs against the curtains, causing them to rise and fall with a breath all their own.

Dimitri remains near the door as I enter the room. Una comes toward me while two Sisters move about in the background. One pours water into a bedside cup. The other shakes out a blanket from the massive wardrobe near the window.

"Lia! I'm so glad you've come." Una leans in, kissing my cheek. She speaks in a low voice that is not quite a whisper. "Lady Abigail woke up about a half hour ago and began asking for you immediately."

"Thank you, Una. I came as quickly as I could." I look over her shoulder at the figure on the bed. "How is she?"

Una's face becomes grave. "The Elders say she may not last the night."

"Let me go to her then." I step around Una and make my way to the bed, nodding at the Sisters tending Aunt Abigail.

As I come closer to the bed, my steps slow involuntarily. I have long waited to meet Aunt Abigail in person. Now it is a moment I do not want to pass. I steel myself and move forward, though, for what else is there to do?

When I finally stop at the side of her bed, the stone around my neck begins to pulse with a vibration I can nearly hear. I pull it from within my robe, cupping it in my hand. It is as hot as if pulled from a fire, yet it does not burn the soft flesh of my palm.

I slip it back inside my robe and look down at my aunt. I have always imagined her vibrant and full of life as she surely was in the time before her illness. Now her skin is as thin and wrinkled as crepe, her form so small it is barely visible under the coverlet. The breath leaves her body in painful rasps, but when she opens her eyes, they are youthful and vibrant, as green as my own, and I recognize her as my grandmother's sister.

"Amalia." She speaks my name almost the moment her eyes open, as if she knew I was standing there all along. "You've come."

I nod, sitting on the edge of her bed. "Of course. I'm sorry it took me so long. I came as quickly as I could."

She attempts a smile, but the corners of her mouth only barely lift. "It is no small journey."

I shake my head. "No. But nothing could have kept me away." I reach for her hand. "How are you feeling, Aunt Abigail? Or shall I call you Lady Abigail as the others do?"

She begins to laugh but it ends in a series of coughs. "Please do me the honor of calling me Aunt Abigail." She sighs, her voice fading with melancholy. "It seems a very long time since I was Abigail. Since I was simply a daughter, a sister, or an aunt."

"To me, you will always be Aunt Abigail." I lean in and kiss her dry cheek, marveling that she can feel so familiar.

The chain holding the adder stone around my neck spills out the neckline of my robe, and Aunt Abigail reaches toward me with one hand, touching the still-hot stone.

"You have it." She lets it fall back against my chest. "Good."

"What is it?" I am unable to hide my curiosity, even in the face of her illness.

"Glain nadredd." I do not understand the words, but they leave her mouth in a sigh of remembrance. When she next speaks, her words are clearer. "It is an adder stone. But not any stone. Mine."

I lift my hand and hold it against the stone as if doing so will unlock its secrets.

"What is it for?" I ask her.

Her eyes drift to my wrist and the medallion that is visible along the sleeve of my robe. "That." She pauses again as if for strength. "All the Sisters on Altus have a stone imbued with their magic. Its strength depends on its owner. Mine has

protected me from harm, healed me when ill, and bolstered my power when required. Now it will protect you from the Souls, even as you wear the medallion of the Gate. Even as your closest friends fall to Samael's power. But it will not work forever, and when its power, *my* power, wanes you must imbue it with your own."

"How long will it last?"

"At least until you reach the pages. If fortune is with us, a bit longer. I..." She licks her dry lips, and I pause in my questioning to offer her water that she refuses. "I emptied myself of all my power, child, and poured it all into the stone."

Regret is like a dagger in my chest as I realize the reason Aunt Abigail has fallen so ill; she has given all of her remaining strength to me via the stone. She must have been aware of Alice's increasing strength, and I wonder if she knew as well about Sonia's betrayal. I cannot bear to ask if I am the cause of her weakness. Cannot bear to know. And in any case, there is no undoing what is already done. It is far smarter, and far kinder, to use our time wisely.

"Thank you, Aunt Abigail, but what if it is not enough? When your power leaves the stone... what if I cannot provide enough to ward off the Souls until I can bring the prophecy to an end?"

Her smile is faint, but it is there. In it, I see the life force that has guided the Sisters for decades. "You are stronger than you know, my child. It will be enough."

Her words ring through my memory. In an instant, I am transported back to the morning at Birchwood when Aunt

Virginia gave me the letter my mother wrote just before her death. *You are wiser than you believe, dear heart. And stronger than you know*, Aunt Virginia had said.

Aunt Abigail closes her eyes for a moment. When she opens them again, they burn with new intensity. "You must uncover the pages."

I nod. "Tell me where they are, and I will use them to end the prophecy."

She grasps my hand tighter. "I cannot... tell you."

I shake my head. "But... that is why I've come. Why you *asked* me to come. Don't you remember, Aunt Abigail?"

"It is not memory that fails me, my child."

I still don't understand.

Aunt Abigail's eyes roam the room, though she is too tired to move her head. She lowers her voice even further so that I must strain to hear her. "There are... many ears in the Sanctuary. Some of them will use that which they overhear to aid the cause of the Sisters. Others will use it to aid a cause of their own."

I look up, noting one Sister folding bedsheets near the window. I do not know where the other has gone, but Una is grinding something with a mortar and pestle and mixing the powder in a glass while Dimitri still leans against the wall by the door.

I turn back to Aunt Abigail. "But how will I find the pages if you cannot tell me where to look?"

Her hand leaves mine, grasping my arm and pulling me closer so that I am mere inches from her dry, cracked lips. "You

will leave the day after tomorrow. Your father's trusted companion, Edmund, will see you safely off the island and to your first meeting point. A new guide will lead you for each segment of travel. Only Dimitri will accompany you the whole way. He has been in my service for some time. I trust him implicitly."

Her gaze meets mine, and I think I see a twinkle of pride. "No one person will know the way of your journey. Rather, each guide will be responsible for only a small portion of it. Even the final guide will not know his segment is the last. He will be told it is only one of many stops."

I sit up, feeling a surge of love and pride for my aunt. Even ill and dying, her mind and will do not fail her. Still, I am not as trusting as I once was.

"What if one of the guides should abandon us or fall to the Souls?"

"The guides have been chosen carefully, but you are wise to allow for every possibility," she rasps. "That is why I am prepared to tell you and only you what you must know."

She motions me toward her, and I lean down.

"Come closer, my dear." I position my ear near her lips, and she whispers only one word. "*Chartres.*"

I straighten, puzzling over the word. I know I have heard it correctly, but I don't know what it means. "I don't—"

She interrupts with a whisper. "*At the feet of the Guardian. Not a Virgin, but a Sister.*" Her eyes dart around the room. "As long as you have crossed the sea, my words will guide you. Should you be forced to continue alone, I trust you have enough now to find your way."

I mouth the single word, liking the feel of it on my tongue, and commit the strange phrase to memory. The faintest sense of familiarity lies within it, though I cannot recall anyone ever speaking it aloud until now.

Una appears on the other side of the bed holding the cup into which she was mixing the ground powder. She smiles sadly.

"I believe Lady Abigail requires rest now."

I look down at my grandmother's sister. She is already fast asleep, and I lean in and kiss her hot forehead. "Sleep well, Aunt Abigail."

Una places the cup on the bedside table. "I am sorry, Lia. Is there anything I can do to ease your sorrow?"

I shake my head. "Just make her comfortable, I suppose."

She nods. "I've brewed something to ease her pain, but I don't want to wake her when she is finally resting comfortably. I'll watch over her, though. When she awakes, I'll make sure she is not in pain." She smiles. "You should rest. You still look quite tired yourself."

I do not realize the truth in her words until she says them, and then, all at once, exhaustion falls over me. "Will you come and get me the moment she is awake? I should like to spend all the time I can with her before..."

Una nods in understanding. "I'll fetch you the moment she regains consciousness. I promise."

I walk on shaking legs to meet Dimitri by the door. He takes my hand, and we step into the hall, closing the door behind us.

"We should get you to bed," he says. "You will need all your strength in the coming days."

I look up at him as we walk. "What do you know about the location of the pages?"

His expression narrows in contemplation. "Very little. I've only been told to prepare for travel and that you and I, together with Edmund as our guide, will be leaving the day after tomorrow."

I nod. Though I trust Dimitri completely, I have already vowed to honor my aunt's confidence. I will not tell him of the words whispered within the sacred walls of her room.

"Dimitri?"

"Hmmm?" We turn a corner, and I recognize the hallway leading to my room.

"I must see Sonia before we leave."

I feel guilty that I have not insisted until now, but I have not been certain of my own strength. I want to believe that my sense of forgiveness is strong enough to overcome anything, but I am still reeling from the shock of Sonia's betrayal. I suppose I will not know, truly, my ability to forgive her until I see her again. And so, see her I must before I leave Altus, perhaps for the last time.

Dimitri stops at the door to my room, and I see the working of his mind behind the shadow of worry in his eyes.

"Are you certain that's a good idea? The Elders *do* say that she has improved, but perhaps it would be better to wait until she is completely well and we have returned from our journey."

"No. I need to see her, Dimitri. I will not rest until I do, and I really should have done so much sooner."

"Nothing could have been gained by seeing her as she was when she arrived on Altus, and the Elders would have forbidden it anyway. But if you feel it necessary to see her before we leave, I will speak to them and arrange for a visit tomorrow."

I stand on tiptoe and wrap my arms around Dimitri's neck. "Thank you," I say, before touching my lips to his.

He returns my kiss with barely contained passion before pulling away. "*You* must rest, Lia. I will see you in the morning."

I lean my forehead against his chest. "I don't want you to go."

His fingers move through the curls at the back of my head. "Then I won't."

I look up at him. "What... what do you mean?"

He shrugs. "I will sleep on your floor if you like, or anywhere else you would like me to stay. There is no shame in it. Not here. And," he says, his eyes twinkling with mischief, "I've already told you that I will honor your society's rules whether or not you wish it."

There is a remnant of my brain, the one that was instructed by Miss Gray at Wycliffe in all matters of propriety, thet wonders at my own lack of shame, but it is only a candle compared to the fire building within. It is not a fire stoked by my growing feelings for Dimitri. Not those alone. It is lit by my own exhilaration at the knowledge that there may be another way,

another path, open to me yet. That my options may not be as limited as I once believed.

I cannot help smiling. "All right, then. I want you to stay."

He opens the door to my room. "Then stay I will."

I do not change for bed. Remembering the state in which I woke up this morning, I am not entirely certain I have a choice. Having a man in my room overnight is scandalous enough, even for my own newly burgeoning sense of freedom. Having a man in my room while I am naked, even under the covers, would be impossible for me to justify, even in the mystical world of Altus.

I make myself comfortable on the bed while Dimitri retrieves blankets and pillows from the wardrobe and spreads them out on the floor. When he crosses the room and parts the curtains over the big window, I discover that it is not a window at all, but a set of double doors like those in Aunt Abigail's room.

He opens one of the doors halfway, turning to me. "Do you mind? I like the breeze off the water."

I shake my head. "I didn't realize it opened."

He comes back to the bed, tucking the thick coverlet around me. "Now you'll be warm while you sleep to the sound of the sea."

He leans in and kisses me chastely on the lips. "Good night, Lia."

I feel shy despite our close proximity. "Good night."

He blows out the candle by the bed, and I hear him settle into the blankets on the floor. It does not last long, though,

for the bed is wide and unfamiliar, and I do not like thinking of Dimitri on the cold floor.

"Dimitri?"

"Hmmm?"

"Would it be possible for you to sleep in my bed while . . . honoring the laws of my society?" I wonder if he can hear the smile in my voice.

"Quite possible."

I am certain I hear the smile in his.

“My goodness!” Luisa’s voice startles me from a deep slumber. “I daresay you have grown quite used to the ways of the island!”

I sit up, untangling myself from Dimitri’s arms. He opens his eyes slowly, not at all startled by Luisa’s abrupt morning greeting.

“Yes, well, for the sake of my remaining sense of propriety, let’s keep this between us, shall we?”

Luisa raises her eyebrows. “I shall keep your secrets if you keep mine.”

“I don’t know any of your secrets. At least not any of the more recent ones.” I stretch, fighting the urge to lay back down with Dimitri.

“A situation I might be able to remedy if you send your

heathen island boy away while you bathe and dress." She marches to the wardrobe.

I do not want Dimitri to leave, not even for a moment. But I do need to prepare for my visit with Sonia, and I would also like to check on Aunt Abigail.

I lean down and kiss Dimitri softly on the lips while Luisa digs through the wardrobe, her back turned to us.

"I'm sorry," I say.

He runs a finger from the messy hair at my temple down my cheekbone and neck, all the way to the point where the neckline of my robe begins. "It's quite all right. I need to dress and speak to the Elders about your meeting with Sonia. I'll be back to fetch you in a while."

I nod. "Thank you for staying."

"Thank *you*," he says, grinning. "It was the best night's sleep I have had in some time." He rises from the bed and turns to Luisa, standing at the foot of the bed with a fresh robe in her arms. "The rest of the island already knows of my feelings for Lia. I couldn't care less if they know where I spent the night, but on her behalf, I thank you for your discretion."

She rolls her eyes. "Yes, yes. Be gone now, will you? I shall never get her out of this room if you don't leave!"

"Very well, then." He smiles, making his way out of the room without further word.

Luisa bursts into laughter the moment he is gone.

"What?" I try to feign innocence, but the heat on my cheeks makes me suspect I have failed.

She throws the robe at me. "Don't be coy with me, Lia Milthorpe. I know you too well."

"I'm not being coy." I shrug. "Nothing happened. He . . . honors the laws of our society."

The laughter begins as a giggle she can contain behind her hand and builds to a full-fledged howl that causes her to fall onto the bed next to me. I am slightly offended by her mocking laughter but cannot manage a word in my defense or Dimitri's. Luisa is too busy gasping for air to hear me anyway, and worse, it is contagious.

I do not want to join her on principle. I am, after all, the subject of the ill-begotten humor. But I cannot help myself, and soon we are both laughing so hard that tears run down Luisa's cheeks and my stomach folds in on itself in pain. Our laughter subsides a little at a time until we are laying side by side atop the coverlet, our breath coming in increasingly slower heaves.

"Now that you have had a good laugh at my expense, why don't you tell me about your night with Rhys?" I say, staring at the ceiling.

"Well, I can tell you one thing: I do not think 'honoring the laws of our society' is"—she begins laughing again—"very high on his list of priorities."

I throw a pillow at her. "Very well. Have a good laugh. But while you and Rhys satisfy your less virtuous desires, I think it very selfless that Dimitri cares about the customs of our society."

"You are quite right, Lia." I can hear her trying to quell the laughter rising yet again. "Dimitri is every bit the gentleman. I only thank God that Rhys is not!"

"Oh... you! You're impossible!" I sit up, grabbing the clean robe and trying to keep a straight face. "Did you say something about a bath? I should very much like to know where to get one."

"You have always been good at changing the subject." I cannot dispute her words, but she lets it go, and for that, I am grateful. She sits up and rises to a standing position. "I will have someone fetch you a tub and fill it with hot water. They will bring it to you, I'm sure, as they did for me."

"Thank you."

"You're welcome." She makes her way to the door and opens it to step into the hallway. Before she closes it behind her, she looks back. "I was only teasing before, Lia."

I smile. "I know that."

The smile she offers me in return is shadowed by melancholy. "Dimitri cares for you a great deal."

"I know that, too."

And somehow, though certain words have not been said between Dimitri and me, I do.

"You do not have to do this, you know," Luisa says.

We are sitting on the bed, waiting for Dimitri to fetch us for the visit with Sonia. Just as Luisa promised, a large copper tub was brought to my room and filled with warm water scented with fragrant oil poured from a clear vial. I do not know if it

is because it has been so long since I have had a proper bath or because it truly was an extraordinary experience, but it was the most memorable bath of my life. Feeling the slippery silk robe fall against my clean, scented skin was heaven.

I turn to Luisa. "If not now, when? I am leaving tomorrow, remember?"

I gave Luisa only the vaguest of details about the next portion of our journey, telling her that Dimitri and I are tasked with retrieving the pages while it is hers to stay and look after Sonia until she is well.

Luisa plays with a fold in her robe, light purple silk shimmering in her fingertips. "You could wait until she is well enough to return to London."

I shake my head. "I cannot. Sonia is one of our closest friends, and I would never forgive myself if I didn't see her before I leave. If it were you, I would do the very same."

Luisa sighs. "Very well, then. I will accompany you."

"It's all right if you wish to wait. I know it will be... difficult, seeing Sonia in such a state."

She reaches for my hand. "I will not abandon you. Now or ever. We're in this together."

I smile and squeeze her hand just as there is a rap at the door. Dimitri's dark head appears in the frame.

"Good morning. Again." He grins.

Luisa rolls her eyes. "Come on, Lia. Let's go before Dimitri makes himself comfortable."

Dimitri holds out an arm for me to grasp. "I see. Lightening the mood at my expense. That's quite all right."

I laugh and kiss him on the cheek as we join him in the hallway, closing the door behind us. We continue down the hall, nodding to those who pass. Many times they glance from me to Dimitri and then to our linked arms, a dark expression crossing their faces. I refuse to voice aloud the resentment still simmering underneath my skin. There are more important things that must be faced this day.

"How is Sonia, Dimitri? Have you heard anything new?" I want to be prepared for our visit.

"I received an update this morning, in fact. It seems the Elders feel they have turned a corner. They are not ready to pronounce her well, but she has not mentioned the Souls or the medallion in over twenty-four hours."

But that doesn't mean they're gone. That they're not lurking in the corners of her mind.

I think it and wonder if I will ever trust Sonia again.

We come to the end of the outdoor hallway. Dimitri surprises me by leading us down a small flight of stairs instead of turning a corner and continuing into the Sanctuary.

"Where are we going?" Luisa says, turning to look back at the building that houses our rooms.

He steps onto the same stone pathway that took us to the grove yesterday afternoon. "To Sonia's chambers."

"Which are?" Luisa prompts.

"Which are," Dimitri says, "in a different building from the one you and I occupy."

Luisa never enjoys waiting for information, so I am surprised

and relieved when she only sighs, gazing as we walk over the rolling fields and out toward the sea.

The sky is the same impossibly deep, clear blue it has been every day since we arrived, and I wonder if I will forever after think of it as Altus blue. We continue walking until I recognize the place where Dimitri pulled me off the path and toward the grove. This time, we continue even as the path begins to descend toward the ocean.

As with yesterday, this part of the island is deserted. For a long while, I do not see anything resembling shelter, and I am beginning to wonder if the Elders are keeping Sonia in a cave when I spot a small stone structure at the edge of a cliff up ahead.

Without meaning to, I drop my hand from Dimitri's arm and stop walking. Looking at the building ahead, it is a wonder it can be there at all, so precariously perched on the cliff does it seem.

Dimitri follows my gaze and reaches for my hand. "It is not as bad as it seems, Lia."

Luisa turns to him, anger written across her exotic features. "Not as bad as it seems? Why... it's perched at the edge of the world! The word *bleak* comes to mind!"

He sighs. "I will admit that from here it looks... austere. But it is appointed with all the amenities of the Sanctuary. It is kept for certain rituals and rites which require privacy and quiet, including those required to banish the Souls. That's all."

It is impossible to explain why I managed to visit Aunt

Abigail at her sickbed just last night without crying while now I feel the sting of tears. Perhaps I simply cannot believe that the prophecy has taken Sonia and exiled her to such a place without even the love and care of her friends. The injustice of it makes me want to shout into the wind, but instead I turn from Dimitri and gaze out over the water trying to compose myself.

After a moment, I feel the butterfly touch of Luisa's fingers on my arm. "Come, Lia. We'll go together."

I nod and turn back to the path, putting one foot in front of the other until the building comes into better view, and I see that it is, in fact, more than one room. It is more of a mini-compound—much, much smaller than the Sanctuary and without the exterior hallway but built with the same blue stone and copper roof.

We follow a smaller pathway that winds through a lush garden, and I begin to breathe easier still. It is more than pleasant. It is beautiful and peaceful, the perfect place to gather one's strength.

The building stands at the end of the pathway. After the serenity of the garden, I am surprised to see that there are two Brothers stationed at either side of the enormous door. They are dressed like any other gentleman on Altus. Like Dimitri, in fact, in the daytime attire of white tunic and trousers. I have no reason at all to think they are guards, and yet I have the distinct feeling that they are here for that very reason.

"Good morning," Dimitri says to them. "We are here to see Sonia Sorrensen."

They bow in deference to Dimitri, eyeing me suspiciously.

"Has the protocol changed on Altus while I have been away? Do we no longer offer greetings to a Sister?" Dimitri's voice is tight with barely controlled anger.

I place a hand on his arm. "It's all right."

"No, it is not," he says without turning to look at me. "Do you know this Sister may be your next Lady? Guardian or Gate as the prophecy dictates is no matter; she is working to do our bidding. And she may well rule over you in the future. Now," he says through clenched teeth, "greet your Sister."

I cannot help feeling badly when they bow their heads. "Good morning, Sister," they say in unison.

I return their bow feeling anger of my own, though none directed at the men in front of me. "Good morning. Thank you for watching over my friend."

Nodding, shame touches their eyes as they open the door and stand back so that we may enter.

We step into a hallway that seems to run the length of the building, ending at a glass door through which I can see a glimpse of the ocean in the distance. I pull Dimitri to the side and look at Luisa.

"Luisa, give us a moment, will you?"

She shrugs, stepping a few feet down the hall and looking at the art on the walls, the only privacy we can hope for in such a small space.

I turn to Dimitri. "Never do that again."

He shakes his head, confusion evident on his face. "What?"

"What?" My voice is a harsh whisper. "*That*. Humiliate me in front of the Brothers or anyone else on this island."

"I was not *humiliating* you, Lia." He is clearly shocked at the insinuation. "Just yesterday you were upset at the treatment we were both receiving by those most ignorant on the island."

"And *you* told *me* to be patient." I am not speaking in a whisper anymore, but I cannot seem to help myself.

He folds his arms across his chest, looking for a moment like a sullen child. "Yes, well... I grew tired of their petty stares and whispers. And you *may* be the next Lady of Altus. They have no right to treat you in such a manner. I will not have it."

The anger leaves my body as quickly as it arrived. How can I be angry that someone cares for me enough to demand my fair treatment?

"Dimitri." I reach up and place my arms around his neck. "I don't know whether I will be the next Lady of Altus, but I think I finally understand that I will always be a Sister. And whether a simple Sister or one who is the Lady, it is up to me to earn the respect of the Brothers, the Grigori, and the other Sisters. It something only I can do, and it may take a very long time." I stand on tiptoe and kiss him quickly on the mouth. "But it will only make them resent me more if they feel forced into showing respect I have not rightly earned."

He exhales as if very tired. "You are far too wise for a Sister so new to the Island. Altus is fortunate to have you—whether

as a simple Sister or the next Lady." He tips his head and kisses me softly. "And so am I."

"Oh, for goodness sake!" Luisa is standing a few feet in front us. "It is nauseatingly sweet that you have just had your first official fight and reconciliation in one swift shot, but the artwork on these walls is not that interesting. Can we go see Sonia now? Please?"

I laugh, pulling away from Dimitri. "Let's go."

We make our way down the hall, turning right into another hallway just before reaching the glass door in the distance. Without question, Dimitri approaches a simple wooden door. An elderly Sister sits on a chair outside the door, a guard of another sort, I imagine. She is working a shimmering green thread through a fine white cloth.

"Sister." Dimitri bows his head, and Luisa and I repeat the greeting.

The Sister bows in return and, this time at least, my eyes are met with kindness and warmth. She does not speak but simply stands and opens the door, ushering us inside before closing it even as she remains out in the hall.

I don't know what I expected, but nothing as warm and inviting as the room Sonia has called hers in the days since our arrival on Altus. It is quite large, with a deeply cushioned sofa at one end and a large bed piled high with plush coverlets at the other. Across the room and directly in front of the door through which we entered is a set of now-familiar double doors, open to a central courtyard filled with flowers. Somehow

I know that I need only step through the doors and Sonia will be there. I make my way to them with some hesitation.

Stepping through the doorway is like stepping into another world. It is a larger version of the plantings along the pathway to the building, and I think I recognize hydrangeas and peonies in addition to the jasmine. The ocean breeze scents and softens the air. It is woven into the fabric of everything on Altus, and I think I will never be at home away from it again.

Underneath the distant murmur of the sea, water of another kind can be heard. Dimitri lifts his eyebrows in silent question, and I step onto a gravel pathway, following it around a corner as I listen for the water. I know it when I come to it—a small fountain at the center of the courtyard. It gurgles over stones piled high at its center. It is lovely, but it is not the urge to let the water run over my hands that causes me to run toward the fountain. It is the bench sitting near it or, more accurately, Sonia sitting *on* the bench.

She rises when she hears our feet crunch over the gravel, and when I look into her eyes I see the hesitation and fear in their ice-blue depths. I do not have to think before running to her. It is instinctual, and I hardly register the seconds between seeing her again for the first time and the moment when we are embracing and laughing and crying all at the same time.

"Oh! Oh, my goodness, Lia! I have missed you!" Her voice is muffled by tears.

I step back and look at her, taking in the dark smudges

under her eyes, the wan skin, and the figure that could hardly stand to lose five pounds and looks as if it has lost ten.

"Are you all right?"

She hesitates before nodding. "Come. Sit." She begins pulling me toward the bench, but stops and looks back at Dimitri and Luisa. "I'm sorry," she says shyly. "I haven't said good morning."

Dimitri smiles. "Good morning. How are you feeling?"

She thinks about his question as if the answer is not so simple. "Better, I think."

He nods. "Good. Would you like me to leave you?"

She shakes her head. "I'm told you are a son of Altus. I imagine you know everything anyway. It is all right with me if you stay. And... Luisa? Will you stay?"

Sonia has never looked more ashamed than when she finally faces Luisa. I do not know if it is because she tried so earnestly to convince me of Luisa's betrayal in the first half of our journey or if it is her own shame, but she can barely meet Luisa's eyes.

Luisa smiles in reassurance and joins us near the bench. Dimitri, ever the gentleman, sits on one of the large stones bordering the fountain. We sit for a few uncomfortable moments, none of us sure where to begin. Once, only once, Sonia's gaze drops to my wrist. I draw my hand farther inside my sleeve in an effort to keep the medallion hidden. When I meet her eyes, she looks quickly away.

Finally Dimitri looks around the garden. "I had forgotten how lovely it is here. Have you been well treated?" he asks Sonia.

"Oh, yes. The Sisters have been very kind under the . . . under the circumstances." Her fair skin flushes in shame, and we grow silent once again.

Dimitri stands up, drying his hands on his trousers. "Have you been out of doors?" He looks up. "I mean well and truly out of doors, without the walls of this courtyard to confine you?"

"Once," Sonia says. "Yesterday."

"Once is not enough. It is too beautiful to see it only once. Let's go for a stroll, shall we?"

26

We step through the glass door at the end of the hall, and in an instant, the sea is spread before us. It glistens in the sunlight, and though it is far below us, the smell of it is stronger and more powerful than at any other time on Altus. Dimitri leans down, placing his lips very near my ear.

"What do you think?"

It takes my breath away. I find I cannot do it justice with words, and so I simply smile in answer.

He reaches to touch my hair, and even now it seems his eyes darken with something like desire. I am surprised when his hand comes away with the ivory comb Father gave me long ago.

"It was slipping," he says simply, handing it to me before turning to the others. "It's a fine day for a walk. I suggest we make use of it."

He promptly hurries ahead, leaving us alone, and I marvel at his ability to do and say exactly the thing that is most needed at any given time.

Luisa, Sonia, and I walk without speaking, the wind whipping our hair and fluttering our robes. I rub the comb between my fingers as we walk. Its smooth surface does nothing to calm the anger that bubbles once again below the surface of my thoughts.

Sonia finally breaks the silence with a soft sigh.

"Lia, I am... I am so sorry. I can hardly remember those last days in the wood." She looks away as if gathering her strength from the water below. "I know I did terrible things. Said terrible things. I was... not myself. Can you forgive me?"

It takes me a moment to answer. "It is not a matter of forgiveness." I hurry ahead of Sonia and Luisa, hoping to stem the rush of bitterness I hear in my voice and feel in my heart.

"Then... what?" Despair is evident in Sonia's voice.

I stop walking, turning to look at the water. I do not hear the sound of feet on gravel and know Sonia and Luisa have stopped behind me. There are so many words, so many questions, so many accusations... They are as numerous as the grains of sand on the beach below. But there is only one that matters now.

I turn back to Sonia. "How could you?"

Her shoulders sag in defeat. Her complacency, her *weakness*, evokes not sympathy, not compassion, but the building fury I have reined in since the night when I awoke to find her

pressing the medallion to my wrist. For one terrible moment I scramble for something to use to unleash my frustration.

"I trusted you. I trusted you with *everything*!" I scream it, throwing the comb at her with every ounce of anger coiled inside my body. "How will we trust you now? How will we trust you ever again?"

Sonia flinches, though the comb is an ineffectual weapon. And I suppose that is the point, for even now, I love her. I am loath to hurt her even as I cannot seem to stop myself.

Luisa steps forward as if to shield Sonia from me. From *me*. "Lia, stop."

"Why, Luisa?" I ask. "Why must I stop asking the questions that must be asked, however much they frighten us?"

There is nothing to say in the silence that follows. I speak the truth, and we all know it. I *have* missed Sonia. I *do* love and care for her. But we cannot ignore those things which might cost us dearly—might cost our very lives—in the name of sentiment.

Luisa steps toward me, bending to pick up a few stones. She inches closer to the edge of the cliff before tossing them into the sea, and I watch them sail through the air. It is a futile diversion. We are too far up to see them drop into the roiling water below.

"Lia is right." I turn to meet Sonia's voice and see that she has retrieved my comb. She studies it as if it holds the answers to all our questions. "I have breached your trust, and there is no sure way to know that I will be stronger the next time

the Souls attempt to use me, though I do hope there won't be a next time. They..." She hesitates, and when she begins speaking again her voice comes as if from far away, and I know she is remembering.

"They did not appear to me as the Souls. They appeared as my...as my mother." She turns to me, and there is naked pain in her eyes. "I met her on the Plane. She was sorry for sending me to live with Mrs. Millburn. She said that she didn't know what to do, that she thought Mrs. Millburn would be able to help me understand my power. It was nice to have a mother again, if only in a world other than this one."

"And then?" My voice is nearly a whisper.

"Then she began worrying for my safety. Saying that I was putting myself in danger by keeping the medallion. That we were all in danger because of your refusal to open the gate. At first, I didn't listen. But after a while, well...I don't know how to explain it except to say that it began to make a strange sort of sense. Of course, I realize now that I was not in my right mind, but it..." She looks into my eyes and even now I see the power the Souls had over her. Even now I see the power in an offer to replace something dear and once lost. "It happened so slowly that I cannot even say when it began."

Her words rise and fall on the breeze off the ocean, echoing through my mind until there is nothing but silence. Finally she reaches toward me, the comb in her hand.

I take it from her. "I'm sorry." I say it because throwing the comb was not kind, but in the deepest parts of myself, I am not sure I mean it.

She turns her palms to the sky as if in surrender to our judgment. "No, *I* am sorry, Lia. But all I can do is beg your forgiveness and swear an oath that I would rather die than betray you again."

Luisa brushes off her hands and goes to Sonia, placing her hands on Sonia's shoulders. "It is enough, Sonia. It is enough for me."

It is not easy, but I cross the uneven ground, placing an arm around each of them so that we are embracing as we did when the prophecy was still just a riddle and not the thing that would both change and possibly end our lives.

For a moment on the hill overlooking the sea, I believe it is as it once was when the three of us could do anything together. But it *does* only last a moment. Because deep down we all know nothing will ever be the same again.

We are halfway up the path to the Sanctuary when we see the person running toward us.

We have said our goodbyes to Sonia, and though nothing is certain, I believe she wants to be well. Wants to be true to our cause. Now there is nothing to do but wait until the Sisters deem her strong enough to return to London.

Dimitri shields his eyes against the sun, gazing at the figure in the distance. "It is a Sister."

The Sister's robe billows in the breeze as she runs, and I catch sight of golden hair streaming behind her, reflecting like glass in the sunlight. When she finally reaches us, I do not recognize her. She is young, perhaps Astrid's age, and she does not speak right away. She is so out of breath that she bends at the waist, gasping for air. A minute or so later, she finally straightens, her breath still coming in short bursts, her cheeks still flushed with exertion.

"I am . . . sorry to tell you that Lady Abigail has . . . passed." It does not immediately register what she has said. My mind is as blank as the unused canvases that line the art room at Wycliffe. But what the young Sister says next breaks through my numbness. "They have sent me for you and bid that you come, my Lady."

My Lady. *My Lady*.

All I can think is, *No*.

And then I run.

"It is not your fault that you were not here, Lia." Una places a hot cup of tea on the table. "It would not have made a difference if you were. She never regained consciousness."

Una has repeated this detail more than once since I rushed in, bedraggled and distraught, from our visit with Sonia and the news of Aunt Abigail's passing. It does nothing to ease my guilt. I should have stayed with her. I should have stayed by her side every moment. I tell myself she would have known I was there, conscious or not.

"Lia." Una sits next to me, taking my hand in hers. "Lady Abigail lived a long and fruitful life. She lived it in peace here on Altus, the way she wanted to live it." She smiles. "And she saw you before she passed. I think that's what she was waiting for all this time."

I bow my head and the tears drip from my eyes straight onto the table. I do not know how to tell Una the many ways and reasons I mourn Aunt Abigail. Aunt Virginia is helpful in matters of support but has acknowledged the weakness of her power and has already told me all she knows.

It was Aunt Abigail on whom I hoped to rely for guidance. When I thought of the prophecy, it was she who stood strong and wise against it. It was she who seemed my closest ally, even across the miles. Now I am as alone as I have ever been.

Now it is just Alice and me.

27

Dimitri and I stand alone on the shore of the ocean, staring across the empty expanse of water. The barge carrying Aunt Abigail's body has long since been pushed into the sea. She is gone, as is everyone else who stood on the beach while my aunt's body was given to the sea surrounding Altus.

It is very quick by modern standards, putting someone to rest the very day they pass, but Dimitri tells me it is the custom on the island. I have no reason to repudiate it other than customs of my own that would seem just as strange to the people of Altus. Besides, Aunt Abigail was a Sister and their Lady. If this is how they say goodbye, I imagine this is how she would have wanted to say goodbye as well.

Dimitri turns from the ocean and begins walking, slipping his hand around mine. "I will see you safely back to the

Sanctuary, and then I must go before the Grigori to address some business."

I look up at him in surprise. Even my grief cannot suppress the curiosity that has always been mine. "What sort of business?"

"There is much to discuss, especially now that Lady Abigail has passed." He looks straight ahead as we walk, and I cannot help but feel that he is avoiding my eyes.

"Yes, but we leave tomorrow. Can't it wait?"

He nods. "That is what I have requested, in a manner of speaking. I still must answer for my interference with the kelpie, but I have asked to defer appearance before the Council until after the missing pages are in hand."

I shrug. "That seems reasonable."

"Yes," Dimitri says. "The Council will send word of their decision before morning. But there is another point of contention. It concerns you."

"Me?" I stop walking as we near the path that will take us to the Sanctuary. The walkway is more populated now, and we pass several Sisters as we near the main compound.

Dimitri takes both my hands in his. "Lia, you are the rightful Lady of Altus."

I shake my head. "But I already told you; I don't want it. Not right now. I cannot..." I look away. "I cannot think about it now with all that is ahead of me still."

"I understand. I do. But in the meantime, Altus is without a leader, and the role is yours to either renounce or accept."

Annoyance ignites my simmering frustration. "And why

doesn't the Grigori speak directly to me? Surely for all of Altus's forward thinking, they are not above addressing a woman?"

I hear the weariness in his sigh. "It is simply not done. Not because you are a woman, Lia, but because the Grigori's Elders keep to themselves except when absolutely necessary for order or discipline. It is a sort of... segregation much like that of the monks in your world. That is why the Grigori occupies quarters on the other side of the island. They rely on emissaries such as myself to provide communication with the Sisters. And trust me, Lia, if you are ever called to an audience with the Grigori it can mean nothing good."

I give up trying to wrap my head around the nuances and politics of the island. There is simply not time to decipher such arcane rules and customs.

"What are my options, Dimitri? All of them."

He takes a deep breath, as if needing extra air for the conversation ahead. "There are only three, really: You may accept the role that is rightfully yours and appoint someone to lead in your stead until you can return. You may accept the role and stay to lead now, though this would mean someone else will have to retrieve the missing pages on your behalf. You may refuse the position."

Chewing my lower lip, I worry over the different alternatives. There is a part of me that wants to renounce the position now. To remove it from my consciousness so that I might concentrate on finding the missing pages. But there is another

part, the still practical and thinking part, that recognizes now is not a time for rash decisions.

"What will happen if I renounce it now?"

His answer is simple. "It will go to Ursula in lieu of Alice who, in violation of the Grigori's laws, is not eligible to assume the position."

Ursula. Just the name causes me disquiet. She may be a strong and wise leader for all I know, but I have learned to trust my instincts, and I am not prepared to entrust something as important as the future of Altus, something to which Aunt Abigail devoted herself wholly, to someone who causes me such unease. No. If I am the rightful Lady, the Grigori will do as I ask if it is in the interest of the island.

And somehow, I'm certain that it is.

I look up at Dimitri, resolve hardening within me. "I neither accept nor reject the position."

He shakes his head. "That is not one of the options, Lia."

"It will have to be." I straighten my shoulders. "I am the rightful Lady, and I am being dispatched to find the missing pages on behalf of the Sisterhood. Since I cannot be in two places at once or be expected to fully concentrate on the journey before me with a role as important as Lady hanging over my head, I request a deferment as well."

I turn, pacing the ground leading away from him a few feet before turning back. The more I think about it, the stronger I feel. "I appoint the Grigori to lead in my stead until I have safely retrieved the pages."

"It has never been done," Dimitri says simply.

"Then perhaps now is the time."

I find Luisa in the library, illuminated in a soft pool of light from a nearby desk lamp. As I note the dark curls that spill against her ivory cheekbones, it hits me that tomorrow, for the first time since we left for Altus, I will be without her companionship. How I will miss her quick wit and good humor.

"Luisa." I try to say it softly to avoid startling her, but I needn't have worried. When she looks up, her face is a sea of calm.

She rises, smiling softly and making her way across the room. Her arms close around me, and for a moment, we do nothing but stand in the embrace of friendship. When she pulls away, she studies my face before speaking.

"Are you all right?"

"I think so." I smile at her. "I've come to say goodbye. We're leaving very early in the morning."

She returns my smile sadly. "I won't bother asking where you are going. I know you cannot speak of it. Instead, I will simply promise that I shall stay here and look after Sonia while you find the pages. We'll be very efficient then, won't we? And we'll be together again in London in no time."

I want to leave now, while we are both in good humor and feeling hopeful about the future, at least outwardly. But I know I will not rest easy if I do not say something about this morning.

I sigh. "I *want* to trust Sonia again."

"Of course you do. And you will." She steps forward to wrap me in a fierce embrace. "Trust will come in time, Lia, as all things do. Now is not the time to worry over Sonia. I will do that for you while you're away. Just focus on your own safety and the journey ahead. Find the pages. We will manage the rest when you return."

We cling to the bond of our friendship a moment more, and all the while I try to blot out the unspoken response forming in the back of my mind: *if I return, Luisa. If.*

I can hardly breathe for the suspense. A full hour has passed since saying goodbye to Luisa, and as I sit on my bed waiting for Dimitri, anxiety over the Grigori's decision winds my nerves so tightly I feel they will snap at any moment.

A soft rap at the door comes none too soon. I cross the room to open it, and it is no surprise that Dimitri is standing in its frame. He steps inside without prompting.

I do not speak until the door is closed behind him. Then I can wait no longer.

"What did they say?"

He puts his hands on my shoulders, and for a moment, I fear he will say they have refused. I fear he will say a decision must be made now. One that will be forever binding.

Thankfully, he does not.

"They have agreed, Lia." He smiles, shaking his head. "I can hardly believe it, but they have agreed to give us both a deferment. It was not easy, but I was able to convince them that you should not be penalized for working on behalf of the prophecy and I should not be penalized for acting as your escort when Lady Abigail bid it done."

Relief washes my anxiety clean. "They will give us until after the pages are found?"

"Better," he says.

"Better?" I cannot imagine what could be better.

He nods. "They will defer it all until after the prophecy itself is resolved, provided you continue to work to its end. If you should change your mind... If you should act as Gate, the position will be given to Ursula."

I shake my head. "That will not happen."

"*I* know that, Lia."

I turn from him, trying to wrap my head around such a swift change in the Grigori's position. "Why would they make such an agreement if it is so unprecedented?"

He sighs, and his eyes drift to the corner of the room as if seeking escape.

"Just tell me, Dimitri." Weariness weighs heavily on my voice.

His eyes find mine once again. "They figure the fates will decide; if you end the prophecy, you will make the decision as is your right. If you fail..."

"If I fail?"

"If you fail, it will be because you have either succumbed as Gate... or because you have not survived the prophecy at all."

28

It is still dark when Una wakes me the next morning.

My heart sinks when she hands me a stack of folded clothing and I realize it is the laundered riding breeches and shirt I wore on the way to Altus. I have grown used to the silk robe while on the isle. I have grown used to many things.

While I wash and dress, Una adds enough food and drink to my knapsack to get Dimitri and me to our first stop. I have already packed my arrows and dagger for the journey. Though I know that Dimitri will be by my side for added protection, Sonia's betrayal was a reminder that it is best to rely on oneself, just in case.

I can think of nothing else I need.

I am comforted by the heat of the adder stone against my skin. It slips easily beneath my shirt, and as I adjust the sleeves, my eyes come to rest on the medallion, still around my wrist.

I have considered leaving it in the care of the Grigori, the Sisters, even Una herself, but I cannot bring myself to believe there is anyone I might trust with the medallion. Not after what happened with Sonia.

Una follows my gaze, glancing down at my wrist. "Is everything all right?"

I nod, buttoning the front of my shirt.

"Would you..." She hesitates before continuing. "Would you prefer to leave the medallion here? I would keep it for you, Lia, if it would help."

I chew my lower lip, considering her offer though I have been over the subject many times over. "May I ask you something?"

"Of course."

I tuck the shirt into my breeches as I consider my words. "Can those of you on Altus—the Grigori, the Brothers, the other Sisters...can you be tempted by the Souls?"

She turns, walking to the small writing table behind her and lifting something from its surface. "Not the Grigori's Council. Not ever. The Brothers and Sisters, well...not in the way you and Alice can. You are the Guardian and the Gate, and because of that, you are far more vulnerable to the Souls."

"I sense there is something you're not telling me, Una."

Turning from the writing table, she makes her way back to me with something in her arms. "I'm not keeping anything from you intentionally. It is simply not easy to explain. You see, a Brother or Sister would not have direct influence over the Souls' ability to cross into this world or over Samael's fate.

But the Souls can tempt the Brothers or Sisters to work on their behalf—to influence those with more power."

Like Sonia and Luisa.

"Has this ever happened here on the island?" I ask her.

She sighs, and I can see that it pains her to continue. "There have been . . . incidents. Times when someone has been caught trying to influence the course of events in aid to the Souls. But it doesn't happen often." This last is added in a rush, as if she wants to reassure me despite the knowledge that is anything but reassuring.

And it is just as I thought. Just as I knew. There is no one whom I may trust with the medallion. No one but myself, and even that I sometimes doubt when I feel the pull of it on my wrist.

I button the sleeves of my shirt, covering up the sliver of black velvet.

Una's gaze drops to my wrist. "I'm sorry, Lia."

Ridiculously, I feel the sting of tears once again, and I try to gather my composure by turning to look at the room that has been mine while at the Sanctuary. I commit to memory the simple stone walls, the warmth of the well-worn floor, the smell both musty and sweet. I do not know if I will ever see it, any of it, again.

I want to remember it always.

Finally I turn to Una. She smiles, holding something out to me.

"For me?"

She nods. "I wanted you to have something . . . something to remember all of us and your time on Altus."

I take the object from her arms, surprised at its softness, and shake it out. My throat goes dry with emotion as the violet silk unfurls. It is a riding cape made of the very same fabric as the Sisters' formal robes.

Una must take my touched silence to mean something else, for she breaks in hurriedly. "I know you did not care for the robes when you first came to us, but I simply..." She looks down at her hands, sighing when she looks up to meet my eyes once again. "I simply want you to remember us, Lia. I have grown used to your friendship."

I lean in to embrace her.

"Thank you, Una. For the cape and your friendship. Somehow, I know we will meet again." I pull back to look at her with a smile. "I will never be able to thank you enough for taking care of Aunt Abigail in her final days. For taking care of me. I shall miss you terribly."

I pick up my bow and knapsack and tie the cape around my neck, wondering if I will ever have the heart to take it off. Then, as it seems I always must, I turn to leave.

❦

The island is lit only by torches along the path as Dimitri, Edmund, and I make our way from the Sanctuary down to the harbor. I have only the vaguest recollection of landing there when we arrived on Altus. Those first moments on solid ground are nothing but a blur followed by the two lost days when I did nothing but sleep.

As we make our way toward the water, my trousers pull at

my thighs and my shirt scratches against my chest. Already the world of silk robes and bare skin on sheets seems very far away.

Dimitri wears a cape similar to mine, though his is black and more difficult to see in the fog. When I came upon him and Edmund in the early morning darkness, Dimitri's gaze lit immediately upon the soft fold of silk about my neck.

A smile touched his lips. "Still lovely in violet."

I know our boat as we arrive at the dock, for a robed Sister sits at either end with an oar in hand. The sleeping island has silenced us, and we climb in without speaking. The Sisters begin to row away from the island as soon as we are settled, Dimitri and I toward the front of the boat and Edmund just behind us.

Aunt Abigail's whispered words float through my mind as if on the mist rising over the ocean. I hope our guides will be trustworthy and that Dimitri and I will not be required to find our way alone, but I feel a renewed commitment to do whatever is necessary.

As I watch the silent Sisters row us farther out to sea, I suddenly remember a question, half-formed and unspoken in the haze of my exhaustion on the way to Altus.

"Dimitri?"

"Hmmm?" His eyes are on the water.

I lean closer to him, keeping my voice low so as to not offend the Sisters rowing the boat. "Why are the Sisters silent?"

He seems surprised, as if he has only just realized how odd it is that we are being transported across the sea by silent women.

"It is part of their vow. They promise silence as protection against giving away the location of the isle."

I look back at the Sister rowing from the front. "So they cannot speak?"

"They can, but they don't do so outside of Altus. It would be a violation of their vow."

I nod, recognizing, perhaps for the first time, just how devoted the Sisters are.

Watching Altus grow smaller, I feel as if something should be said, something to mark its significance and the significance of my time there. But in the end, I say nothing. In the end, speaking of it will only dilute the memory of the jasmine-scented air and the soft breeze drifting off the water and the night spent in Dimitri's arms with nothing to worry over save being thought inappropriate by those who occupy a different world entirely.

I do not take my eyes from the island until it fades into the mist. One moment it is there, a small, dark speck in the distance, and the next it is gone.

The trip across the water is uneventful. I remain close to Dimitri, my leg touching his, and this time feel no compunction to put my hands in the water.

As before, I lose all track of time. At first, I try to gauge our direction in the hopes of gaining some idea of where we are going. But the mist feeds the voracious apathy brought on by the rhythmic rocking of the boat, and I give up after a while.

The adder stone is a comfort against my skin, its pulsing proof that the power of Aunt Abigail's protection is still with me. That the Souls cannot make use of the medallion even as I wear it in such close proximity to the mark. I let my mind wander as I doze in and out of sleep against Dimitri's shoulder.

We do not speak, to each other or to Edmund, something I regret when the bottom of the boat bumps up against a beach I do not see until we are upon it. Dimitri and I step into the water and make our way to the shore, Edmund right behind us as the Sisters remain in the boat. Only now do I realize Edmund does not have a single piece of gear. Most notably absent is the rifle that was ever-present in our journey through the woods leading to Altus.

"Where are your things, Edmund?" My voice, too loud after the long silence of the boat ride, is a bell ringing through the early morning.

He bows his head. "I am afraid this is where I must leave you."

"But... we only left a few hours ago! I thought we had time to say goodbye."

His answer is simple. "We do. There's no need for goodbye now. I will return to Altus and see to the other girls. When Miss Sorrensen is well, I will escort her and Miss Torelli safely back to London. I will see you there again in no time at all." He sounds cavalier, but I see the ghost of sorrow in his eyes.

I don't know what else to say. The fog is still thick, even now that we are off the water. The topography of the beach is

lost; it is all I can do to decipher the swaying grass somewhere in the distance.

I glance back at Edmund. "What are we to do now?"

He looks around, as if the answer to my question might be found in the thick gray haze blanketing the beach. "I suppose you should wait. I was told to get you to this beach and then return to Altus. Another guide will find you here." He looks back at the Sisters in the boat and seems to catch a signal that I do not. "I must go."

I nod, and Dimitri steps forward, extending a hand. "Thank you for your services, Edmund. I look forward to seeing you again in London."

Edmund shakes his hand. "I trust you will see to Miss Milthorpe's safety?" It is the closest he comes to acknowledging his concern.

Dimitri nods. "With my very life."

There is no goodbye. Edmund simply nods, making his way down the beach and through the shallow water with hardly a splash. He is back inside the boat in moments.

The sadness that settles around my shoulders is no longer unfamiliar. It is like an old friend, and seconds later, Edmund and the boat fade into the mist. Yet another person gone as if he never existed at all.

"Where do you suppose we are?" I ask Dimitri.

We are sitting on a sand dune, gazing at the gray nothingness. Dimitri studies our surroundings as if he might determine our location by the thickness of the fog that surrounds us in every direction.

"I think we may be somewhere in France. I believe the boat ride was too long to have carried us back to England, but it is impossible to know for sure."

I think about what he said, trying to guess where the missing pages might be hidden in France. It is no use, though. I haven't a clue, and I turn to matters of more immediate importance.

"What will we do if the guide doesn't show up?"

I try to keep the whine out of my voice, but I am already tired, cold, and hungry. We have the meager supplies packed for us in Altus, but neither Dimitri nor I is anxious to make use of them if we can avoid it. It is only wise to preserve our resources as long as possible.

Dimitri speaks from the sand beside me. "I am certain the guide will be here soon."

Though the utter faith of his statement and the conviction with which he makes it gives me some confidence, it is not in my nature to offer blind trust. "How do you know?"

"Because Lady Abigail said the guide would meet us, and while she might not be able to guarantee the results of our journey, she would choose none but the most trusted for such an important task, to say nothing of the safety of her great-niece and the future Lady of Altus."

"I have not said I would accept the appointment," I remind him.

He nods. "I know."

I am pondering the merit of challenging the smugness in his voice when a low huffing comes from somewhere ahead in the mist. Dimitri hears it, too, and he lifts his head in the direction of the sound, placing a finger to his mouth.

Nodding, I listen, peering through the fog until a figure begins to take shape there. It is monstrous, huge, and many-headed. At least, I think it is before the figure breaks through the haze and comes closer. Then I see that it is just a man on horseback leading two other horses behind him.

"Good morning." His voice is strong and confident. "I come in the name of the Lady of Altus, may she rest in joy and harmony."

Dimitri rises from the beach, approaching the man cautiously. "And you are?"

"Gareth of Altus."

"I have not heard tell of you on the isle." Suspicion is evident in Dimitri's voice, at least to me.

"I have not lived on Altus for many years," the man says. "Yet it remains my home. It has that effect on one, does it not? In any case, there are those of us in service to the Sisterhood who are best used with discretion. I'm sure you understand."

Dimitri seems to give this some thought before nodding. He gestures me over, and I scramble off the sand, eager to have a better look at our next guide.

I don't know why I expect him to be dark, but it is with surprise that I see he is very fair. His hair is not the spun gold of Sonia's but a shade so light as to be nearly white. In contrast, his pale skin is unnaturally tan, as if he has been taking too much sun. I imagine, then, that he has not been here long, for it would be nearly impossible to get any color in a place like this.

He tips his head in my direction. "My Lady. I would bow if I were not atop this beast."

I laugh, put at ease by his informal manner and obvious good humor. "It's quite all right. I am not the Lady of Altus yet."

He raises his brows. "Really? That shall make for interesting conversation on the journey ahead." He pulls the two horses forward and I nearly squeal with happiness when I realize it is Sargent and the horse Dimitri rode on the way to Altus.

I hurry forward to pet Sargent's smooth neck. He nuzzles my hair, making the chuffing noise I recognize as one he makes when content.

"How did you get them here? I thought I wouldn't see Sargent again until I returned to London!"

Gareth leans down. "A gentleman never tells his secrets, my Lady." Rising straight in the saddle once again, he grins. "I'm only trying to be clever to detract from my own ignorance. I really have no idea how the horses came to be here. I didn't even realize they were yours until just now. They were simply waiting right where I was told they would be."

Dimitri approaches his house. "Shall we depart then? This fog makes me wary. I'd like to get out into the open."

"Quite right," Gareth says. "Come along then. Mount up and let us begin. We need to make our first stop by nightfall."

"And where is our first stop?" I put my foot in the stirrup and lift myself onto Sargent's back.

Gareth turns and calls out, "A river."

"A river?" I ask. "How very descriptive."

We follow Gareth off the beach and up a steep sand dune. My fears are unfounded that Sargent will have trouble with such unfamiliar terrain. He performs as if he were born on this very beach, and before I know it, we are back in a meadow and traveling through a field of tall grass. The way ahead looks to be mostly flat with occasional rolling hills, and I am grateful to see not a wood in sight.

The fog lessens as we move farther away from the beach and, miraculously, the sky is at last blue overhead. It is impossible

to imagine that it has been there the whole time we were enveloped in the mist on and near the water, and my spirits lift immediately as the sun casts its gilded light over the tall grass.

It is a luxury to have so much open space after the confining forest that led us to Altus. Now we ride abreast of one another, making it easier to converse.

"So, if you are not the Lady, then who is now that Lady Abigail has passed?" Gareth asks.

"It is a rather long story." I am stalling, unsure how much I should say.

"As it happens, I have time." He smiles. "And if I may say, Altus would be very lucky to have such a beautiful Lady at her helm."

Dimitri breaks in. "I am not sure Miss Milthorpe wishes to speak of such a private matter." The note of jealousy in his voice causes me to stifle a giggle. *Miss Milthorpe?*

I look at Dimitri. "Is it all right to speak of it? Or is it forbidden?"

Surprise wars with hostility on Dimitri's face. "It is not *forbidden*, per se. That you are the heir to the title of Lady is no secret. I simply imagined you might not want to share such private details with a stranger."

I force myself not to smile at his boyish petulance. "If it is no secret, then surely it cannot be very private. Besides, it sounds as if we have a long ride ahead. We may as well pass the time in conversation, don't you agree?"

"I suppose," he says, his tone grudging.

When I turn back to Gareth, he is not even trying to stifle the victorious grin spreading across his bronze face.

I attempt to keep my explanation as abstract as possible. "This business," I say, gesturing to the fields around us, "is such that it supersedes my appointment as Lady. I cannot accept such responsibility until it is resolved, so I have been given the privilege of time to finish this journey before I make my decision."

"Do you mean to say that you might not accept the appointment?" Gareth's voice is incredulous.

"She *means*—" Dimitri break in, but I stop him before he can continue.

I try to make my voice gentle. "Pardon me, Dimitri. But might I speak for myself?" He looks chastised, and I sigh, turning my attention back to Gareth's question. "I mean that I cannot even consider it until I finish what must be finished."

"But that would mean Sister Ursula would rise to the position, would it not?"

"That is correct." I wonder how privy to island politics the average Brother and Sister are.

"Well, I for one shall never return to Altus if Ursula is in charge!" I think he might spit, so obvious is the disdain in his voice.

"And might I ask why you feel so strongly about Ursula?"

He glances at Dimitri before answering, and for the first time I see a thread of kinship between them. "Ursula and that power-grubbing daughter of hers—"

"Astrid?" I ask.

He nods, continuing. "Ursula and Astrid don't care about Altus. Not really. They seek their own authority and power. I don't trust either of them for a moment, and neither should you." His expression grows serious as he gazes out over the fields. When he meets my eyes once again, all humor is gone. "I believe you would be doing the island and her people a great service if you were to assume the role of Lady."

My cheeks grow warm under the scrutiny of his gaze, and Dimitri sighs beside me with something like annoyance. "You honor me with your words, Gareth. But you don't know me at all. How do you know I would be a wise leader?"

He smiles, tapping his temple. "It is in the eyes, my Lady. They are as clear as the sea that cradles the island."

I smile in return, though I can practically hear Dimitri roll his eyes.

The fields stretch on and on, morphing from grass into shimmering wheat as the day passes. We stop only once at a small brook that babbles over smooth, gray rock. Drinking from the icy water and replenishing our canteens, we ensure that the horses, too, have their fill. I take a moment to close my eyes, stretching back onto the grassy bank and sighing deeply with pleasure as the sun warms my face.

"It is nice to feel the sun again, is it not?" Dimitri's voice comes from beside me, and I open my eyes, shielding them from the sun as I smile at him.

"*Nice* is too mild a word, I think."

Dimitri nods, his face brooding as he stares out over the moving water.

I sit up, leaning over and kissing him full on the mouth. When we pull apart, he is pleased, if a bit surprised. "What was that for?"

"It is a reminder that my feelings for you are far too strong to falter in the short time since we have been away from Altus." I smile, teasing him. "And far too deep to waver in the face of a handsome man, however charming and friendly."

For a moment, I wonder if I have wounded his pride, but it soon passes and his face breaks into a wide smile before faltering just a little.

"Do you think Gareth handsome then?"

I shake my head in mock exasperation, kissing him once again before rising and dusting off my breeches. "You are very silly, Dimitri Markov."

His voice drifts to me on the breeze as I make my way to the horses. "You didn't answer! Lia?"

Gareth is already atop his mount, and I double-check Sargent's bit before lifting myself onto the saddle. "This was a beautiful place to stop. Thank you."

"You're welcome," he says, eyeing Dimitri as he makes his way to his horse. "I imagine you're tired. It is said you have had quite a journey."

I nod. "I'm quite happy now that we are out of the woods. It was harrowing, traveling through so dark and closed a forest to get to Altus."

He looks at Dimitri to make sure he is saddled and ready to ride. When it seems all is in order, Gareth turns his horse.

"You needn't worry. I believe you will be in the open from here."

And then we are moving, though once again, my destination is a closely guarded secret.

❦

We pass the rest of the day in pleasant camaraderie. Our brief time by the stream seems to have reassured Dimitri, and he is friendlier toward Gareth as we make our way across several fields, some planted with crops and others swaying with wheat or grass.

The sun moves across the sky and is beginning to cast long shadows by the time we come to yet another stream. This one is much bigger than the last and winds through the verdant hills and a small grove of trees at its bank. Gareth reins his horse to a stop and jumps to the ground.

"Right on schedule," he says. "This is where we make camp for the night."

We find basic supplies inside the packs strapped to our horses and set about making a small camp. Gareth lights a fire, and as he and Dimitri raise the tents, I put together a simple dinner. It is not at all strange to share a camp with Gareth. Already he is like an old friend. He and Dimitri entertain me with tales of common acquaintances from Altus. They grow rambunctious in their familiarity and it is not difficult to do my part by laughing in all the right places. The fire has burned low when Gareth finally rises with a yawn.

"We should sleep if we are to make an early start tomorrow as we must." He nods toward Dimitri and me. I am sure I catch a glimmer in his eye even by the failing light of the fire. "I'll leave you to say good night in peace."

He heads for one of the tents, leaving Dimitri and me alone in the chill night air.

Dimitri's chuckle is a low and knowing rumble. He holds out a hand and helps me to my feet, pulling me against him. "Remind me to thank Gareth later."

I do not need to ask him why he wishes to thank Gareth. He lowers his mouth to mine, his lips tender but insistent, and my mouth opens under his until everything else falls away. In Dimitri's arms, I find the peace that eludes me in every coherent, thinking moment. I allow myself to be lost, to fall beneath the power of Dimitri's body against mine and the tenderness in his kiss.

When we finally pull apart, it is Dimitri's doing.

"Lia... I must escort you to your tent now." He rubs his cheek against mine, and I marvel that the soft stubble can feel both prickly and sensuous.

"Can you stay?" I am not ashamed to ask. Not anymore.

"I should like nothing more, but I will not sleep in these strange surroundings." He lifts his head, gazing at the darkness that becomes total beyond the light of the fire. "Not while we are on our way to the pages. It would be wise, I think, to keep watch outside your tent."

"Can't you ask Gareth?" I am being bold, and I do not care.

He looks into my eyes, before leaning in to press his lips, hard this time, to mine. "I trust no one else with your safety, Lia." He smiles. "We have all the time in the world. As many nights as you wish in our future. Come now, let's get you to bed."

But while I am comforted all that night by the shadow of Dimitri's presence outside my tent, I still cannot sleep. His words ring through my mind and I know that he is wrong.

We do not have all the time in the world. Only the time the prophecy allows us. The time we take from it. And the time between now and the moment when I will have to reconcile the promised future with Dimitri and my past with James.

Our camp is small and packed quickly. In no time at all, we are back on our horses, making our way through the fields once again.

After the fog at the beach where we first landed, the sun is a blessing. I close my eyes to it for long moments at a time, tipping my face back and letting the warmth of it seep into my skin. I feel the presence of those who have gone before me in the prophecy. I feel the oneness of us all, though we are not together in this world. It fills me with serenity, and for the first time in days, I feel at peace with my fate, whatever it may be.

It is just such a moment when I realize the total silence surrounding me. No horses' hooves. No chuffing of their great mouths. No easy banter between Gareth and Dimitri. When I open my eyes, we are amid a grove of trees so small that it does not even block out the sun.

Both Dimitri and Gareth have reined their horses to a stop, though neither has dismounted. I pull on Sargent's reins.

"Why are we stopping?" I ask.

Gareth's gaze takes in the surrounding field and trees. "I am afraid we must say goodbye, though I wish a more sheltered location had been arranged as a meeting place for your next guide." He shrugs. "I suppose out of the confines of the woods, this is the best that can be done."

I try to hide my disappointment, for I have grown to trust Gareth.

"When will our next guide arrive?" I ask him.

He shrugs. "I imagine he will be here shortly, though I cannot say for certain. Our identities and schedules are kept secret from one another on tasks such as this one." He digs around in his pack, tossing two extra bags to the ground. "Remain here until your guide arrives. The packs are well supplied and will last you a couple of days at least."

"Will we ever see you again?" This time I am sure my disappointment can be heard.

He grins. "One never knows."

"Gareth." Dimitri looks up at him. "Thank you."

He smiles. "You're welcome, Dimitri of Altus."

He trots his horse over to me and holds out a hand. I place mine in his. "Regardless of whether you accept the title in name, in my eyes, you will always be the rightful Lady of Altus." He bends his lips to my hand, kissing it gently before he turns his horse and gallops away.

Dimitri and I stand in the stillness left by Gareth's departure.

It happened so quickly, neither of us is immediately sure what to do. Finally, Dimitri dismounts, leading his horse to a tree before coming back for mine.

We pitch the tent and create a makeshift dinner from the odds and ends found in the packs. By the time darkness falls, we have come to accept that our new guide will not arrive this night. Dimitri once more stands guard outside the tent while I, too cold to be comfortable, huddle under the blankets and pass a fitful night.

Several times, I believe I hear rustling amid the trees surrounding the camp, boot steps on the hard-packed ground. Dimitri must hear it as well, for he rises from the ground, his figure casting eerie shadows over the tent as he paces outside. I call to him several times, asking if everything is all right, but after a while he tells me sternly to go to sleep. To let him do the guarding without the distraction of my worry. Chastised, I will myself quiet.

I lay in the dark, my body tense for a long while before blackness finally claims me.

30

Our new guide is nothing at all like Gareth.

The first thing that catches my eye is his brilliant red hair. When he turns to greet me the sun sets it on fire in a blaze of gilded rust.

"Good morning." Dimitri tips his head without introducing himself.

"Emrys, your guide." He appears to be significantly older than Gareth, though not as old as Edmund.

"Good morning. I'm Lia Milthorpe." I extend a hand and Emrys briefly shakes it before stuffing both hands back into his pockets.

I expect him to make conversation, to get to know us before we depart, but he does no such thing. He simply turns and heads for his horse, a chestnut mare tied to a tree near Sargent and Dimitri's mount.

"We should be going," he says as he unties the horse. "We have a long day ahead of us."

I look at Dimitri, raising my eyebrows in silent question, and he shrugs and heads to the tent. Together we break camp, shoving the tent haphazardly into Dimitri's pack and the blankets into mine while Emrys stays atop his horse with not an offer of help. I look at him once and find him gazing off into the woods. We've only just met, and already it is difficult not to think him as strange.

The camp cleared of our debris and looking as if we were never there at all, Dimitri strides to his horse, tightening his saddle and placing a foot in the stirrup. After a quick check on Sargent, I do the same.

Emrys nods and spurs his horse forward, and so begins our second day, with little fanfare and even less conversation.

I don't know if it is because we are growing closer to the missing pages or if it is simply paranoia, but I spend the day with a growing sense of foreboding. I cannot explain it or blame it on Emrys who, though not as talkative as Gareth, is not unpleasant.

As we make our way over a large hill, a town comes into view, nestled into the bowl of a valley. In the distance, elegant spires reach, it seems, nearly to the sky. It has been a very long time since I have seen a town of any sort, and I feel a sudden urge to continue on, to sleep at an inn with a soft bed, to eat hot food prepared by someone other than myself, to walk the streets and purchase something from an inviting shop or take tea in a quaint hotel.

But we do not continue toward the town. Instead, Emrys hesitates briefly as if considering his options before veering to the left. We continue through a field of wheat, haloed in the golden sun, and travel toward a charcoal smudge in the distance. As we come closer to it, I realize it is a stone farmhouse sitting at the edge of a forest. Age-old trees seem to touch the sky beyond the house and barn.

As we continue toward the farm, I wonder if it will be one of our stops or perhaps a meeting place for a more talkative guide. It is neither, and we continue past the house and a small boy who stands outside it, feeding chickens that strut in circles, pecking seed from the ground beneath his feet. He watches us curiously as we pass.

"Bonjour, mademoiselle." A smile touches the boy's mouth as his eyes meet mine.

France, I think, smiling in return. "Bonjour, petit homme."

His smile widens to a grin, and I am grateful for even my questionable ability to speak French.

The shadows begin just past the house, and the sun disappears almost entirely as we enter the wood. It is not as dense as the one through which we traveled to reach Altus. The light finds its way through the trees, creating a lacy patchwork over the forest floor. It is beautiful, but even still, my chest grows heavy with anxiety. This is too much a reminder of the dark trip to Altus, of those few days when the world seemed to stand still and I lost all sense of time and myself.

We come across only one point of interest—a moss-covered stone pillar that rises bizarrely from the forest floor. It is not unusual, really, for stone tributes and sacred sites are plentiful throughout Europe. But this one reminds me of Avebury, the ancient stone circle mentioned in the prophecy.

My eyes follow it as we pass. Emrys is as quiet and uninterested as ever, and Dimitri is silent behind me. I do not bother asking them about the stone.

Some time later, Emrys slows, looking back over his shoulder at us. "There's water up ahead. It will be a good place to break."

It is the most he has said since departing camp this morning, and I nod in agreement. "A break would be lovely." I add a smile for good measure, and though I think he means to return it, it seems almost painful for him to do so.

Unlike most of those we have come across in our journey, the stream is not in a clearing but is half-hidden within the shade of the forest. It is rather small and winds through the trees not with a roar or a rush but with a merry gurgle. We dismount, drinking from the stream and filling our canteens.

I am surprised when Emrys looks over and speaks directly to me. "I would be happy to care for the horses while you take a rest, Miss. I imagine the journey leading to this day has been long. We will make our destination by nightfall. There is time for a break."

"Oh! Well...that is all right. I can care for my horse. I shouldn't like to be a burden." I don't tell him that a rest, even a small one, does sound lovely.

Dimitri's surprise gives way to agreement. "Emrys is right, Lia. You look tired. We can manage the horses."

The energy seeps out of my body, seeming to leak into the ground at the simple thought of a rest. "If you're certain it's okay..."

Dimitri leans over and kisses my cheek. "It is. Close your eyes for a bit while we water the horses."

I wander over to a patch of sun not far from the water and lower myself to the dry grass growing there. Lying back, my restless night's sleep soon catches up to me, and I am sung to sleep within moments by the river's lullaby.

I am not aware of anything until the touch of Dimitri's hand pulls me from slumber. The stroke of his fingers is gentle on my wrist, and I smile, wanting to delay the moment when we will have to mount our horses once again.

"This is no way to get me moving." My voice is still lazy with sleep.

He picks up my hand, and I feel the slide of something soft against the soft underside of my wrist.

"You're not listening," I tease.

The voice, when it answers, is quiet, as if trying not to be heard. "It will be so simple, if only you will do as they say."

This voice is not Dimitri's.

I open my eyes, pulling my hand back as I see Emrys, on his knees and holding something in his hand. Something trailing black velvet. The medallion.

"What are you...what are you doing? Give that to me! That doesn't belong to you."

I look down at my unmarked wrist to be sure, but, yes, it has been removed while I slept. Glancing around, I try to find Dimitri without taking my eyes off Emrys, but the riverbank behind him is empty.

"I don't want to hurt you. I'm only doing what I was told." Emrys doesn't flinch, and his lack of concern over the possibility of being interrupted by Dimitri scares me more than anything.

It makes me wonder what Emrys has done with him.

I scramble backward over the hard-packed earth until my back comes up against a tree trunk. For all its solidity, I do not feel safe. There is nowhere to go from here.

"Please leave me alone." I sound weaker than I intend but am too frightened to be angry at myself for it.

I have a moment, only a moment to curse myself inwardly. It is only then that I remember Gareth's words: *You will be in the open from here*. And yet we are not in the open. We have been in the forest for most of the day and even now are well-shielded by its ageless trees.

We should have known.

Emrys stands, advancing on me with a purposeful stride. This time, there is no talking. This time, he grabs ahold of my wrist with force, falling to the ground beside me and leaning over my body as he tries to place the medallion on my marked wrist. Pulling back with all my might, I try to keep it from him. But he is too strong, even as I kick and struggle.

He has my wrist in his hand. The dry velvet crackles against my skin and the medallion, as cool and terrifyingly inviting as

the sea in which I almost drowned, pushes against my flesh. Emrys's big hands fumble with the clasp, locking it into place even as someone comes into view behind him, racing toward us with single-minded fury.

I almost don't recognize Dimitri for the rage in his eyes and the trail of blood dripping from his forehead, but I know it is him as he pulls Emrys away, dragging him from me and dropping him into the dirt. I do not have time to feel shock as Dimitri strikes Emrys with more anger than I have ever seen displayed from one human being to another.

I am too busy pulling the medallion from my wrist.

It takes me a moment to get it off. When I do, I am so shocked that my body begins to shake, and I drop the medallion where it falls. I do not worry about losing it. It is mine. Only mine. It will find its way back to me whatever I do.

Leaving the medallion on the ground, I rush to Dimitri, pulling at his shoulders as he continues to kick Emrys, now sprawled on the ground, moaning and holding his stomach.

"Stop! Stop it!" I scream. "Dimitri! We don't have time for this!"

His breath comes so fast that his back and chest heave with the effort of it. When he turns to me, his eyes are filled with things wild and dangerous. He looks at me as if I am a stranger, and for one panic-filled minute I wonder if he has lost his mind completely. If he will not remember who I am at all. But then he pulls me to him, holding me tightly against his body and burying his face in my hair.

When his breathing finally slows, I pull back, looking at the gash that drips blood at his hairline. I reach up to check it, but pull back before touching him, afraid of causing him pain.

"What happened?" I ask.

He lifts a hand to his temple, wiping away some of the blood and looking at it as if he does not recognize it as his own. "I don't know. I think he hit me with something. I was by the river and the next thing I knew I was waking up on the bank and hearing your scream. I came as fast as I could."

Before I have time to say anything, the rustle of leaves a few feet away catches our attention. We turn our heads to the source of the noise and see Emrys, rising from the ground and making his way to the horses. He moves quickly for a man who has taken such a beating, mounting his horse and tearing off into the forest without a word or a glance back.

We do not try to stop him. There is nothing to be gained, and clearly, we can no longer use his services as guide.

I look up at Dimitri. "Was he one of the Souls?"

Dimitri shakes his head. "I don't think so. If he had been, he would have been far more dangerous. It is more likely that he intercepted our original guide to do the Souls' bidding for a far simpler purpose. It would be an easy matter to offer a peasant money in exchange for leading us astray."

I remember the words of the man who called himself Emrys: *I'm only doing what I was told.*

Taking a deep breath, I look at the surrounding forest. "Do you have any idea where we are?"

He shakes his head. "Not really, but I think it is safe to say that Emrys was probably not leading us the right way all this time."

Overcome with frustration, I turn away from him and pace toward the river. Picking up the medallion and placing it back on my wrist, I can hardly contemplate the possibility that our journey will end here. That after all we have been through, all we have overcome, we will have to turn back because of a weak-spirited guide whom the Souls were able to turn to their cause. Worse, we may never find the missing pages now that Aunt Abigail is dead. Only she was the keeper of the pages' secrets. Only she was able to set up such a careful journey.

And now she is gone.

Dimitri's hands grasp my shoulders from behind. "Lia. It will be all right. We'll figure this out."

I whirl on him, a surge of hopelessness filling me up until I am overflowing.

"How will we do that, Dimitri? How? We are lost in the middle of an unknown wood. And if that is not enough—" I turn from him, laughing aloud. It sounds as bitter as it tastes in my throat. "And if that is not enough, *we do not even know where we are going*! We have nothing, Dimitri. Nothing to guide us from here save a cryptic word." I drop to a large boulder by the side of the stream. Anger slips through my pores like water, leaving me only with despair.

"What word?" Dimitri asks.

I look up at him. "Pardon me?"

He walks toward me, lowering himself so that we are eye

to eye. "You said 'nothing to guide us from here save a cryptic word.' What word?"

I am still hesitant to give over the words passed privately to me from Aunt Abigail on her deathbed. Still, it is not as if I have a choice, and if I cannot trust Dimitri, then who is left?

I take a deep breath. "Just before Aunt Abigail died, she told me to remember a word that would lead me to the pages if we should become lost. But there is not much point to it now. Our guide is gone, Dimitri, and even if he were not, the word may be nothing more than the sickbed musings of a dying woman."

He looks into my eyes. "What was the word, Lia?"

"Chartres." I say it, though I am no surer of its meaning now than I was when it was whispered from Aunt Abigail's dying lips.

I remember Aunt Abigail's other words: *At the feet of the Guardian. Not a Virgin, but a Sister.* I don't share them with Dimitri. Not yet. They seem meant only for me. After all, I may be the next Lady of Altus. As such, it seems fitting that Aunt Abigail's secrets become mine.

Dimitri's eyes take on a far-off glaze as he rises and paces away from me.

I stand up and call after him. "Dimitri? What is it?"

It takes him a moment to turn around, but when he does, something in his expression gives me cause to hope. "The word... *Chartres.*"

"What about it?"

He shakes his head. "When we were young and growing

up on Altus, the Elders would tell us stories. That is how our history is passed, you see. The culture of the Sisters and the Grigori does not believe in written history. Ours is told, passed from generation to generation."

I nod, trying to be patient though I would dearly like for him to get to the important part.

"Chartres was . . . a church, I think . . . No! That is not right. Chartres is a town, but there *is* a cathedral there. One that is important to the Sisterhood." He makes his way back to me, fire in his eyes. I know he is remembering. "There is a . . . a cave there. A grotto, I think, underground."

"I don't understand what this has to do with anything."

He shakes his head. "I don't know. But there is said to be a sacred spring there, as well. Our people revered it in ancient times. They thought there was a sort of . . . energy or current running underneath the building."

I look up. "Dimitri?"

"Yes?"

"Where is Chartres?" I have to ask even as I think I already know.

His eyes meet mine, shared knowledge already in their depths. "France."

I try to make sense of the things we know and how to use them to our advantage, but even the small hope we have seems futile. "France may not be a big country, but it is too big to cover every corner on horseback, at least without a guide. Even if Chartres is the hiding place of the pages, and there is still no proof that it is, we could be days and days away from it."

He shakes his head. "I don't think so. Wherever the pages are hidden, I don't think we are more than a day off track. The supplies that Gareth gave us are already running thin, which makes me believe that our journey was never meant to be a long one. And I think we may count on the fact that Gareth, at least, was leading us in the right direction. If we backtrack to the places we passed while in his company or shortly after parting, we will likely be somewhat close to the planned route."

Everything he says makes a mysterious and perfect kind of sense. I can think of no other course of action, and I feel a smile light my lips for the first time in hours.

"Well, then. What are we waiting for?"

31

As we travel back through the woods, I am increasingly grateful for Dimitri's sense of direction. He seems sure of the way while I am disoriented shortly after leaving the site of Emrys's betrayal. The sun is directly above us and we are still in the forest when we decide to stop to water the horses.

Dismounting, Dimitri ties his horse near the river. The animal dips his head, drinking greedily from the stream as Dimitri heads for the cover of the forest, presumably to tend to personal matters. I lead Sargent to the small brook winding through the trees, and he slurps at the clear water as I uncap my canteen.

It is there, bending over the crystal water of the small stream, that I see them.

At first, there is nothing but the river. But as I lean toward it, preparing to replenish my water supply, the reflective surface distorts into a relatively clear image.

I peer closer, fascinated. My ability to scry was discovered shortly after arriving in London and has never come easily. I have always had to call on it in the past. But not this time. This time the image appears clearly and without effort. It only takes a moment to see that it is not one person reflected in the water, but many. They are on horseback, tearing through the woods against the backdrop of thunderous horses' hooves that I cannot actually hear but somehow know are there simply from the vision in the water.

I strain for a better look as they draw nearer within their watery world, beating a path across the forest floor on steeds of white. Soon enough I know exactly who they are, though they do not look as they do on the Plane. There the Souls are bearded, their hair flowing behind their backs like torn silk. They wear tattered clothing and raise swords of fiery red. But to cross into this world, they must take possession of a physical body.

Even in the scrying water, they look like men I might pass on the streets of London, though with a particular fierceness I would know in any world. They wear trousers and waistcoats and hunch over their horses rather than sit upright bearing swords. But I know them for who they are.

I cannot tell how many they number. Countless, and all riding with single-minded purpose. Though the horde frightens me, both with their number and their intent, it is the man in the front that causes the blood to freeze in my veins.

Fair-haired and beautiful, he is perfectly at ease in his rage. It is not a mask or an emotion of the moment. While the others behind him ride with urgency I can see, even in the warped water-mirror, he is confident of his destination and his success once there. But it is the mark of the serpent, visible in the gap left by his open collar, that makes me realize how very, very much trouble Dimitri and I are in.

The Guard. Samael has sent the Guard to stop us from reaching the pages.

Or to take them from us once we do.

I don't know how far away they are, but I know that they are coming. And they are coming for me.

I do the only thing I can; I rise from the water and run.

"Dimitri! Dimitri!" I shout, scanning the riverbank for him. "We have to leave! Now!"

He emerges farther downstream, worry creasing his face. "What is it? What's the matter?"

"The Guard. They're coming. I don't know how far away they are or when they will catch us, but they're coming."

Dimitri does not question me. He talks while striding to his horse. "How many are there?"

I shake my head. "I don't know. Many."

He mounts his horse in an instant. "On horseback?"

I nod.

"Mount up and give me your cloak." He says this as he is already untying his own.

"What?" The command is so sudden, I am not certain I have heard him correctly. Even still, I put a foot into one stirrup and lift myself into the saddle.

He holds his black cloak out to me. "You and I have different colored cloaks, but our horses are both dark."

He doesn't have to say more. I know what he means to do, and I won't have it. "No. We are not splitting up, Dimitri. It is too dangerous, and I'll not have you exposed to the Souls to protect me."

"Listen to me, Lia. There is no time to argue. This is the only hope we have of safely retrieving the pages. We will trade cloaks, raising the hoods to hide our faces, and continue back to the small town we saw in the valley. I will get you as far as I can. When the Souls are near enough, make for the town while I lead them in the opposite direction.

"The Guard are known for their cruelty, but they cannot use their magic for anything but shifting while in this world. With any luck, it will take them a while to realize they're following me and not you. Besides, you have Lady Abigail's stone. That will offer you an added measure of protection."

Even as he says it, I feel the warmth of the adder stone against my chest. "But... what about you? What will you do if they catch you?" The thought of leaving Dimitri behind makes my heart weigh heavy in my chest.

His face softens. "Don't worry about me. I am strong enough to take care of the Souls. Besides, it is not me they want, and launching an attack against the Grigori's own would be a violation of our laws."

I nod, untying my cape. I hand it to Dimitri in exchange for his black one and tie the dark cloak around my neck while I continue speaking.

"What will I do once I get to the town?" I raise my hood and glance around the forest, knowing we are losing precious time but terrified of leaving something out. Of forgetting a question in this one moment when I might still ask it.

He walks his horse over to me, and the other horse sidles up next to Sargent so that Dimitri and I are as close as possible on horseback. "If you have time, ask someone for directions to Chartres. If you don't, make for a church, any church, and wait for me there. No Soul can enter a holy place, in any form, and live."

There are so many things I want to say, but I have time for none of them before Dimitri leans in, kissing me hard on the lips.

"I will come for you, Lia."

Then he slaps Sargent's flank. The horse jolts forward and Dimitri moves into place behind me. As we fly back through the woods, I cannot help wondering if I will ever see him again. Or if all the soft words I have been saving will go unsaid forever.

As with the Hounds, I feel the presence of the Guard before I see or hear them. I cannot deny our horrifying connection, however much I detest all that they stand for. For a time, I speed through the forest, Dimitri close on my heels, with nothing but the certainty that the Souls are coming closer.

Then, all at once, I *do* hear them.

They tear through the forest behind me, and I lean over Sargent's neck, begging him to go faster, to get us to the clearing leading to the small town that may or may not be Chartres. For a time, Dimitri is still behind me, and then, just as the crashing through the trees behind us grows nearer and louder, just as I realize that the Souls truly are right behind us, the sound of Dimitri's horse veers to the right and I know he has gone.

I force myself not to think too long or too hard about his safety and the possibility of our never seeing one another again. Instead, I continue through the forest, trying to focus on finding my way back to the clearing.

Not at all sure I am headed in the right direction, I come upon the strange rock standing solidly on the leaf-covered ground and feel tremendous relief. I suddenly do not feel alone, and I speed past the stone toward the clearing that I know will come. All the while, I begin to hope. To believe I will make it to the safety of the church in the village.

But that is before I hear the horse gaining speed behind me. Before I dare a glance back and nearly freeze in terror.

It is no longer the Souls as a pack that give chase. No. They have likely lived up to Dimitri's expectations and followed him in the other direction. But there is one Soul who has not followed Dimitri. One who has found me even through the woods and our charade.

It is the fair-haired man, the one who was leading the pack in my vision at the river. His horse rattles behind me with

renewed vigor, and I lean over Sargent's neck, trying to pick up enough of a lead that I might have time to find a place to hide.

It works. He drops behind me, and I break into the clearing at the edge of the field, spotting the stone farmhouse up ahead. This time, I do not dare look back. I make for the rear of the house and ride past it toward the barn. I do not have time to breathe a sigh of relief when I see that the big doors stand open.

Heading straight into the shadowy confines of the barn, I jump off Sargent's back even before he comes to a complete stop. A quick glance around tells me there are only three horses in the barn.

Three horses and six stalls.

I usher Sargent into one of the empty stalls and have his saddle off and lying in the dirt in less than a minute. Latching the door behind me, I stand in the walkway between the stalls, scanning the barn for a place to hide. It only takes a moment to find the loft.

My breeches make climbing the ladder easy. I am up it in seconds, wedging myself behind crates of tools and stacked horse blankets as the sound of the Guard's horse draws nearer and nearer outside the barn. I take advantage of the extra time to remove the knapsack from my back and pull out the dagger. Wrapping my fingers around the jeweled hilt, I feel better for its presence in my hand. The Guard is in a man's body now. He will bleed like any other if cut.

Dust motes shimmer in the dim afternoon light, leaking in

between the wooden slats of the barn. The barn is quite dark, and I try to render myself invisible while still maintaining a view, however small, of the barn floor below. If I am going to be found and trapped aboveground, I would prefer to have some notice. I focus on calming my breathing as the horses chuff and shuffle below. Beyond shifting, I know the Souls do not have supernatural powers. Not in my world, at least. But it is difficult not to believe that the Guard will hear me or somehow know that I am here.

I have finally caught my breath when I hear footsteps, light and careful, below me. Peering from between the crates and craning my neck for a view of the barn floor, I am surprised to see the boy who was feeding the chickens. He surveys the barn calmly, his gaze resting on Sargent in one of the stalls. Lifting his chin, he turns in a slow circle until his eyes come to rest on me. I meet his gaze and lift a finger to my lips, mentally begging him not to give me away. At the same time, I want to scream at him to run, for though the Souls are after me and me alone, I have no confidence in their mercy for a passing child.

It is too late, though. I do not have time to say anything before the barn door creaks further open. I can see only a sliver of the Guard's blond form as he stands, backlit by the sun, in the doorway. He is still for only a moment before stepping into the barn and becoming lost in its shadows. I can no longer see him, though I still hear his stealthy boot steps making their way across the floor below.

His steps are not hurried. They sound softly at first, growing

slightly louder until they come to a stop in front of the boy below me. I ease forward for a better view, mindful of old buildings and their many creaks and groans. But it is no use. Within the confines of my hiding place, I cannot move enough to gain more than a glimpse of the Guard's black riding boots and legs. His upper body and face are hidden in shadows.

I can see the boy clearly, however. He stands, perfectly still, in front of the blond Guard. I have the strangest feeling that the boy is not afraid.

The Guard stands in silence for a moment. When he speaks, his voice is guttural and twisted. It seems to require effort, and I don't know why I am surprised that he questions the boy in French.

"Où est la fille?" *Where is the girl?*

It is a simple question, but the wrongness of the voice that asks it raises the hair on my arms. It is the voice of one who does not know how to coax sound from within its own body.

The boy's voice is small within the expansive space of the barn. "Venez. Je vous montrerai." *Come. I'll show you.*

My heart nearly stops beating, the adrenaline coursing through my veins as I scan the loft frantically for possible escape routes.

But the boy does not lead the Guard to the loft. Instead he begins walking toward the front of the barn and another set of open doors.

The Guard does not follow immediately. He stands in silence for a moment, and I have the distinct feeling that he is gazing around the barn. I lean farther back into the shadows, hardly daring to breathe. The boot steps start up again. They carry the Guard closer to the bottom of the ladder, and I try to judge the distance from the loft to the barn floor. I am contemplating the risk of jumping should the Guard climb the ladder after me when the footsteps become softer and grow farther away.

The boy's voice startles me in the silence of the barn. "Elle est partie il y a quelque temps. Cette voie. À travers le champ."

She left awhile ago. That way. Across the field.

I lean forward just enough to get a glimpse of the boy, pointing the man to the fields in the distance.

There is a moment of utter silence. One moment when I wonder whether the Guard will turn and search the barn, bit by bit. But it doesn't last long. The footsteps start up again, coming closer for a time as the Guard walks toward the back of the barn. I do not understand at first why he would waste the time. Why he would not start out across the field from the front of the barn. Then the horses shuffle below me and I understand. His horse. He left his horse at the back of the barn.

I almost weep with relief as he passes the ladder to the loft, but I continue to hold myself still, keeping my breath shallow and silent until I hear him reach the back of the barn. The sounds of him mounting his horse are muffled, coming from outside, but the rattle of the animal's hooves are unmistakable as they race away from the barn. I wait a couple of minutes in the silence left by his departure, trying to calm my galloping heart.

"Il est parti, mademoiselle. Vous pouvez descendre maintenant," the boy calls from below, telling me it is safe to come down.

I take one last look around the barn, my paranoia getting the better of me, before I manage to drop the dagger back in my knapsack and coax myself down the ladder. When I drop to the ground, the boy is waiting for me. I turn and embrace him. His shocked body is small and stiff in my arms.

"Merci, petit homme." I pull back to look at him, hoping my French is passable enough that I might at least know which direction the Guard was headed. "Que voie lui avez-vous envoyé?"

The boy turns to look at the open front door of the barn. "À travers le champ. Loin de la ville." *Across the field. Away from town.*

The town with the church.

Bending down, I look into the boy's deep brown eyes. They remind of Dimitri's, and I push the thought aside. I cannot afford to be sentimental when I might discover the name of the town in the distance.

"Quel est le nom de la ville? Celui avec l'église grande?" I can hardly breathe as I wait for his answer.

He replies with only one word, but it is the only one I need.

"Chartres."

32

Sitting astride my horse just outside the barn, I survey the field and my options.

The boy did say that he sent the Guard in the opposite direction of the town, but even so, there is no guarantee that the Guard has not changed course and gone looking for me in Chartres. Especially if he thinks the pages are hidden there.

Twisting atop the horse, I gaze into the forest behind the stone farmhouse. Its leafy shade provides more places in which to take cover than does the open field that stretches toward Chartres, but I don't know what has happened to Dimitri or where the rest of the Guard may be. I could very well walk right into their hands should I reenter the wood. At least in Chartres there is the sanctuary of the church.

And the possibility of finding the missing pages. If there is any way at all, any way in the world, to see them in my hands, I will do it.

I fix the town in my sights, pressing my heels into Sargent's flank. He lurches forward, his hooves a bolt of thunder against the ground. He carries us across the field as if propelled by the wind itself.

As if he knows well the danger we are in.

The field's openness is terrifying, though the sun shines brightly, turning gold the wild grass and swaying wheat that stretches in every direction. For all its beauty, the field leaves me no place to hide. My heart hardens on the heels of the thought. *I am done hiding*, I think.

Still, I feel as if I will jump out of my skin every step of the way. I am half surprised to make it across the field without hearing the sounds of the Guard's horse behind me. The town grows nearer until I am finally upon it, and I veer onto what looks to be a main street.

Chartres is not as small as it seemed from a distance, but there are still only a few people walking its dusty streets. They seem to be in no hurry, and they watch me pass with equal parts curiosity and annoyance. Observing their tranquil countenance, I can only gather that I have disturbed what was likely one in a string of endlessly serene and uneventful days.

But my afternoon in Chartres will be anything but uneventful, for as I turn down a small street, trying to follow the cathedral's spires, I come upon the blond Guard speaking to an old woman on the corner. He is still atop his mount, and even from my position some distance away, I hear the animal undertone

in his voice. He stops speaking at once and, as if he senses my presence, swivels his head in my direction.

I do not know how long it takes me to get moving. Everything seems to speed up and slow down at the very same time. I only know that as I turn Sargent toward the church, the Guard spurs his horse forward, leaving the old woman standing on the corner, her mouth still hanging open in mid-sentence.

He is right behind me as I bolt through the village, zigzagging down one street and up another in a desperate attempt to make my way to the cathedral. It takes me a few such turns to get it right. I am twice misled by small roads that seem to lead toward the church but that in the end lead me away from it entirely. My pursuer, ruled by the same earthly limitations as I, does not seem to know the town any better. He follows me every which way, even when I am sure he will find a place to cut me off.

I finally turn down a dusty road that leads to a hill, and it is then that I see a sign reading NOTRE-DAME CATHEDRAL CHARTRES. I round a bend in the road and see the cathedral sitting regally atop the hill. Its spires rise above the ancient stone walls of the church, seeming to touch heaven itself. Sargent, his breath coming loud and fierce, clambers up the road with the Guard in close pursuit.

I prepare to dismount and make a run for the safety of the church as we approach the front of the cathedral. It draws closer and closer until I am right upon it. Once at the foot of its imposing facade, I barely slow before dropping to the ground with more force than I expect. It takes my breath away, and I stumble, trying to right myself even as I see my pursuer enter the final stretch of road behind me.

I have never been more grateful for breeches than I am now as I race up the stairs toward the cathedral's massive, arched wooden doors. I take the steps two at a time. My bow smacks at my back as I try to move as quickly as possible while also ensuring I do not fall on the ancient stone. If I stumble it will be the last time I do, for I hear the Guard behind me. His footsteps fall faster than mine, growing nearer until I am sure he must be right behind me.

I do not look back when I arrive at the doors. I simply reach forward, grasping an enormous iron handle and pulling until the door opens a crack. It is all I need. I slip through it, pushing it shut behind me as I step into the cool sanctuary of the cathedral.

Sliding immediately away from the door, I lean back against the wall. After the frenzied journey through town and up the hill to the church, the quiet in the nave is deafening. My breath, noisy and labored, echoes off the stone walls, and I stand for a moment, eyeing the door and trying to breathe normally. Despite Dimitri's assurances, I half-expect the Guard who gave chase to burst through the door. He doesn't, and after a moment I dare to move away from it and into the cavernous church.

The church is immense, the ceiling rising so high that its end is barely a shadow above my head. Intricate stained glass windows cast a rainbow of dim light over the cathedral's walls and floor, and I catch glimpses of elaborate stone carvings depicting saints and biblical scenes. Darkness lurks in the rooms beyond the altar, but I move quickly toward them. The Guard may not be able to enter the church, but the enormity of it makes me feel vulnerable. There is too much mystery here. I want only to find the sacred grotto and determine if it is where the missing pages lie.

Passing the altar, I come to a great hall. I know from the many times I traveled with Father that historical sites often have signs guiding visitors to places of importance, and I search the walls for direction as I make my way quickly toward the back of the church. There are a few closed doors along the way, but I do not dare open them.

Instead, I turn onto a smaller hallway and discover a faint beam of sunlight coming from a door at the side of the church. I follow the light to the door, and am relieved to see that it is open just an inch. I push it open a little more and peer through the crack.

At first, I am disappointed to find myself looking out on a small street. It seems foolish to waste time in an area that is not even within the sanctuary proper, but something catches my eye. Something on a smaller building not far from the cathedral.

A sign reading MAISON DE LA CRYPTE.

House of the Crypt.

There is, of course, no way of knowing if the pages really are hidden in the crypt, but I have not come this far to sit by while the Guard stalks me outside the church. I contemplate for a moment the possibility of waiting for Dimitri, but it only takes me seconds to discount the notion. Dimitri may have helped me through the woods leading to Altus, but I have traversed alone many dark and frightening paths to this place.

If I hurry, it should take less than a minute to travel along the small street to the entrance. I am doubtful of any protection offered by sheer proximity to the cathedral, but I have no choice, and I look around to be sure there is no one on the street before slipping through the crack of the open doorway.

It must be growing late, for the sun is already fading behind the buildings on either side of the alley. I feel as though the temperature has dropped in the short time I have been in the church. Night will soon fall. The thought spurs me onward, and I reach the entrance to the crypt quickly and without incident, pulling open a door that, while large, would be dwarfed by those of the cathedral itself.

Closing the door behind me, I find myself standing in a small, humble room. There are no ornate carvings or stained glass windows, and yet a deep sense of peace settles into my soul. Somehow this place, without all its pretense and glory, feels more like home than any place save Altus. A now-familiar heat grows against the skin of my bosom, and when I reach a hand to it, the adder stone is hot against my palm.

Moving farther into the room, I am relieved to see that it is quite small. There are very few doors and only one hallway, and I imagine the building was erected haphazardly over the grotto while the cathedral received more glorious attention. Reaching the back of the room, it does not take me long to come upon a narrow doorway atop a winding staircase. The stairs are stone, and I step onto them without hesitation, the adder stone growing hotter beneath my shirt as I make my way toward the bottom.

I touch the walls for stability on the way down, marveling at the dank smell that rises from the depths of the crypt. It is the scent of the earth itself on every side. Descending the stairs is like coming home, and I somehow know that these walls have seen much over thousands of years. That they have protected and hidden things precious to our cause.

When I finally step to the floor of the grotto, I am surprised at its size. The walls are stone on all sides, and though the ceiling is not nearly as tall as those in the cathedral, they still rise well above my head. The crypt itself is quite wide, stretching a good distance from end to end. It is larger, in fact, than the room above it. Lit only by torches along either wall, it takes a moment for my eyes to adjust to the faint light.

When they do, it is the altar at one end that catches my attention.

I make my way down the length of the crypt, trying to keep my footsteps as quiet as possible. I doubt one would be reprimanded for paying tribute to such a site, but one would certainly be reprimanded for what I may have to do to find the pages, and when I reach the altar, I take a moment to observe the statue there. It is the beautiful, if fairly common figure of a robed woman I imagine must be the Virgin Mary.

At the feet of the Guardian. Not a Virgin, but a Sister.

Taking one last glance around, I move toward the statue,

dropping to my knees at her feet. The stone is cold and hard. It bites into my skin even through my trousers.

I study the floor, looking for anything that might indicate a hiding place, but it does not take me long to discount the notion. Despair rushes in as I look at the floor beneath the altar and statue. It is all the same. An endless stretch of gray stone with no distinguishing characteristics in the dim light.

This is what I think at first. Before I see the line of darkness, no more than a smudge, really, running through one of the stones.

I lean back, trying to get a better view and wondering if my proximity only makes it more difficult to decipher whatever is there. And then, yes, I see the same line running through the stone next to it and the one up from that. Beginning to understand, I use my sleeve to wipe away some of the dirt before jumping to my feet. Then I take a few steps back to test my theory.

I can feel the smile break out over my face even as there is no one to see it and even as I never imagined I would smile to see such a symbol.

There, on the ground at my feet, is the same symbol that is on my medallion. The dark line, curving across seven large stones to form the Jorgumand. And though it is dark and faded and covered with centuries of grime, I can still make out the "C" at its center.

"C" is for *chaos*. Chaos of the ages.

I drop hurriedly to the ground, feeling around the mark of the Jorgumand for a loose stone. It does not take me long to realize that it is no use; every stone bearing a piece of the snake is solid. My fingertips soon ache from trying to pry them loose. But there is one last stone at its center, the stone bearing the "C," and when I feel it shift under my fingers, I wonder at my stupidity.

I should have known it was there all along.

Reaching into my knapsack, I remove my dagger. The many-colored jewels on its hilt glimmer, even in the dim light of the cavern. I remember finding it in Alice's room at Birchwood, wood shavings still clinging to its shimmering blade. Wood shavings from my floor and the spell of protection Alice worked to undo in order to leave me vulnerable to the Souls on the Plane.

This time it will be used for a more noble purpose.

Loosening the marked stone is not easy. For a long while, I scrape away at the dirt, debris, and old mortar, pushing the dagger deeper and deeper into the crevices surrounding the stone on every side. I stop to test my progress every few minutes, frustrated when time and again I can do nothing more than wiggle it back and forth. I lose all track of time until, finally, the stone begins to move more easily, and I believe I might just be able to free it.

Returning the dagger to my knapsack, I push my fingers into the openings around the stone. There is not much room in which to work, but I try to move the stone back and forth in an effort to lift it out of the ground. I push and tug for some time to no avail. The angle is all wrong. There is not enough room to get a good grip, though I try to pull straight up rather than at an angle. The stone breaks what little is left of my nails, and my fingers bleed with the effort, but soon I begin to feel that there is more room on either side of the stone. Pressing my fingertips deeper into the narrow spaces at the side of the stone, I bite my lip to keep from crying out as the neighboring stones scrape and cut my already tender flesh. Knowing I will not have an unlimited number of opportunities before my hands give out, I grip with every ounce of strength I have.

Then I pull.

The stone is heavier than it looks. My hands shake as I lift it from the ground, and for a moment, I think I will drop it. But I don't.

By some miracle, I manage to keep a hold of it until it is clear of the abyss revealed by its absence. I do not bother catching my breath. Setting the stone aside, I peer into the seemingly infinite chasm. It is black as pitch. I reach my hand into its dark, moist depths and feel around. Beyond worrying about insects, mold or dirt, I do not even wonder at the strange things my hand bumps up against on its way to the bottom of the hole.

It is far deeper than I expect. My arm is engulfed nearly to the shoulder before I reach the bottom, but when I do, my hand immediately touches upon something softer and warmer than the surrounding stone. I grasp for it and lift my arm, bringing with it a small square of leather.

Putting the stone back in its rightful place, I ensure that everything looks as it did when I arrived. When it does, I rise

to the altar and open the fragment of leather that has been lying in wait far beneath the ground.

The breath catches in my throat as my eyes light on a remnant of thin, crackly paper. Lifting it from the leather, I unfold it gently. It feels as old as time. Even flat, it is still lined with creases, and I smooth it carefully, peering at the words written across its surface.

It is then that I see it is not one, but two pieces of worn paper.

I hold one in each hand, peering first at one and then the other in the dim light of the grotto. It does not take me long to understand.

One piece of paper is an even rectangle with a perfectly smooth edge and words printed carefully in Latin. I recognize the format from the Librum Maleficii et Disordinae—the Book of Chaos found in father's library at Birchwood Manor nearly a year ago. Latin has never been my strong suit. It was only James's translation that allowed me to read that first, harrowing glimpse of the prophecy.

Which is why I gasp with relief when I see the second page nestled behind the first. A page clearly torn from something else, for it is not as neat and clean as the page of the book itself. No. This is a small piece of paper. A piece of paper that also holds the words of the prophecy, though this time in cramped and hurried writing.

But that is not the important part.

The important part is that these words, these cramped and hurried words, are in English, translated long ago as if someone knew I would be the one standing in the crypt at Chartres needing desperately to read the words of the final page of the prophecy.

Breathing a sigh of relief, I tuck the page of the book behind the translation. Then I bend my head to the dim light of the torches.

And I read.

Yet from chaos and madness One will rise,
To lead the Ancient and release the Stone,
Shrouded in the sanctity of the Sisterhood,
Held safe from the Beast, and
Setting free those bound by Prophecy's
Past and impending doom.
Sacred Stone, released from the temple,
Sliabh na Cailli',
Portal to the Otherworlds.
Sisters of Chaos
Return to the belly of the Serpent
At the close of Nos Galon-Mai.
There, in the Circle of Fire
Lit by the Stone, bring together
Four Keys, marked by the Dragon
Angel of Chaos, mark and medallion
The Beast, banished only through
Sisterhood at Guardian's door
With the rite of the Fallen.

Open your arms, Mistress of Chaos
To usher in the havoc of the ages
Or close them and
Deny His thirst for eternity.

Coming to the end of the page, I realize it *is* a page. There are no missing pages of the prophecy. Only one. But even as it is impossible to decipher its meaning here and now, I am sure it is all I need.

I do not have the luxury of taking the page with me. Not while one of the Souls may be waiting for me outside the crypt. So I read. I read until I am positive I have it memorized. Until I know I will be able to recite the words even when I am on my own deathbed, hopefully many years from now.

And then I hold both versions to one of the torches and watch them burn.

33

"Bonsoir. Puis-je vous aider à trouver quelque chose?" the priest asks.

Good evening. Can I help you find something?

I eye him warily as I approach him in the room leading to and from the crypt. I have just ascended the stairs, though he did not come upon me until I was well away from the entrance to the grotto. As I come closer, I glance at his neck, relieved to see that he bears no mark of the Guard.

"Non, Père. Je me promenais la cathédrale et suis devenu perdu." I offer him a nervous smile and the excuse of being lost. Then, just to be safe, I assure him that I can find my own way out. "Je peux trouver ma voie en arrière d'ici, merci."

The priest nods, eyeing my breeches with disdain. I had forgotten all about them and feel an inappropriate urge to laugh aloud. For a brief moment, I forget that I may still be in mortal danger, and I want nothing more than to share my amusement with Luisa and Sonia. The thought brings a smile to my lips, for I know they would also have to fight to contain their laughter.

I move past the priest toward the door. He stands in the center of the room, eyeing me as if I am a common criminal, though with my disheveled appearance and men's attire, I suppose I cannot blame him.

Forced to make a move, I open the big door and look up and down the alley, cautiously at first and then more openly as I become surer that no one lingers outside. When I am as certain as possible that the path back to the cathedral is clear, I slide out of the door and hurry down the street. I reach the door of the church with a sigh of relief, but when I try to pull it open, I find that it is locked.

I try again, pulling as hard as I am able, but it does not budge. I am trying to slow the blood racing through my veins when I hear a sound behind me. Turning to see who is there, it is not what I expect. Not at first.

A large, white cat jumps from atop the stone wall that runs along the street. The animal makes its way toward me languidly, and though I would like to be relieved that it is only a cat, something about its manner makes me uneasy. I know what it is a moment later when the cat's jewel-green eyes find mine just before he shimmers on the ground, becoming in seconds the fair-haired Guard. Changing form seems effortless, and he hardly slows in his movement toward me, a sinister smile taking root on his mouth. The unhurried manner with which he approaches does nothing to decrease my fear. His very leisure terrifies me, as if he is so sure of his eventual triumph that he need not even rush to make it so.

Sliding along the wall of the church, I inch my way toward the only entrance I know for certain will not be locked—the one at the front where I first entered the cathedral. I do not dare take my eyes from the man. I try to gauge whether I have a better chance of escape if I turn and run or continue playing the game of which he seems to be in charge.

I am still some distance away from the end of the small street when he picks up his pace, his footsteps coming more purposefully. The movement causes his collar to open ever so slightly, and I see the serpent, coiled around his neck like a choker. I feel the pull of it even as fear tightens my stomach.

I do not consciously make the decision to run. I simply do it, instinct screaming it is the only chance for escape from Samael's Guard and my own dark affection for the snake that is his mark.

The stone is slippery underfoot, and I cannot run as fast as I would like for fear of falling. Even still, the footsteps hurry in their pace behind me. It is not far to the front of the church, though time seems to stretch and twist in the moment of my attempted escape. I think I have made it to safety as I round the corner toward the front of the cathedral. But I underestimate the slickness of the stone and fall hard, slamming into the ground with a force that makes my teeth rattle.

It only takes me seconds to get up and continue running, but it is not fast enough. The stumble has closed my lead, and

as I race up the stairs to the church, the scent of the Guard's tangy sweat drifts to me on the evening breeze.

Finally reaching the top of the stairs, I lunge for the handle of the great wooden door just as the man lunges for me. This time we both go down, the man holding tightly to my foot while I reach for the door to the church that is my only sanctuary. My bow and knapsack slip from my shoulder, landing some distance away.

"Give... me... the... pages." His voice is a growl. It slithers toward me until I feel that his words themselves crawl across my skin.

"I don't have them!" I scream at him in a desperate bid for freedom, hoping it is only the pages he desires and not simply my death as I fear. "Let me go! I don't have them!"

He does not answer. His utter silence terrifies me more than anything he could say. As he pulls on my leg, drawing me nearer to him, the snake coiled around his neck seems to slither, reaching toward me until I believe I can hear it hiss.

I scan the front of the church for Dimitri or anyone who might help. But this time there will be no salvation. Not from Dimitri. Not from the Sisters. Not from my Otherworldly gifts.

And then I see my knapsack. My arrows stick halfway out of the bag, but it is not this that gives me cause to hope. No. It is Mother's dagger lying a couple of feet from the bag that stems my despair. It is a reminder that my salvation is up to me.

Me and the strength and will I have gained in this world.

I swing my free leg, landing a ferocious kick to the Guard's

face. It sends him sprawling backward, though he takes me with him a few inches even as his grip loosens on my other leg. I reach for my knapsack, using my arms to pull me closer to it and dragging the man along with me in the moment before he regains his wits and grabs more tightly onto my leg. This time, as he pulls me back toward him once again, he lets out a guttural howl.

It is primal and pained, and it connects with some lost part of me that remembers my place in the prophecy and my role in fighting the Souls. I kick again, this time with all my might, and my free foot connects once again with the man's face. The force of it shakes my body to its very core, and I can't help but feel that I have Aunt Abigail and her adder stone to thank for the slight loosening of the Guard's hands on my leg. A loosening that allows me to stretch just enough for my fingers to close around the dagger's hilt.

I cannot say for sure if the heat of the stone imbues me with added strength, or if perhaps it simply makes me feel less alone. As if Aunt Abigail and all her power and wisdom are with me. I suppose it doesn't matter, for I swing the dagger in an arc toward the Guard's face, hitting his neck with such force that he lets go of my foot entirely.

Surprise registers in his eyes in the moment before the blood rushes in a spreading stain across his white shirt. The snake around his neck writhes as if alive, licking angrily but ineffectively toward me in the moment before the man's face morphs into that of the cat in the alleyway, a laborer, a gentleman, and finally, back to his own frighteningly beautiful countenance.

I register dimly that they are all of the forms he has assumed since crossing into my world through some former Gate.

This time, I do not crawl. I run. I scramble to my feet and bolt for the door, barely feeling the weight of it under my hand as I heave it open. Slamming it behind me, I do not stop to catch my breath. I walk backward toward the interior of the church, putting some distance between me and the door without taking my eyes off it. For a long while, I watch, half-expecting the man to come bursting through. Half-expecting him to submit to death in order to follow me into this place that is held sacred from the Souls.

I don't know how long it takes to be certain he isn't coming, but after a while I sink to the floor in relief, my back against a wall, my eyes still on the door.

Dimitri will come. I don't know when, but I know as sure as the sun rises and sets that he will come. I wrap my arms around my knees, whispering the words of the lost page and further committing them to memory.

In the darkened church, I whisper. And I wait.

❦

This time, Alice comes to me.

I am asleep in the cathedral, my back still against the wall, when I feel her presence. I open my eyes to find her standing at the end of the aisle leading from the door to the altar. From a distance, she looks as translucent as she did the night on the stairs at Milthorpe Manor, but as she approaches, I am horrified to watch her grow more and more solid. By the time she

stands before me, her presence is almost as substantial as if it were her physical body and not a spirit figure of the Plane. I am not surprised to find she has grown yet more powerful.

She surveys me with an expression I have never seen before. I think perhaps it is some vile mixture of hatred and admiration.

"So," she finally says. "You have found what you were looking for."

Even in her spirit form, my sister strikes something sinister and fearful in my heart. I lift my chin, trying to sound unafraid. "Yes, and it is too late for you or the Souls to take it. It has already been destroyed."

She does not flinch, and I wonder if she already knew. If she has been watching me from the Plane. "The missing pages were never material to us except where they would help you to end it. We desire only one end to the prophecy, and the pages are not required to see it done."

"So it was all to keep me from finding the pages, not to steal them yourself." It is not a question. I think of the Hounds, the kelpie, Emrys . . . all working on behalf of the Souls to keep me from reaching Chartres.

All working in concert to keep me from ending the prophecy.

"Of course." She smiles, tipping her head. "And I suppose you think you've won. That by finding the pages, you will be able to unlock the prophecy and end it to your liking." All traces of amusement leave her eyes. "But you're wrong, Lia. So very wrong."

"I don't know what you mean, Alice."

She comes closer until she is right in front of me, dropping to her heels so that we are eye to eye.

"You will, Lia." Fire licks behind her emerald eyes. "You may have found what you were looking for, but there are things still lost. Things that require even more answers. Even more danger. Most importantly of all, there is one thing you need that you will never, ever have."

"What might that be, Alice?"

She hesitates for just a moment, before answering with one simple word. "Me."

She smiles, and it is filled with such emptiness that a chill runs up my backbone. I have no idea what she means, but I do not have time for contemplation. Our eyes meet for a split second, and then she is gone, and I am alone in the darkness of the cathedral once again.

34

I keep close to the doorways as I make my way across the busy streets, warily eyeing the other pedestrians.

One would think I would be unafraid on a city street after the long and threatening journey to the missing page, but it has only heightened my suspicion. I remember the Guard at the church in Chartres, his countenance changing from cat to laborer to gentleman, and know that other Guards could be around me at any time, in any place. It is instinctive to drop my eyes to the collar of any unfamiliar man or woman. I am always looking for the twisted serpent around the necks of strangers.

Crossing the cobblestone street, I make my way past the old iron fence, breathing a sigh of relief as I enter the park and continue toward the pond at its center. I have spent many afternoons walking its leafy grounds since returning from France. It reminds me the smallest bit of the rolling hills of Altus.

I think of Dimitri as I walk. He accompanies me on occasion, though I am just as content to walk alone. Thinking of him, his infinite eyes and the dark hair that curls at his neck, I cannot help but be grateful that he returned with me to London, pledging to stay by my side until the prophecy is at rest, whatever it may bring. His presence is a comfort, though I would not like to admit it aloud.

Dimitri did not arrive at the cathedral in Chartres until the morning after I found the missing page. I was still waiting against the wall, though a priest had offered to find me quarters elsewhere. I wanted to be right there when Dimitri arrived. I wanted to be the first thing he saw when he came through the door.

After riding to a seaside town and boarding a ship back to London, we returned to Milthorpe Manor, where I was barely able to stumble to my chamber before falling into a deep sleep that lasted nearly twenty-four hours. When I awoke, it was to Dimitri, keeping watch over me from a chair by the bed.

He has been with me every day since, taking a room at the Society's brownstone under the maternal, if overly attentive, eye of Elspeth. Though he has spoken freely of his devotion, I have not yet reconciled my feelings for him with the ones that still stalk my heart for James. I add it to the list of things I avoid thinking about in the name of the prophecy.

Besides, I find I am reluctant to contemplate the future. There are too many questions in the past and far too many still ahead. Perhaps I am becoming superstitious, but it seems foolish to tempt fate by assuming I will have any future at all.

And for all of my pleasure in Dimitri's company, there are times, whole moments and days, when I wish only to be alone. When I wish to contemplate all that has happened and all the things still to come.

There can be no doubt that change is on its way.

Immediately upon return from Chartres, I received word from Philip that he has found Helene Castilla, the third key. He is on his way back with a plan for bringing her to London, and I cannot help but wonder how the addition of another girl will impact my now-fragile alliance with Sonia and Luisa.

Thinking about Sonia still casts a shadow over my heart. There are times when I remember the old Sonia, the shy, trusted friend who was my closest companion during the darkest hours following Henry's death and my flight from New York. In those moments, I miss her and want to see her again. To embrace her and sit by the fire and tell her everything that has happened since that horrifying moment when I awoke to see her eyes glazed with the madness of the Souls.

But it is difficult to ignore the newly cynical part of my mind.

The one that whispers: *What if it happens again?*

Yet I will have to find a way. A way to bring everyone together once more and a way to manage the many demands of the prophecy, for even as Philip makes his way back to London, Sonia, Luisa, and Edmund are en route from Altus. I have received no details of Sonia's recovery and can only assume she is well, but that does not mean I rest easy in the certainty of her loyalty.

For now, I am surprised to realize that it is Dimitri I trust most.

Shortly after returning to London, I wrote down the words of the missing page so that he and Aunt Virginia could study them by the glow of the library lamp at Milthorpe Manor. When they were finished, when they were certain they would not forget a single word, I burned it yet again.

Since then, we have spent hours trying to decode the enigmatic words on the final page. The answers come rarely and with much effort, but there is one part I finally understand.

The Beast, banished only through Sisterhood at Guardian's door.

I whispered it in the quiet of my chamber over and over, knowing it held the key to an unwelcome knowledge. I saw Alice in the church at Chartres, her eyes afire with something dark and unnameable.

Most importantly of all, there is one thing you need that you will never, ever have.

And my foolish, foolish question. *What might that be, Alice?*

Me.

It came to me in the dark of night and with such horror that I sat straight up in bed, whispering the words of the missing page, understanding at last.

Ending the prophecy will somehow require us both. Alice and me.

The Guardian and the Gate.

I have not dared to contemplate how it might be done.

How Alice and I might work in concert to bring the prophecy to an end when we are on opposing sides. But for now, I work with Dimitri to hone the gifts that are mine. With his assistance, I practice my craft as Spellcaster, though not for a dark purpose as my sister does. I continue my work with the bow while attempting, with the help of Dimitri and Aunt Virginia, to decipher the words of the prophecy's last page.

Most of all I try to close my mind—and my heart—to my sister. I try not to think of her as I saw her the last time we met at the cathedral in Chartres. I try not to see her fiery eyes, shining with the fevered desire of the Souls.

For while I do not know what the future will bring, I now know one thing is certain: Alice was right.

When the prophecy finally ends, one of us will be dead.

ACKNOWLEDGMENTS

It seems impossible to properly thank everyone who has supported me in seeing this book make its way from first draft to polished book, but I keep trying!

First, to my agent, Steven Malk, my sincerest advocate in all things. I would be lost without your support and wisdom. To my incomparable editor, Nancy Conescu, who ensures that every sentence, every word, is polished to perfection. You make me a better writer. For that—and so much more—I am eternally grateful. To Andrew Smith, Melanie Chang, and the entire Little, Brown and Company Books for Young Readers marketing team. Your passion, creativity, and determination are unrivaled. I feel so fortunate to have you on my side. To Rachel Wasdyke, the best publicist EVER and a fantastic traveling companion besides. To Amy Verardo and the LBYR subsidiary rights group who continue to conquer the world with the Prophecy series on your banner. To Alison Impey who somehow knows exactly the cover everyone wants to see before they know it themselves.

In addition to the contingent of talented people on the business end of things, there are many people whose love and support allow me to write with single-minded passion. At the top of that list is my mother, Claudia Baker. Thank you doesn't seem big enough for everything you do and everything you mean, but it's all I have. Thank you again to my father, Michael St. James, for passing on his love of well-written words. To David Bauer and Matt Ervey, lifelong, true-blue friends. To Lisa Mantchev, whose companionship and shared love of ice cream gets me through revisions, criticism, and mountains of self-doubt. To the 2009 Debutantes for sharing my joy and neurosis. To the many online review bloggers who spread the word with incomparable enthusiasm and energy, especially Vania, Adele, Laura, Steph, Alea, Mitali, Devyn, Nancy, Khy, Lenore, and Annie. Whatever anyone says—you guys count. I wish I could name every one of you!

Lastly, to Morgan Doyle, Jacob Barkman, and the many young people who allow me to be a part of their lives. You honor me by sharing your passion for life. It's a privilege to know you as you truly are. To Anthony Galazzo...I love you like my very own son. Everything else is too big for words. And again to Kenneth, Rebekah, Andrew, and Caroline—the reason for everything I do and everything I am. You have my heart, always.